Henry James

SHORT STORY CLASSICS

CLASSICS

(AMERICAN)

VOLUME
THREE

EDITED BY

William Patten

WITH
AN INTRODUCTION
AND NOTES

P. F. COLLIER & SON
NEW YORK

CONTENTS—VOLUME III

THE SOUL OF THE GREAT BELL

BY LAFCADIO HEARN

Lafcadio Hearn (born in the Ionian Islands, of an English father and Greek mother, June 27, 1850; died in Tokio, Japan, 1904) may be claimed as an American author, since all but his very latest works were produced in this country. He first displayed his picturesque power of description as a reporter on a Cincinnati newspaper. Then he drifted down to New Orleans, where Creole life and character afforded his peculiar genius rich and congenial material for books as well as newspaper sketches. Coming to New York, he devoted himself wholly to the highest and most artistic forms of literature. "The Soul of the Great Bell" has been selected to represent the author's work for its simple beauty of legendary form, and because it reveals the attraction the Orient always had for the author. Hearn finally abandoned Occidental civilization and went to Japan, where he died, probably the only unreconstructed "old Japanese" in the country

She hath spoken, and her words still resound in his ears.
—Hao-Khieou-Tchouan: c. ix.

THE SOUL OF THE GREAT BELL

BY LAFCADIO HEARN

THE water-clock marks the hour in the *Ta-chung sz'*, in the Tower of the Great Bell: now the mallet is lifted to smite the lips of the metal monster—the vast lips inscribed with Buddhist texts from the sacred *Fa-hwa-King,* from the chapters of the holy *Ling-yen-King!* Hear the great bell responding!—how mighty her voice, though tongueless!—*KO-NGAI!* All the little dragons on the high-tilted eaves of the green roofs shiver to the tips of their gilded tails under that deep wave of sound; all the porcelain gargoyles tremble on their carven perches; all the hundred little bells of the pagodas quiver with desire to speak. *KO-NGAI*—all the green-and-gold tiles of the temple are vibrating; the wooden goldfish above them are writhing against the sky; the uplifted finger of Fo shakes high over the heads of the worshipers through the blue fog of incense! *KO-NGAI!*—What a thunder tone was that! All the lacquered goblins on the palace cornices wriggle their fire-colored tongues! And after each huge shock, how wondrous the multiple echo and the great golden moan, and, at last, the sudden sibilant sobbing in the ears when the immense tone faints away in

By permission of Little, Brown & Co. From "Some Chinese Ghosts," copyright, 1887, by Roberts Brothers.

broken whispers of silver, as though a woman should whisper, *"Hiai!"* Even so the great bell hath sounded every day for wellnigh five hundred years—*Ko-Ngai:* first with stupendous clang, then with immeasurable moan of gold, then with silver murmuring of *"Hiai!"* And there is not a child in all the many-colored ways of the old Chinese city who does not know the story of the great bell, who can not tell you why the great bell says *Ko-Ngai* and *Hiai!*

Now, this is the story of the great bell in the *Ta-chung sz'*, as the same is related in the *Pe-Hiao-Tou-Choue*, written by the learned Yu-Pao-Tchen, of the City of Kwang-tchau-fu.

* * *

Nearly five hundred years ago the Celestially August, the Son of Heaven, Yong-Lo, of the "Illustrious" or Ming dynasty, commanded the worthy official Kouan-Yu that he should have a bell made of such size that the sound thereof might be heard for one hundred *li*. And he further ordained that the voice of the bell should be strengthened with brass, and deepened with gold, and sweetened with silver; and that the face and the great lips of it should be graven with blessed sayings from the sacred books, and that it should be suspended in the centre of the imperial capital, to sound through all the many-colored ways of the City of Pe-King.

Therefore the worthy mandarin Kouan-Yu assembled the master-molders and the renowned bellsmiths of the empire, and all men of great repute and cunning in foundry work; and they measured the materials for the alloy, and treated them skilfully, and prepared the molds, the fires, the instruments, and the monstrous melting-pot for fusing the metal. And they labored exceedingly, like giants, neglecting only rest and sleep and the comforts of life; toiling both night and day in obedience to Kouan-Yu, and striving in all things to do the behest of the Son of Heaven.

But when the metal had been cast, and the earthen mold separated from the glowing casting, it was discovered that, despite their great labor and ceaseless care, the result was void of worth; for the metals had rebelled one against the other—the gold had scorned alliance with the brass, the silver would not mingle with the molten iron. Therefore the molds had to be once more prepared, and the fires rekindled, and the metal remelted, and all the work tediously and toilsomely repeated. The Son of Heaven heard and was angry, but spake nothing.

A second time the bell was cast, and the result was even worse. Still the metals obstinately refused to blend one with the other; and there was no uniformity in the bell, and the sides of it were cracked and fissured, and the lips of it were slagged and split asunder; so that all the labor had to be repeated even a third time, to the great dismay of Kouan-Yu. And when the Son of Heaven heard these things, he was angrier than before; and sent his messenger to Kouan-Yu with a letter, written upon lemon-colored silk and sealed with the seal of the dragon, containing these words:

"From the Mighty Yong-Lo, the Sublime Tait-

Sung, the Celestial and August, whose reign is called 'Ming,' to Kouan-Yu the Fuh-yin: Twice thou hast betrayed the trust we have deigned graciously to place in thee; if thou fail a third time in fulfilling our command, thy head shall be severed from thy neck. Tremble, and obey!"

* *
*

Now, Kouan-Yu had a daughter of dazzling loveliness whose name—Ko-Ngai—was ever in the mouths of poets, and whose heart was even more beautiful than her face. Ko-Ngai loved her father with such love that she had refused a hundred worthy suitors rather than make his home desolate by her absence; and when she had seen the awful yellow missive, sealed with the Dragon-Seal, she fainted away with fear for her father's sake. And when her senses and her strength returned to her, she could not rest or sleep for thinking of her parent's danger, until she had secretly sold some of her jewels, and with the money so obtained had hastened to an astrologer, and paid him a great price to advise her by what means her father might be saved from the peril impending over him. So the astrologer made observations of the heavens, and marked the aspect of the Silver Stream (which we call the Milky Way), and examined the signs of the Zodiac—the *Hwang-tao,* or Yellow Road —and consulted the table of the Five *Hin,* or Principles of the Universe, and the mystical books of the alchemists. And after a long silence, he made answer to her, saying: "Gold and brass will never meet in wedlock, silver and iron never will embrace, until the flesh of a maiden be melted in the crucible; until the blood of a virgin be mixed with the metals in their fusion." So Ko-Ngai returned home sorrowful at heart; but she kept secret all that she had heard, and told no one what she had done.

* * *

At last came the awful day when the third and last effort to cast the great bell was to be made; and Ko-Ngai, together with her waiting woman, accompanied her father to the foundry, and they took their places upon a platform overlooking the toiling of the molders and the lava of liquefied metal. All the workmen wrought at their tasks in silence; there was no sound heard but the muttering of the fires. And the muttering deepened into a roar like the roar of typhoons approaching, and the blood-red lake of metal slowly brightened like the vermilion of a sunrise, and the vermilion was transmuted into a radiant glow of gold, and the gold whitened blindingly, like the silver face of a full moon. Then the workers ceased to feed the raving flame, and all fixed their eyes upon the eyes of Kouan-Yu; and Kouan-Yu prepared to give the signal to cast.

But ere ever he lifted his finger, a cry caused him to turn his head; and all heard the voice of Ko-Ngai sounding sharply sweet as a bird's song above the great thunder of the fires—*"For thy sake, O my father!"* And even as she cried, she leaped into the white flood of metal; and the lava of the furnace roared to receive her, and spattered monstrous flakes of flame to the roof, and burst over the verge of the earthen crater, and cast up a whirling fountain of many-colored fires, and subsided quakingly, with lightnings and with thunders and with mutterings.

Then the father of Ko-Ngai, wild with his grief, would have leaped in after her, but that strong men held him back and kept firm grasp upon him until he had fainted away, and they could bear him like one dead to his home. And the serving-woman of Ko-Ngai, dizzy and speechless for pain, stood before the furnace, still holding in her hands a shoe, a tiny, dainty shoe, with embroidery of pearls and flowers— the shoe of her beautiful mistress that was. For she had sought to grasp Ko-Ngai by the foot as she leaped, but had only been able to clutch the shoe, and the pretty shoe came off in her hand; and she continued to stare at it like one gone mad.

But in spite of all these things, the command of the Celestial and August had to be obeyed, and the work of the molders to be finished, hopeless as the result might be. Yet the glow of the metal seemed purer and whiter than before; and there was no sign of the beautiful body that had been entombed therein. So the ponderous casting was made; and lo! when the metal had become cool, it was found that the bell was beautiful to look upon and perfect in form, and wonderful in color above all other bells. Nor was there any trace found of the body of Ko-Ngai; for it had been totally absorbed by the precious alloy, and blended with the well-blended brass and gold, with the intermingling of the silver and the iron. And when they

sounded the bell, its tones were found to be deeper
and mellower and mightier than the tones of any other
bell, reaching even beyond the distance of one hundred
li, like a pealing of summer thunder; and yet also like
some vast voice uttering a name, a woman's name, the
name of Ko-Ngai.

* *
*

And still, between each mighty stroke there is a long
low moaning heard; and ever the moaning ends with
a sound of sobbing and of complaining, as though a
weeping woman should murmur, *"Hiai!"* And still,
when the people hear that great golden moan they
keep silence, but when the sharp, sweet shuddering
comes in the air, and the sobbing of *"Hiai!"* then,
indeed, do all the Chinese mothers in all the many-
colored ways of Pe-King whisper to their little ones:
*"Listen! that is Ko-Ngai crying for her shoe! That
is Ko-Ngai calling for her shoe!"*

Henry Cuyler Bunner (born in Oswego, N. Y., 1855; died 1896) was one of the most gifted editors of his generation. From its early days until shortly before his death he was the editor of "Puck," developing it from a weekly joke times in journalism to a position in which it became a real force in American politics as well as a vehicle of lighter verse and fiction. None of his editorials or contributions excelled those of the editor. He was a rare temperamental personality—his short stories reflect it, and few makers succeeded in imparting a more affectionate appreciation in the minds of their readers. His extraordinary versatility is exemplified in the parody given herewith. "There are two kinds of parody," says Brander Matthews—"one is a mere imitation of the external form, and it expressly deprecative and insincere; the other is parody and calls for an exception of the internal spirit. In this Bunner excelled."

A SUCCESSFUL FAILURE

BY H. C. BUNNER

Henry Cuyler Bunner (born in Oswego, N. Y., 1855; died 1896) was one of the most gifted editors of his generation. From its early days until shortly before his death he was the editor of "Puck," developing it from a mere free lance in journalism to a position where it became a real force in American politics as well as a vehicle of clever verse and fiction. None of its editorials or contributions excelled those of the editor. His was a rare temperamental personality—his short stories reflect it, and few authors have succeeded in inspiring a more affectionate appreciation in the minds of their readers. His extraordinary versatility is exemplified in the parody given herewith. "There are two kinds of parody," says Brander Matthews—"one is a mere imitation of the external form, and is commonly inexpensive and tiresome; the other is rarer and calls for an evocation of the internal spirit. In this Bunner excelled."

New York, June 12th, 1887.

MY DEAR MR. STOCKTON:

   When I asked you to write a story for "The Midsummer Puck," you told me that your engagements forbade your making a promise. I told you that if you did not write your story for me, I should write it for you. You told me that that arrangement satisfied you completely. You never wrote your story. I did. This is it. And I am sincerely yours,

H. C. BUNNER.

A SUCCESSFUL FAILURE

BY H. C. BUNNER

I T was on the 27th of January, a number of years
ago, that I sent my petition for a vacation to the
Board of Directors of the Royal Toronto and
Extra-Colonial Fire Insurance Company, in whose
Albany Branch office I was employed. It was received, and forwarded to Toronto, by the Secretary,
who was an English Canadian, very stiff and formal,
and given to the worship of English manners and of
English ways of doing everything. I do not think
you could have wounded him more than by telling him
that something he had done was not strictly English.
There were four other clerks, besides myself, who were
as much like the head of the office as it was possible
for them to make themselves after many years of assiduous practice. The letter paper of the Company
bore the principal English flag crossed with the other
English flag on a background of the coat-of-arms of
England, and the flag of the United States peeped
modestly out of the middle distance. I was the only
American in the office except the office-boy, and I
often said to my wife that if it were not for the office-
boy, I should feel myself an exile in a foreign land.

Although I had not been married long, I had been in

the employ of the Royal Toronto and Extra-Colonial
Fire Insurance Company for nearly twelve years; and
although I had been promised a vacation of one week
every year when I entered the Company's employ, it
had never been found convenient to let me off, except
for three days when I got married.

This seemed to me to be unjust, and my wife thought
so too. She suggested that, as we had a little money
laid up, and as we both wanted to go to Europe, and
as the Company owed us at least eleven weeks of vacation, less the three days of our honeymoon, making
just ten weeks and four days, I should ask the Board
of Directors to compound for this time and for such
time as would be due me in the four years that were
to elapse before I should receive my promotion to a
senior clerkship in the regular course, by giving me
one long vacation of four months, deducting the three
days.

I have observed that my wife's advice is generally
sound, and so I drew up the petition, and, as I have
said, presented it on the 27th of January.

I got an acknowledgment the next week, saying
that the petition would be considered at the next semi-
annual meeting of the Board, on the 15th of June, and
the decision would be promulgated in September. It
was in the fall, therefore, that I received a reply, in-
forming me, in language that I thought somewhat
cold, that, in spite of the extraordinary character of
my request, the Board had concluded to grant it, and
that I was to have three months' leave of absence, less
three days, beginning on the 15th of the following

June. I suppose they took off one month on account of the extraordinary character of my request.

When I told my wife, which I did as soon as I reached home that evening, she was overjoyed, and flung her arms about my neck.

"We will not mind about the month less, dear," she said: "perhaps we might have got tired of it if we had stayed so long."

It is my wife's habit to look on what I might call the consolatory and compensatory side of things, and I consider this a very happy faculty, although, perhaps, difficult of acquirement except under those agreeable circumstances when it is not needed.

"But," she said, when her first transports were subsided, "if we are going to Europe, we ought to know the European languages, and neither of us speaks anything but English."

I reminded her that I had learned a little Latin at school; but she observed, quite justly, that my Latin would be of very little use to us unless we were traveling in Roumania, where it is still spoken, or unless we were going to associate with the people in and about the Vatican, which it was hardly likely we should, especially as we attended the Congregational Church.

"Now, French," she continued, "is the universal language. It is spoken in all the courts, and I presume also among the common people. You know that all the nice dishes on the bills of fare are in French, so I suppose the waiters speak it fluently."

Her arguments appeared to me unanswerable, and

I cast my deciding vote for the French language. The next question was how to acquire it. We could not afford to employ a French teacher without encroaching upon the money we had laid up for our traveling expenses, and as we lived in a remote suburb of Albany, we could hardly expect a good teacher to come out to us in the evening except at an exorbitant price. We thought, also, it would be much more agreeable to study by ourselves, without having a stranger about, who might not be interested in our trip, which was all we cared to talk about just then.

We discussed the various methods of learning a foreign language, and finally decided upon the Natural Method. That is, we determined, instead of beginning with the grammar and the rules of syntax, to learn by building up simple sentences, exactly as a child learns his mother-tongue. We had both observed that while a child finds little difficulty in learning to speak well and freely the language which he hears spoken about him, he may pass many years of labor in making himself master of a language which he learns by rule. My wife knew of a girl, in the school where she was educated, who studied French for three years, and then was unable to write it with real fluency and correctness.

The next day I bought, for reference, a French-and-English grammar and a French-and-English pronouncing dictionary. We spent most of the first week in learning how to pronounce according to the dictionary, and then we began our course of mutual instruction.

We took turns at being teacher and pupil. First I

would sit down, and my wife, with the dictionary in her hand, would indicate some object in the room, and would speak the French name of it, which I would repeat until I thought I had it fixed in my mind. Then she would name other objects until she thought I had forgotten the first one, when she would suddenly recall it to my attention, asking me if I knew what it was. If I failed to tell her correctly, she took my place, and I became the teacher. Thus we made a sort of game of it, which we found extremely enjoyable.

Our progress, however, was not as rapid as we could have wished; and finally I pointed out to my wife that a child learns because his mind is free from other impressions, and receives only the impression of the moment, while we were naturally thinking of other matters—of the to-morrow's dinner or of the temperature of the room, for example. It was evident, I told her, that to succeed we must reduce our minds to the blankness of childhood—in fact, that the one of us who was being taught must, for the time, imagine himself or herself (as the case might be) actually to be a child. I admitted that this would require an effort of the imagination; but I saw no way to avoid it.

After some thought, my wife came to our rescue with a scheme which I at first ridiculed, but at last accepted provisionally. The scheme was to stimulate the imagination by the influence of material surroundings. The one of us who was playing the pupil was to sit on a chair elevated on a box or a trunk, to wear some garment suggestive of infancy, and to possess his or her mind with the idea of being a baby. At first, as I have mentioned, I did not like the plan; but I consented to try it.

My wife began at once to lay out the garment. At first she said she would send to a neighbor for the pattern; but on mature reflection she abandoned this idea, and sent to New York for a dressmaker's guide, or something of the sort. By multiplying ten times the figures on the pattern there shown, she was enabled to construct a white cotton frock, or slip, as she told me it would be called, which buttoned in the back and had ruffling at the neck and down the shoulders. It was nine feet long, and fitted me snugly and my wife very loosely. It was supplied with two sets of bows to pin on the shoulders—a pink set to be used when I wore it, and a blue set for my wife.

When she first saw me attired in this garment, and seated upon a dining-room chair placed upon a soap-box, my wife laughed heartily; but I could not wholly agree with her that there was any occasion for laughter, for when she came to try it on, I thought she looked unusually pretty in it.

I found, indeed, that the dress was of great practical value. Before I had worn it ten minutes, I felt that my mind was reduced to the vacuity of a child's. In this way we readily learned *un table, le vase, le chaise*, and many other words. At the end of a month, with the aid of the Grammar, we began on short and easy sentences. We both felt that our progress was entirely owing to the slip.

"I shouldn't like to have any one know of it, though," said my wife.

On the afternoon of the 14th of June, I did not go home from the office, but joined my wife at a small and modest hotel where I had taken a room for the day. We were to leave on the nine o'clock boat, and as we lived so far out of town, we had thought it better to dismiss our one servant, close up our little house, and wait in Albany till the time for the boat to start. We had no intimate friends in the town, and so we indulged ourselves in the luxury of a room at a hotel for the few hours we had to wait. Our tickets had been taken for Liverpool by the "Carnival of Venice," a steamer belonging to a small but well-conducted line, for we could not afford to travel, even second class, by any one of the great lines. The "Carnival" was a good, stanch, seaworthy vessel, and had been recommended to us as thoroughly comfortable, although her cargo was mostly freight, and she carried only a few passengers. The Captain was reputed to be a most agreeable man.

Our baggage had gone down the day before, and we only carried our hand-bags, in which we had put all that we thought necessary for a night's travel. We were to go on board the steamer as soon as we arrived at New York, which would be at six o'clock in the morning. The "Carnival" was to sail at seven sharp, taking advantage of the outgoing tide.

I have said that we carried only our hand-bags; but I should have added that we had also a package containing a can of deviled ham, a can of crystallized lemonade, a can-opener, a knife and a loaf of bread. It had occurred to us that we might be too late for breakfast on the "Carnival," and that, by this means, whatever might be the accidents of travel, we had at hand a plentiful supply of food in the most compact form. As my wife remarked, we had sandwiches and lemonade reduced to their original principles.

After a very good dinner at the hotel, we took a French lesson in our room, to pass away the time, packed our hand-bags neatly, and, as it was a fine summer night, began to stroll leisurely down toward the steamer dock, which lay at some distance from the quiet hostelry which we had chosen. But before we had gone a block, my wife stopped suddenly, and I saw that she was agitated.

"I am sure I left it on the bed," she said, as though to herself.

I asked her what she meant, and she told me hastily that she had just remembered leaving our slip on the bed, where she had thrown it at the close of the French lesson.

"Very well," I said: "let us leave it there. We probably would not use it much on the steamer, and you can make a new one when we get to Liverpool."

"Oh, no," she replied, excitedly, "that would never do. We would not get used to a new one. And, besides, what will people think if they find it?"

I offered to go for it; but she preferred to go herself.

"I should attract attention if I stood here in the street with these two satchels," she explained, "and there is no reason why both of us should go back to the hotel. Now I can slip back and get the chambermaid to open the door for me, and I can be back here in a few moments."

She hurried off, and returned in even less time than I had expected, carrying the slip rolled up in a newspaper.

"It was lucky I went back," she said. "Do you know that we left the room door open? And just as I got there a man was walking down the corridor, and trying all the doors. I suppose he was what they call a hotel sneak thief."

"Very likely," said I; "and if this had been a diamond necklace instead of a cotton slip, he would have stolen it."

"I'm glad I have not a diamond necklace," said my wife.

We were the first people on board the steamer, and we amused ourselves, after putting our baggage in our stateroom, by leaning over the rail and watching the other passengers come over the gangplank. Most of them came very late, giving themselves just time to catch the boat, and arriving very hot and uncomfortable. Indeed, two men came rushing down the dock together just as the gangplank was drawn in, and had to jump to reach the deck. My wife and I agreed that we would make it a rule to be ahead of time in our traveling, rather than behind.

Later in the evening, when my wife had retired to our stateroom, and I was smoking a cigar on the upper deck, a man came leisurely up and took his position

close by me. I was leaning on the rail, and looking at
the gray hills past which we were rapidly slipping.

I recognized the stranger as one of the two men who
had almost lost the boat. He was a large man, with a
heavy black mustache. I could not see very well in the
moonlight; but I thought the mustache was dyed. He
wore a flashy watch-chain and a bright-colored necktie, and his clothes were somewhat extravagant in their
cut. I thought he looked like a theatrical man, or
perhaps an auctioneer.

After a little while, the stranger addressed me with
some remark about the beauty of the scenery, and then
began to tell me the names of the mountains we were
passing, and of the towns whose lights we could see
along the water's edge.

"You see," he said, "I know about these things, for
my business requires me to travel a great deal. I am
in the show business."

I did not know what to say to this, so I merely remarked that it must be a very interesting business.

"It *is* a very interesting business," he said, "and
my branch of it is especially interesting. I am a
purveyor of freaks."

My curiosity was now aroused, and I asked him to
tell me exactly what was the business of a purveyor
of freaks.

"A freak," he said, "is a curiosity, a live curiosity
of any sort, such as a bearded lady, a five-legged cow
or a living skeleton. They are so called because they
are frequently referred to as freaks of nature, in the
lectures that are delivered about them. Some of my

freaks are happy discoveries; but most of them, such
as fat women, living skeletons, and bearded ladies, I
manufacture. I select likely subjects, and put them
through a strictly scientific course of training, calculated to make them perfect specialties. As there are a
great many dime museums and as the number is increasing, I am kept pretty busy."

I thought that it must be a profitable business, as
well as an interesting one, and I said so to the stranger, who turned and looked me sharply, and I thought
suspiciously, in the face.

"It *is* a profitable business," he said, "when I am
not troubled with thieves. But when a man's freaks
are stolen from him—yes, stolen—you can not call his
business profitable, can you?"

I said I thought that under such circumstances a
business might be called anything but profitable.

"I have just lost," he said in a somewhat loud and
excited tone of voice, "one of the most valuable freaks
I have ever had—a natural freak—a fat child, weighing two hundred and forty-nine pounds."

He seemed very much moved by emotion, and I said
I was sure it must have been a heavy loss to him.

He looked at me as if he had some doubt as to
whether I was speaking seriously, and continued:

"That theft was not only dishonest, but it was cruel.
She was stolen from the hotel in my absence. Her
name is Amanda Belasco. She is only three years
old, and she weighs two hundred and forty-nine
pounds. She lives on the bottle exclusively, and she
has to have her milk mixed at a certain strength—

one part of milk to four of water. She can not stir
hand or foot to help herself. Think of taking that
child away from her natural parents and guardians,
whom I have under salary, and exposing her to the
chance of indigestion and death. She needs, when in
a normal state of health, three gallons and a half a
day. The man who abducted that child is a villain,
sir. Think of it!"

I thought of it, and it seemed to me that he must be
a very great villain indeed. A man who steals an
ordinary small baby, weighing perhaps ten or eleven
pounds, is generally considered a villain, and I felt that
a man who would steal two hundred and forty-nine
pounds of infant must proportionately surpass him in
iniquity. I told the stranger so; but he paid no attention to me.

"If there is a law in the land," he said, "I will pun-
ish that man." He paused a moment and then added,
very mysteriously, it seemed to me:

"I will leave you to think of that."

He turned away and walked toward the cabin door;
but as he reached it he looked over his shoulder and
said sternly:

"My name is Dockshaw."

I did not care what his name was, and I was greatly
puzzled by his manner, and as I could make nothing of
it, I thought it best to go to bed, which I did.

We arose early the next morning, in order to be on
board of the "Carnival of Venice" in good season. As
soon as we were dressed, we went on deck, and I was
surprised to see my acquaintance of the night before

standing by the gangplank that led from the steamboat to the wharf, engaged in earnest conversation with his friend, who also had a black mustache and a bright-colored necktie. I was surprised, because it was only seven o'clock, and breakfast was not yet ready on board the steamboat.

I was still more surprised, however, when the friend approached me and asked permission to speak to me privately. When I stepped aside with him he said to me in a low tone:

"I am a detective from Albany, and you are my prisoner. Will you come quietly with me, or shall I call a New York policeman and give you in charge? I have one waiting on the wharf."

"But for what—" I stammered—"for what am I arrested?"

"For the theft," he replied, sternly, "of Mr. Dockshaw's fat infant."

I saw it all, with mortification and annoyance. It was that wretched slip which Mr. Dockshaw had noticed in our room at the hotel, and which he had supposed must belong to the mammoth infant. Mr. Dockshaw, then, was my wife's sneak thief. I explained, as briefly as I could, the situation; but when I had finished, the detective and Mr. Dockshaw, who had joined us, shook their heads.

"It is a very good story," said Mr. Dockshaw; "but it is too much like what I hear in my own line of business."

"Very well," I answered, for I was now provoked, "you may arrest me; but if you cause me to lose my ship, I shall recover damages from you for my passage money and the loss of my holiday, as I can easily prove my innocence. But if you will go with me to the New York office of my company, I can at once establish my respectability."

After some discussion, Mr. Dockshaw accepted this proposition, and I informed my wife of what had happened, and told her to wait on the steamboat until I should return. At first she was alarmed, but presently took a more hopeful view of the matter.

"Think how much worse it would be," she observed, "if you were really guilty."

I remembered that Mr. Weatherwick, the manager of our New York branch, whom I knew quite well, was a methodical and assiduous business man, and was always at his desk by eight o'clock, and often earlier, so I proceeded at once, with my two companions, to the company's office. They were evidently much impressed by the place, for it was a large marble building, old-fashioned, but of notable solidity and respectability. The porter was sweeping out the office, and none of the clerks were on hand; but he told us that Mr. Weatherwick would soon be in. It was nearly eight o'clock, however, before he arrived.

Mr. Weatherwick was accustomed to command many subordinates, and he had, although a small man, a tone of precision and determination which evidently had a great effect upon Mr. Dockshaw and the detective. He was not long, with the help of the general reports of the Albany branch (which were always transmitted in duplicate to the sister establishment), in convincing them that I was not the sort of man to filch a two-hundred-and-fifty-pound baby, even if I had ever desired so large and voracious an addition to my family.

When this was made clear to Mr. Dockshaw, he murmured a hasty apology, and started for the door.

"Hold on," I said, "this will not do. It is now ten minutes past eight and the 'Carnival of Venice' has certainly sailed. My tickets, which are return tickets for two, are of no use to me. Even if the steamer people would allow me to use them now, there is no boat on their line for a month, which would give me only two weeks in Europe."

It should be remembered that this was a number of years ago, when only the fastest steamers made the passage in fourteen days, and three weeks was a good trip for a boat like the "Carnival of Venice."

"You must," I continued, "pay for tickets for my wife and myself by some other line, or I shall remain in New York and sue you."

Upon this a discussion ensued, which was conducted with considerable acrimony, until Mr. Weatherwick interposed.

"The arrest was a mistake," he said to Mr. Dockshaw, "but you must do what you can to save this gentleman from any consequent annoyance. Now you would have to pay several hundred dollars for the tickets; but you can hire a tug to overtake the steamer for twenty-five or thirty dollars. The 'Carnival of Venice' is a slow boat, and may easily be caught by a lively tug before she reaches Sandy Hook."

This suggestion was gratefully received by Mr. Dockshaw, and after I had signed a promise not to hold him further responsible for any detention, we started for the riverside. Before I left, however, Mr. Weatherwick drew me to one side, and said:

"I do not wish to interfere in your private affairs; but, as an officer of the company, I would advise you to prosecute any further studies of foreign languages you may intend to make without the aid of underwear."

I remembered that Mr. Weatherwick was not a family man; so I did not correct him; but thanked him, and set off for the river.

When we got to the wharf, we inquired of the policeman where we could find a tug.

"You are in luck," he answered: "there is a steamtug lying alongside now, which will start in a few minutes for Fire Island, to assist in getting a wreck off the sands. She is one of the fastest tugs in the bay, and I will introduce you to her captain, who is a friend of mine."

While Mr. Dockshaw was making a bargain with the captain, I went on the steamboat, and found my wife, who was delighted at my return; and in a short time we were both seated, with our hand-bags in our laps, on the deck of the "John B. Smiler."

We saw several ocean steamers as we puffed swiftly down the bay; but nothing resembling the "Carnival of Venice." We were sure of this, for they were all going the other way. After an hour or two, and while we were looking at a long, low strip of land, with a lighthouse at the end, which we had just passed, Captain Smiler came up to us and told us that we had reached Sandy Hook, and that the "Carnival of Venice" was nowhere to be seen.

When we had got over our first disappointment, we observed that the captain had gone below, and that the "John B. Smiler" was still steaming on, with the land on one side, and the open sea on the other. I sought out the captain, and suggested that he should take us back to New York; but to this he roughly demurred.

It was not his fault, he said, that he had failed to catch the steamer; and he had his engagement at Fire Island, and was going there. The most he would do to accommodate us was to set us down at Kilper's. Kilper, he said, kept a sportsman's tavern at the end of Jamaica Bay.

I consulted with my wife, and we agreed that there was no better course to pursue. Our European trip was a failure even before it began, as my wife remarked. Fate had decreed that we should get no further than Kilper's, and when the captain put us ashore, and we saw Kilper himself sitting in the doorway of a tumble-down frame inn on a bare sandbank, we concluded that if the discomforts of our journey were to increase in the proportion already established, as we got further and further out into the world, it was well that our outing should terminate at Kilper's.

Kilper was not at all glad to see us. I do not think he had ever been glad to see anybody. This disinclination to sociability and hospitality was quite strongly marked, and it seemed to us that it qualified Kilper rather for a hermit than for an innkeeper, whose profession is generally supposed to be of a genial character. Kilper told us that his inn was not open for the season, and that he had no bed for us, and no food in the house. We believed this last statement, for from Kilper's appearance we judged that food was a secondary consideration to him, so long as he had whiskey in the house; and it was evident that there was whiskey.

The next question was: how to get back to New York? At first Kilper seemed to think that the only way was for us to walk; and he did not know how far it was, or what road to take. At last he remembered, when my wife took him in hand, that he had a brother who lived on the inland side of Jamaica Bay, and who also kept an inn. This inn differed from the inn of the first Kilper in being open all the year around. If we wanted to row ourselves across the bay, in one of the boats of the first Kilper, of which he had a number, the second Kilper would probably let us have a team to take us to the railroad. It would cost us one dollar to hire a boat, and we might leave the boat with the fraternal Kilper.

We accepted this offer, for the reason that no other course was open to us; and my wife thought that it would be delightful to anchor our boat in the shadow of the first clump of trees we came to, and make our luncheon on sandwiches and lemonade. We were ravenously hungry, having had no breakfast, and having been in the open air since seven o'clock. It was now past one. Perhaps, my wife further suggested, we might find a cooling spring near the shore, with the

waters of which we might make our lemonade. I had
not much faith in the opportune appearance of the
cooling spring, and so I prevailed upon Kilper to lend
us a stone jug of water.

Kilper gave us elaborate directions as to the course
to pursue to reach the abode of the other Kilper, and
then he took us down to the shore, and established us
in a large flat-bottomed boat, such as is used by
sportsmen.

When we shoved off, and put out into the water, we
found ourselves somewhat puzzled, for Kilper had
spoken of our crossing the bay; but we could see no
bay. There was a multitude of islands, and there was
water between them; but that, according to the school
geographies, does not constitute a bay. If the islands
had been in the middle of an ocean, they would have
been an archipelago; but as they were, so to speak, inland, we felt at a loss where to consider ourselves, in
a geographical sense.

Kilper's directions, however, were specific, and as I
pulled steadily along we looked for a convenient place
to land, for we were hungry.

It was necessary, in following the directions we
had received, to row nearly half way around one of
the larger islands, which did not seem to be so much
an island as a sort of thick swamp, with clumps of
brush here and there. Between two of these clumps
my wife noticed a peculiar opening into the marsh, as
if a small canal had been made through the marsh-
grass. Into this she proposed that we should turn.

"Who knows?" she said, "perhaps it may lead to

some pleasant place where we may sit down and eat a comfortable meal."

I turned the boat in, although I had not much faith in my wife's theory; but after rowing a hundred yards or so we came upon a real island, covered with grass and bushes. We had not seen it from outside, because the tall reeds and brush hid it from sight. We landed at once, and, after pulling the boat safely up on the beach, we walked through the bushes toward the interior of the island, carrying our satchels with us.

In a short time we came in sight of a small hut or cabin, evidently very recently built; but apparently empty. We peeped in at the door, which was open, and saw that it was composed of two rooms, a kitchen and a sleeping room, and that it was inhabited, for there was a bunk in which the bed was made up, and there was a fire in the kitchen stove. It all looked very neat and cosey, and we decided that we would search at once for the owners, and ask them if they could not give us something to eat and drink more satisfying than sandwiches and lemonade in their original principles. My wife was greatly delighted at the prospect. "Perhaps," she said, "they will even take us to board. Since our European trip must be given up, we might as well be here, where it is cool and pretty; and you would have a good chance to finish your novel."

I had been writing a novel for some years; but I had never got it near enough to completion to send to a publisher; and I had understood that publishers had a prejudice against accepting an unfinished work.

As my wife was speaking we turned the corner of the hut, and came upon a man busily at work upon a boat. He was at work; but he was not building the boat, which was already built, nor repairing her. In fact, he seemed to be trying to put her in need of repairs. He had a wooden mallet, with which he was beating the paint off her, and hammering dents in her sides. When he saw us, he appeared a good deal startled, and somewhat angrily inquired what we wanted.

"We want," I said in a dignified manner, "to know if we can have some luncheon at your house."

"Well, you can't," he replied, "now you know."

"But we have brought our luncheon with us," I returned, falling back upon the lemonade and sandwiches.

"Well," he said, "take it away with you," and he turned his back on us and went on hammering at the boat.

Discouraged by this rude reception of a perfectly proper inquiry, we moved away; but before we had got very far my wife stopped me.

"Don't you know who he is?" she asked.

"No," I replied, severely, "I do not know who he is, and, from what I have seen of his manners, I shall not cultivate his acquaintance."

"Why," she went on, without noticing my tone, "I remember him perfectly. He is Captain James Pringleberry, the Great International Sea Voyager, who left Albany last month to cross the Atlantic in a boat fourteen feet long. He has shaved off his big beard, and he is not in sailor clothes; but I know it is he. Don't you recollect how we went down to see him off, and how they gave him a celebration on the wharf?"

As soon as my wife said this a great flood of light burst upon me, and I went back promptly to the man.

"You are Pringleberry," I said, "and I am going to New York to expose you."

He turned as white as a ghost and looked thoroughly discomfited.

"Don't be too hard on me, Captain," he began; and, seeing perhaps that I looked pleased at being called Captain, he went on hurriedly:

"I will tell you the whole truth and throw myself upon your mercy. This whole affair is got up for exhibition purposes. I left Albany in this little boat, sailed around here, and put in. I shall stay here the whole summer hammering paint off my boat, and washing her with sulphuric acid and walnut juice to make her look weather-beaten. Arrangements have been made with my brother, who is captain of a brig bound for Oporto, to have me reported spoken in mid-ocean. At the time when I ought to arrive on the other side, a man answering to my description, with a boat like this, will sail into Southampton from a hiding-place near by, and will exhibit himself through England. Then a return trip will be arranged in the same way, and I will sail out from here in my weather-beaten boat, and enter New York as a hero. Then I shall show myself all through the country, and lecture on the dangers of the trip."

"Then you do not really cross the ocean?" I inquired.

"I wouldn't go on them waves, sir," he replied, "for two hundred and fifty dollars a wave."

"Do you want to take us to board here for the summer?" I asked, in a suggestive manner.

Captain Pringleberry looked at me very carefully, and finally concluded that he did.

We had a good luncheon, prepared by Pringleberry, and also a good dinner; and we slept very comfortably in the hut; Pringleberry, who was something of a carpenter, having put up a bunk for himself in the kitchen. The next day he sent Kilper's brother, who, he said, "stood in" with him, to New York for our trunks, which we thought might have been left behind by the "Carnival of Venice." They had been left behind; the passenger list of the "Carnival" being small, our absence had been observed, and the steamer had waited an hour for us. In fact, she had gone down the Bay some time after we left on the "John B. Smiler," which probably accounted for our not having seen her.

We were not, however, so sorry for this mishap as we might have been. The steamship company gave us back the price of our tickets, less ten per cent, and we had a very pleasant time on the island. The mosquitoes bothered us somewhat; but we had excellent bathing and fishing. My wife found enough to occupy her in taking care of the house, or hut, and in helping me with my novel, on which I made great progress, for the place was really retired and quiet.

I gave my afternoons to my novel, and I noticed that Pringleberry was also busy with writing. He worked hard; but did not seem to cover many pages. One afternoon he came to me and said, in a deferential way:

"I judge you are a literary man."

I could not say that I was; but I had not moral courage enough to deny the imputation. Pringleberry went on:

"I am writing my lecture to be delivered on my return trip. I am not a literary man, and I find great difficulty in making it sound right. I wish you would go over it and give me the benefit of your suggestions. I am to lecture in the principal dime museums, and Mr. Dockshaw, who employs me, is very particular. He will be here shortly to see how I am getting on."

"I know Mr. Dockshaw," I said, "and I shall be happy to revise your lecture."

I soon found that Pringleberry's lecture could be improved by various grammatical corrections, and by the addition of certain imaginative details. In the end, I threw his manuscript away, and wrote a wholly new lecture for him, with which he seemed to be greatly pleased.

When Mr. Dockshaw arrived, he did not appear overjoyed at seeing me; but as soon as he had read my lecture he changed his mind.

"This is what I have been looking for," he said: "I will pay one hundred dollars for every lecture you will write like this."

As I had a great deal of time to spare from my

novel, I accepted this liberal offer, and wrote a number
of lectures for Mr. Dockshaw, for which he paid
promptly. I went further than this, and invented a
number of freaks to fit lectures which I had in my
mind. Some of my new freaks were great popular
successes. The Red-Headed Albino and the Mil-
dewed Hairy Man from the Mines of Siberia were
among my great successes.

Thus the summer passed away. When we went
back to Albany, at the expiration of my leave of
absence, I presented myself to the Secretary of the Insurance Company, who asked me, very kindly, if I
had had a pleasant trip to Europe. I answered that
I had had a pleasant trip. He remarked that England
was a great country.

I replied that it was a great country, and offered
him my resignation, explaining that I had found a
line of business which paid me better than being a
clerk in an insurance office. He accepted my resignation with much politeness, and expressed the hope that
I would be more successful in my new business than
I had been as a clerk in an insurance office.

My novel, which I had completed on the island, was
published in the spring. It was accepted by the first
publisher to whom I sent it. It was received, as I
may say without immodesty, with a whirlwind of
approbation. The press notices, of which there were
many, spoke of it as a wonderfully witty and sharply
satirical travesty on the old-fashioned conventional
fiction, and praised it highly as a delicately humorous
burlesque, the irony of which excused its extravagant

caricature of exaggerated sentiment. It was hailed as a masterpiece of caustic humor.

This was very gratifying, especially as the book sold so well that it enabled us to buy a nice house in the suburbs of Albany. Only one thing clouded our pleasure in these expressions of favorable opinion. The book, when I wrote it, was intended to be serious. My wife and I had both been deeply moved by the pathetic passages, when we read them over.

But then, as my wife said, perhaps it was as well that it was misunderstood, after all. "For you see," she said, "if you were a serious writer, you would have to write a better book next time, whereas a funny man can do anything he wants to. I should call it a very successful failure."

THE LIAR

BY HENRY JAMES

It is one of the obvious points of biographical criticism that Henry James, the novelist (born in New York, April 15, 1843), is as truly a scientific psychologist as is his brother, Professor William James, the eminent student of the human mind who holds a chair at Harvard University. In "The Liar" we have a searching study of congenital mendacity, the painter's art of portraiture, more penetrating than X-ray photography, being employed by the author to supply a skiagraph of the soul.

THE LIAR

BY HENRY JAMES

THE train was half an hour late and the drive
from the station longer than he had supposed, so that when he reached the house
its inmates had dispersed to dress for dinner and he
was conducted straight to his room. The curtains
were drawn in this asylum, the candles were lighted,
the fire was bright, and when the servant had quickly
put out his clothes the comfortable little place became
suggestive—seemed to promise a pleasant house, a
various party, talks, acquaintances, affinities, to say
nothing of very good cheer. He was too occupied with
his profession to pay many country visits, but he had
heard people who had more time for them speak of
establishments where "they do you very well." He
foresaw that the proprietors of Stayes would do him
very well. In his bedroom at a country house he always looked first at the books on the shelf and the
prints on the walls; he considered that these things
gave a sort of measure of the culture and even of the
character of his hosts. Though he had but little time
to devote to them on this occasion, a cursory inspection assured him that if the literature, as usual, was
mainly American and humorous, the art consisted
neither of the water-color studies of the children nor

of "goody" engravings. The walls were adorned with old-fashioned lithographs, principally portraits of country gentlemen with high collars and riding gloves: this suggested—and it was encouraging—that the tradition of portraiture was held in esteem. There was the customary novel of Mr. Le Fanu, for the bedside; the ideal reading in a country house for the hours after midnight. Oliver Lyon could scarcely forbear beginning it while he buttoned his shirt.

Perhaps that is why he not only found every one assembled in the hall when he went down, but perceived from the way the move to dinner was instantly made that they had been waiting for him. There was no delay, to introduce him to a lady, for he went out in a group of unmatched men, without this appendage. The men, straggling behind, sidled and edged as usual at the door of the dining-room, and the *dénouement* of this little comedy was that he came to his place last of all. This made him think that he was in a sufficiently distinguished company, for if he had been humiliated (which he was not) he could not have consoled himself with the reflection that such a fate was natural to an obscure, struggling young artist. He could no longer think of himself as very young, alas, and if his position was not so brilliant as it ought to be he could no longer justify it by calling it a struggle. He was something of a celebrity and he was apparently in a society of celebrities. This idea added to the curiosity with which he looked up and down the long table as he settled himself in his place.

It was a numerous party—five and twenty people;

rather an odd occasion to have proposed to him, as he thought. He would not be surrounded by the quiet that ministers to good work; however, it had never interfered with his work to see the spectacle of human life before him in the intervals. And though he did not know it, it was never quiet at Stayes. When he was working well he found himself in that happy state —the happiest of all for an artist—in which things in general contribute to the particular idea and fall in with it, help it on and justify it, so that he feels for the hour as if nothing in the world can happen to him, even if it come in the guise of disaster or suffering, that will not be an enchancement of his subject. More-over there was an exhilaration (he had felt it before) in the rapid change of scene—the jump, in the dusk of the afternoon, from foggy London and his familiar studio to a centre of festivity in the middle of Hert-fordshire and a drama half acted, a drama of pretty women and noted men and wonderful orchids in silver jars. He observed as a not unimportant fact that one of the pretty women was beside him: a gentleman sat on his other hand. But he went into his neighbors little as yet: he was busy looking out for Sir David, whom he had never seen and about whom he natu-rally was curious.

Evidently, however, Sir David was not at dinner, a circumstance sufficiently explained by the other cir-cumstance which constituted our friend's principal knowledge of him—his being ninety years of age. Oliver Lyon had looked forward with great pleasure to the chance of painting a nonagenarian, and though the old man's absence from table was something of a disappointment (it was an opportunity the less to observe him before going to work), it seemed a sign that he was rather a sacred and perhaps therefore an impressive relic. Lyon looked at his son with the greater interest—wondered whether the glazed bloom of his cheek had been transmitted from Sir David. That would be jolly to paint, in the old man—the withered ruddiness of a winter apple, especially if the eye were still alive and the white hair carried out the frosty look. Arthur Ashmore's hair had a midsummer glow, but Lyon was glad his commission had been to delineate the father rather than the son, in spite of his never having seen the one and of the other being seated there before him now in the happy expansion of liberal hospitality.

Arthur Ashmore was a fresh-colored, thick-necked English gentleman, but he was just not a subject; he might have been a farmer and he might have been a banker: you could scarcely paint him in characters. His wife did not make up the amount; she was a large, bright, negative woman, who had the same air as her husband of being somehow tremendously new: a sort of appearance of fresh varnish (Lyon could scarcely tell whether it came from her complexion or from her clothes), so that one felt she ought to sit in a gilt frame, suggesting reference to a catalogue or a price-list. It was as if she were already rather a bad though expensive portrait, knocked off by an eminent hand, and Lyon had no wish to copy that work. The pretty woman on his right was engaged with her

neighbor, and the gentleman on his other side looked
shrinking and scared, so that he had time to lose himself in his favorite diversion of watching face after
face. This amusement gave him the greatest pleasure
he knew, and he often thought it a mercy that the
human mask did interest him and that it was not less
vivid than it was (sometimes it ran its success in this
line very close), since he was to make his living by
reproducing it. Even if Arthur Ashmore would not
be inspiring to paint (a certain anxiety rose in him
lest if he should make a hit with her father-in-law Mrs.
Arthur should take it into her head that he had now
proved himself worthy to *aborder* her husband) ; even
if he had looked a little less like a page (fine as to
print and margin) without punctuation, he would still
be a refreshing, iridescent surface. But the gentleman
four persons off—what was he? Would he be a subject, or was his face only the legible door-plate of his
identity, burnished with punctual washing and shaving
—the least thing that was decent that you would know
him by? This face arrested Oliver Lyon : it struck him
at first as very handsome. The gentleman might still
be called young, and his features were regular : he had
a plentiful, fair mustache that curled up at the ends, a
brilliant, gallant, almost adventurous air, and a big
shining breastpin in the midde of his shirt. He appeared a fine satisfied soul, and Lyon perceived that
wherever he rested his friendly eye there fell an influence as pleasant as the September sun—as if he could
make grapes and pears or even human affection ripen
by looking at them. What was odd in him was a

certain mixture of the correct and the extravagant: as if he were an adventurer imitating a gentleman with rare perfection or a gentleman who had taken a fancy to go about with hidden arms. He might have been a dethroned prince or the war correspondent of a newspaper: he represented both enterprise and tradition, good manners and bad taste. Lyon at length fell into conversation with the lady beside him—they dispensed, as he had had to dispense at dinner parties before, with an introduction—by asking who this personage might be.

"Oh, he's Colonel Capadose, don't you know?" Lyon didn't know and he asked for further information. His neighbor had a sociable manner and evidently was accustomed to quick transitions; she turned from her other interlocutor with a methodical air, as a good cook lifts the cover of the next saucepan. "He has been a great deal in India—isn't he rather celebrated?" she inquired. Lyon confessed he had never heard of him, and she went on, "Well, perhaps he isn't; but he says he is, and if you think it, that's just the same, isn't it?"

"If *you* think it?"

"I mean if he thinks it—that's just as good, I suppose."

"Do you mean that he says that which is not?"

"Oh dear, no—because I never know. He is exceedingly clever and amusing—quite the cleverest person in the house, unless indeed you are more so. But that I can't tell yet, can I? I only know about the people I know; I think that's celebrity enough!"

"Enough for them?"

"Oh, I see you're clever. Enough for me! But I have heard of you," the lady went on. "I know your pictures; I admire them. But I don't think you look like them."

"They are mostly portraits," Lyon said; "and what I usually try for is not my own resemblance."

"I see what you mean. But they have much more color. And now you are going to do some one here?"

"I have been invited to do Sir David. I'm rather disappointed at not seeing him this evening."

"Oh, he goes to bed at some unnatural hour—eight o'clock or something of that sort. You know he's rather an old mummy."

"An old mummy?" Oliver Lyon repeated.

"I mean he wears half a dozen waistcoats, and that sort of thing. He's always cold."

"I have never seen him and never seen any portrait or photograph of him," Lyon said. "I'm surprised at his never having had anything done—at their waiting all these years."

"Ah, that's because he was afraid, you know; it was a kind of superstition. He was sure that if anything were done he would die directly afterward. He has only consented to-day."

"He's ready to die then?"

"Oh, now he's so old he doesn't care."

"Well, I hope I shan't kill him," said Lyon. "It was rather unnatural in his son to send for me."

"Oh, they have nothing to gain—everything is theirs already!" his companion rejoined, as if she took this

speech quite literally. Her talkativeness was system-
atic—she fraternized as seriously as she might have
played whist. "They do as they like—they fill the
house with people—they have *carte blanche.*"

"I see—but there's still the title."

"Yes, but what is it?"

Our artist broke into laughter at this, whereat his
companion stared. Before he had recovered himself
she was scouring the plain with her other neighbor.
The gentleman on his left at last risked an observation, and they had some fragmentary talk. This personage played his part with difficulty: he uttered a
remark as a lady fires a pistol, looking the other way.
To catch the ball Lyon had to bend his ear, and this
movement led to his observing a handsome creature
who was seated on the same side, beyond his interlocutor. Her profile was presented to him and at first
he was only struck with its beauty; then it produced
an impression still more agreeable—a sense of un-
dimmed remembrance and intimate association. He
had not recognized her on the instant only because he
had so little expected to see her there; he had not
seen her anywhere for so long, and no news of her
ever came to him. She was often in his thoughts,
but she had passed out of his life. He thought of
her twice a week; that may be called often in relation
to a person one has not seen for twelve years. The
moment after he recognized her he felt how true it was
that it was only she who could look like that: of the
most charming head in the world (and this lady had
it) there could never be a replica. She was leaning

forward a little; she remained in profile, apparently listening to some one on the other side of her. She was listening, but she was also looking, and after a moment Lyon followed the direction of her eyes. They rested upon the gentleman who had been described to him as Colonel Capadose—rested, as it appeared to him, with a kind of habitual, visible complacency. This was not strange, for the Colonel was unmistakably formed to attract the sympathetic gaze of woman; but Lyon was slightly disappointed that she could let *him* look at her so long without giving him a glance. There was nothing between them to-day and he had no rights, but she must have known he was coming (it was of course not such a tremendous event, but she could not have been staying in the house without hearing of it), and it was not natural that that should absolutely fail to affect her.

She was looking at Colonel Capadose as if she were in love with him—a queer accident for the proudest, most reserved of women. But doubtless it was all right, if her husband liked it or didn't notice it: he had heard indefinitely, years before, that she was married, and he took for granted (as he had not heard that she had become a widow) the presence of the happy man on whom she had conferred what she had refused to *him,* the poor art student at Munich. Colonel Capadose appeared to be aware of nothing, and this circumstance, incongruously enough, rather irritated Lyon than gratified him. Suddenly the lady turned her head, showing her full face to our hero. He was so prepared with a greeting that he instantly

smiled, as a shaken jug overflows; but she gave him
no response, turned away again and sank back in her
chair. All that her face said in that instant was, "You
see I'm as handsome as ever." To which he mentally
subjoined, "Yes, and as much good it does me!" He
asked the young man beside him if he knew who that
beautiful being was—the fifth person beyond him.
The young man leaned forward, considered, and then
said, "I think she's Mrs. Capadose."

"Do you mean his wife—that fellow?" And Lyon
indicated the subject of the information given him by
his other neighbor.

"Oh, is he Mr. Capadose?" said the young man, who
appeared very vague. He admitted his vagueness and
explained it by saying that there were so many people
and he had come only the day before. What was definite to Lyon was that Mrs. Capadose was in love with
her husband; so that he wished more than ever that he
had married her.

"She's very faithful," he found himself saying
three minutes later to the lady on his right. He added
that he meant Mrs. Capadose.

"Ah, you know her then?"

"I knew her once upon a time—when I was living
abroad."

"Why then were you asking me about her husband?"

"Precisely for that reason. She married after that
—I didn't even know her present name."

"How then do you know it now?"

"This gentleman has just told me—he appears to
know."

"I didn't know he knew anything," said the lady, glancing forward.

"I don't think he knows anything but that."

"Then you have found out for yourself that she is faithful. What do you mean by that?"

"Ah, you mustn't question me—I want to question you," Lyon said. "How do you all like her here?"

"You ask too much! I can only speak for myself. I think she's hard."

"That's only because she's honest and straightforward."

"Do you mean I like people in proportion as they deceive?"

"I think we all do, so long as we don't find them out," Lyon said. "And then there's something in her face—a sort of Roman type, in spite of her having such an English eye. In fact, she's English down to the ground; but her complexion, her low forehead and that beautiful close little wave in her dark hair makes her look like a glorified *contadina*."

"Yes, and she always sticks pins and daggers into her head, to increase that effect. I must say I like her husband better: he is so clever."

"Well, when I knew her there was no comparison that could injure her. She was altogether the most delightful thing in Munich."

"In Munich?"

"Her people lived there; they were not rich—in pursuit of economy, in fact, and Munich was very cheap. Her father was the younger son of some noble house; he had married a second time and had a lot of little mouths to feed. She was the child of the first wife and she didn't like her stepmother, but she was charming to her little brothers and sisters. I once made a sketch of her as Werther's Charlotte, cutting bread and butter while they clustered all round her. All the artists in the place were in love with her, but she wouldn't look at 'the likes' of us. She was too proud—I grant you that; but she wasn't stuck up nor young ladyish; she was simple and frank and kind about it. She used to remind me of Thackeray's Ethel Newcome. She told me she must marry well: it was the one thing she could do for her family. I suppose you would say that she *has* married well."

"She told *you?*" smiled Lyon's neighbor.

"Oh, of course I proposed to her, too. But she evidently thinks so herself!" he added.

When the ladies left the table the host as usual bade the gentlemen draw together, so that Lyon found himself opposite to Colonel Capadose. The conversation was mainly about the "run," for it had apparently been a great day in the hunting field. Most of the gentlemen communicated their adventures and opinions, but Colonel Capadose's pleasant voice was the most audible in the chorus. It was a bright and fresh but masculine organ, just such a voice as, to Lyon's sense, such a "fine man" ought to have had. It appeared from his remarks that he was a very straight rider, which was also very much what Lyon would have expected. Not that he swaggered, for his allusions were very quietly and casually made; but they were all too dangerous experiments and close

shaves. Lyon perceived after a little that the attention paid by the company to the Colonel's remarks was
not in direct relation to the interest they seemed to
offer; the result of which was that the speaker, who
noticed that *he* at least was listening, began to treat
him as his particular auditor and to fix his eyes on
him as he talked. Lyon had nothing to do but to look
sympathetic and assent—Colonel Capadose appeared to
take so much sympathy and assent for granted. A
neighboring squire had had an accident; he had come
a cropper in an awkward place—just at the finish—
with consequences that looked grave. He had struck
his head; he remained insensible, up to the last ac-
counts: there had evidently been concussion of the
brain. There was some exchange of views as to his
recovery—how soon it would take place or whether it
would take place at all; which led the Colonel to confide to our artist across the table that *he* shouldn't despair of a fellow even if he didn't come round for
weeks—for weeks and weeks and weeks—for months,
almost for years. He leaned forward; Lyon leaned
forward to listen, and Colonel Capadose mentioned
that he knew from personal experience that there was
really no limit to the time one might lie unconscious
without being any the worse for it. It had happened
to him in Ireland years before; he had been pitched
out of a dogcart, had turned a sheer somersault and
landed on his head. They thought he was dead; but
he wasn't; they carried him first to the nearest cabin,
where he lay for some days with the pigs, and then to
an inn in a neighboring town—it was a near thing

they didn't put him under ground. He had been completely insensible—without a ray of recognition of any human thing—for three whole months; had not a glimmer of consciousness of any blessed thing.　It was touch and go to that degree that they couldn't come near him, they couldn't feed him, they could scarcely look at him.　Then one day he had opened his eyes—as fit as a flea!

"I give you my honor it had done me good—it rested my brain."　He appeared to intimate that with an intelligence so active as his these periods of repose were providential.　Lyon thought his story very striking, but he wanted to ask him whether he had not shammed a little—not in relating it, but in keeping so quiet.　He hesitated, however, in time to imply a doubt—he was so impressed with the tone in which Colonel Capadose said that it was the turn of a hair that they hadn't buried him alive.　That had happened to a friend of his in India—a fellow who was supposed to have died of jungle fever—they clapped him into a coffin.　He was going on to recite the further fate of this unfortunate gentleman when Mr. Ashmore made a move and every one got up to adjourn to the drawing-room.

Lyon noticed that by this time no one was heeding what his new friend said to him.　They came round on either side of the table and met while the gentlemen dawdled before going out.

"And do you mean that your friend was literally buried alive?" asked Lyon, in some suspense.

Colonel Capadose looked at him a moment, as if he

had already lost the thread of the conversation. Then his face brightened—and when it brightened it was doubly handsome. "Upon my soul, he was chucked into the ground!"

"And was he left there?"

"He was left there till I came and hauled him out."

"*You* came?"

"I dreamed about him—it's the most extraordinary story; I heard him calling to me in the night. I took upon myself to dig him up. You know there are people in India—a kind of beastly race, the ghouls—who violate graves. I had a sort of presentiment that they would get at him first. I rode straight, I can tell you; and, by Jove, a couple of them had just broken ground! Crack—crack, from a couple of barrels, and they showed me their heels, as you may believe. Would you credit that I took him out myself? The air brought him to and he was none the worse. He has got his pension—he came home the other day; he would do anything for me."

"He called to you in the night?" said Lyon, much startled.

"That's the interesting point. Now *what was it?* It wasn't his ghost, because he wasn't dead. It wasn't himself, because he couldn't. It was something or other! You see, India's a strange country—there's an element of the mysterious: the air is full of things you can't explain."

They passed out of the dining-room, and Colonel Capadose, who went among the first, was separated from Lyon; but a minute later, before they reached the drawing-room, he joined him again. "Ashmore tells me who you are. Of course I have often heard of you—I'm very glad to make your acquaintance; my wife used to know you."

"I'm glad she remembers me. I recognized her at dinner and I was afraid she didn't."

"Ah, I daresay she was ashamed," said the Colonel, with indulgent humor.

"Ashamed of me?" Lyon replied, in the same key.

"Wasn't there something about a picture? Yes; you painted her portrait."

"Many times," said the artist; "and she may very well have been ashamed of what I made of her."

"Well, I wasn't, my dear sir; it was the sight of that picture, which you were so good as to present to her, that made me first fall in love with her."

"Do you mean that one with the children—cutting bread and butter?"

"Bread and butter? Bless me, no—vine leaves and a leopard skin—a kind of Bacchante."

"Ah, yes," said Lyon; "I remember. It was the first decent portrait I painted. I should be curious to see it to-day."

"Don't ask her to show it to you—she'll be mortified!" the Colonel exclaimed.

"Mortified?"

"We parted with it—in the most disinterested manner," he laughed. "An old friend of my wife's—her family had known him intimately when they lived in Germany—took the most extraordinary fancy to it: the Grand Duke of Silberstadt-Schreckenstein, don't you know? He came out to Bombay while we were there and he spotted your picture (you know he's one of the greatest collectors in Europe), and made such eyes at it that, upon my word—it happened to be his birthday—she told him he might have it, to get rid of him. He was perfectly enchanted—but we miss the picture."

"It is very good of you," Lyon said. "If it's in a great collection—a work of my incompetent youth—I am infinitely honored."

"Oh, he has got it in one of his castles; I don't know which—you know he has so many. He sent us, before he left India—to return the compliment—a magnificent old vase."

"That was more than the thing was worth," Lyon remarked.

Colonel Capadose gave no heed to this observation; he seemed to be thinking of something. After a moment he said, "If you'll come and see us in town she'll show you the vase." And as they passed into the drawing-room he gave the artist a friendly propulsion. "Go and speak to her; there she is—she'll be delighted."

Oliver Lyon took but a few steps into the wide saloon; he stood there a moment looking at the bright composition of the lamplit group of fair women, the single figures, the great setting of white and gold, the panels of old damask, in the centre of each of which was a single celebrated picture. There was a subdued lustre in the scene; and an air as of the shining trains of dresses tumbled over the carpet. At the fur-

thest end of the room sat Mrs. Capadose, rather iso-
lated; she was on a small sofa, with an empty place
beside her.　Lyon could not flatter himself she had
been keeping it for him; her failure to respond to his
recognition at table contradicted that, but he felt an
extreme desire to go and occupy it.　Moreover, he
had her husband's sanction; so he crossed the room,
stepping over the tails of gowns, and stood before his
old friend.

"I hope you don't mean to repudiate me," he said.

She looked up at him with an expression of unal-
loyed pleasure.　"I am so glad to see you.　I was delighted when I heard you were coming."

"I tried to get a smile from you at dinner—but I
couldn't."

"I didn't see—I didn't understand.　Besides, I hate
smirking and telegraphing.　Also I'm very shy—you
won't have forgotten that.　Now we can communicate
comfortably."　And she made a better place for him
on the little sofa.　He sat down and they had a talk
that he enjoyed, while the reason for which he used
to like her so came back to him, as well as a good
deal of the very same old liking.　She was still the
least spoiled beauty he had ever seen, with an absence
of coquetry or any insinuating art that seemed almost
like an omitted faculty; there were moments when she
struck her interlocutor as some fine creature from an
asylum—a surprising deaf mute or one of the opera-
tive blind.　Her noble pagan head gave her privileges
that she neglected, and when people were admiring her
brow she was wondering whether there were a good

fire in her bedroom. She was simple, kind and good;
inexpressive, but not inhuman or stupid. Now and
again she dropped something that had a sifted, selected air—the sound of an impression at first hand.
She had no imagination, but she had added up her
feelings, some of her reflections, about life. Lyon
talked of the old days in Munich, reminded her of
incidents, pleasures and pains, asked her about her
father and the others; and she told him in return that
she was so impressed with his own fame, his brilliant
position in the world, that she had not felt very sure
he would speak to her or that his little sign at table
was meant for her. This was plainly a perfectly truthful speech—she was incapable of any other—and he
was affected by such humility on the part of a woman
whose grand line was unique. Her father was dead;
one of her brothers was in the navy and the other on
a ranch in America; two of her sisters were married
and the youngest was just coming out and very pretty.
She didn't mention her stepmother. She asked him
about his own personal history, and he said that the
principal thing that had happened to him was that he
had never married.

"Oh, you ought to," she answered. "It's the best
thing."

"I like that—from you!" he returned.

"Why not from me? I am very happy."

"That's just why I can't be. It's cruel of you to
praise your state. But I have had the pleasure of
making the acquaintance of your husband. We had a
good bit of talk in the other room."

"You must know him better—you must know him really well," said Mrs. Capadose.

"I am sure that the further you go the more you find. But he makes a fine show, too."

She rested her good gray eyes on Lyon. "Don't you think he's handsome?"

"Handsome and clever and entertaining. You see I'm generous."

"Yes; you must know him well," Mrs. Capadose repeated.

"He has seen a great deal of life," said her companion.

"Yes, we have been in so many places. You must see my little girl. She's nine years old—she's too beautiful."

"You must bring her to my studio some day—I should like to paint her."

"Ah, don't speak of that," said Mrs. Capadose. "It reminds me of something so distressing."

"I hope you don't mean when *you* used to sit to me—though that may well have bored you."

"It's not what you did—it's what we have done. It's a confession I must make—it's a weight on my mind! I mean about that beautiful picture you gave me—it used to be so much admired. When you come to see me in London (I count on your doing that very soon) I shall see you looking all round. I can't tell you I keep it in my own room because I love it so, for the simple reason—" And she paused a moment.

"Because you can't tell wicked lies," said Lyon.

"No, I can't. So before you ask for it—"

"Oh, I know you parted with it—the blow has already fallen," Lyon interrupted.

"Ah, then you have heard? I was sure you would! But do you know what we got for it? Two hundred pounds."

"You might have got much more," said Lyon, smiling.

"That seemed a great deal at the time. We were in want of the money—it was a good while ago, when we first married. Our means were very small then, but fortunately that has changed rather for the better. We had the chance; it really seemed a big sum, and I am afraid we jumped at it. My husband had expectations which have partly come into effect, so that now we do well enough. But meanwhile the picture went."

"Fortunately the original remained. But do you mean that two hundred was the value of the vase?" Lyon asked.

"Of the vase?"

"The beautiful old Indian vase—the Grand Duke's offering."

"The Grand Duke?"

"What's his name?—Silberstadt-Schreckenstein. Your husband mentioned the transaction."

"Oh, my husband," said Mrs. Capadose; and Lyon saw that she colored a little.

Not to add to her embarrassment, but to clear up the ambiguity, which he perceived the next moment he had better have left alone, he went on: "He tells me it's now in his collection."

"In the Grand Duke's? Ah, you know its reputation? I believe it contains treasures." She was bewildered, but she recovered herself, and Lyon made the mental reflection that for some reason which would seem good when he knew it the husband and the wife had prepared different versions of the same incident. It was true that he did not exactly see Everina Brant preparing a version; that was not her line of old, and indeed it was not in her eyes to-day. At any rate, they both had the matter too much on their conscience. He changed the subject, said Mrs. Capadose must really bring the little girl. He sat with her some time longer and thought—perhaps it was only a fancy—that she was rather absent, as if she were annoyed at their having been even for a moment at cross-purposes. This did not prevent him from saying to her at the last, just as the ladies began to gather themselves together to go to bed: "You seem much impressed, from what you say, with my renown and my prosperity, and you are so good as greatly to exaggerate them. Would you have married me if you had known that I was destined to success?"

"I did know it."

"Well, I didn't."

"You were too modest."

"You didn't think so when I proposed to you."

"Well, if I had married you I couldn't have married *him*—and he's so nice," Mrs. Capadose said. Lyon knew she thought it—he had learned that at dinner—but it vexed him a little to hear her say it. The gentleman designated by the pronoun came up, amid the prolonged handshaking for good-night, and Mrs.

Capadose remarked to her husband as she turned away,
"He wants to paint Amy."

"Ah, she's a charming child, a most interesting little creature," the Colonel said to Lyon. "She does
the most remarkable things."

Mrs. Capadose stopped, in the rustling procession
that followed the hostess out of the room. "Don't tell
him, please don't," she said.

"Don't tell him what?"

"Why, what she does. Let him find out for himself." And she passed on.

"She thinks I swagger about the child—that I bore
people," said the Colonel. "I hope you smoke." He
appeared ten minutes later in the smoking-room, in a
brilliant equipment, a suit of crimson foulard covered
with little white spots. He gratified Lyon's eye, made
him feel that the modern age has its splendor too and
its opportunities for costume. If his wife was an an-
tique, he was a fine specimen of the period of color: he
might have passed for a Venetian of the sixteenth cen-
tury. They were a remarkable couple, Lyon thought,
and as he looked at the Colonel standing in bright
erectness before the chimney-piece while he emitted
great smoke-puffs, he did not wonder that Everina
could not regret she had not married *him*. All the
gentlemen collected at Stayes were not smokers, and
some of them had gone to bed. Colonel Capadose remarked that there probably would be a smallish muster, they had had such a hard day's work. That was
the worst of a hunting-house—the men were so sleepy
after dinner; it was devilish stupid for the ladies, even

for those who hunted themselves—for women were so
extraordinary, they never showed it. But most fellows revived under the stimulating influences of the
smoking-room, and some of them, in this confidence,
would turn up yet. Some of the grounds of their confidence—not all of them—might have been seen in a
cluster of glasses and bottles on a table near the fire,
which made the great salver and its contents twinkle
sociably. The others lurked as yet in various improper
corners of the minds of the most loquacious. Lyon
was alone with Colonel Capadose for some moments
before their companions, in varied eccentricities of uni-
form, straggled in, and he perceived that this wonderful man had but little loss of vital tissue to repair.

They talked about the house, Lyon having noticed
an oddity of construction in the smoking-room; and
the Colonel explained that it consisted of two distinct
parts, one of which was of very great antiquity. They
were two complete houses in short, the old one and
the new, each of great extent and each very fine in its
way. The two formed together an enormous struc-
ture—Lyon must make a point of going all over it.
The modern portion had been erected by the old man
when he bought the property; oh, yes, he had bought
it, forty years before—it hadn't been in the family:
there hadn't been any particular family for it to be
in. He had had the good taste not to spoil the original house—he had not touched it beyond what was
just necessary for joining it on. It was very curious
indeed—a most irregular, rambling, mysterious pile,
where they every now and then discovered a walled-up

room or a secret staircase. To his mind it was essentially gloomy, however; even the modern additions, splendid as they were, failed to make it cheerful. There was some story about a skeleton having been found years before, during some repairs, under a stone slab of the floor of one of the passages; but the family were rather shy of its being talked about. The place they were in was of course in the old part, which contained, after all, some of the best rooms: he had an idea it had been the primitive kitchen, half modernized at some intermediate period.

"My room is in the old part, too, then—I'm very glad," Lyon said. "It's very comfortable and contains all the latest conveniences, but I observed the depth of the recess of the door and the evident antiquity of the corridor and staircase—the first short one—after I came out. That paneled corridor is admirable; it looks as if it stretched away, in its brown dimness (the lamps didn't seem to me to make much impression on it), for half a mile."

"Oh, don't go to the end of it!" exclaimed the Colonel, smiling.

"Does it lead to the haunted room?" Lyon asked.

His companion looked at him a moment. "Ah, you know about that?"

"No, I don't speak from knowledge, only from hope. I have never had any luck—I have never stayed in a dangerous house. The places I go to are always as safe as Charing Cross. I want to see—whether there is, the regular thing. *Is* there a ghost here?"

"Of course there is—a rattling good one."

"And have you seen him?"

"Oh, don't ask me what *I've* seen—I should tax your credulity. I don't like to talk of these things. But there are two or three as bad—that is, as good! —rooms as you'll find anywhere."

"Do you mean in my corridor?" Lyon asked.

"I believe the worst is at the far end. But you would be ill-advised to sleep there."

"Ill-advised?"

"Until you've finished your job. You'll get letters of importance the next morning, and you'll take the 10.20."

"Do you mean I will invent a pretext for running away?"

"Unless you are braver than almost any one has ever been. They don't often put people to sleep there, but sometimes the house is so crowded that they have to. The same thing always happens—ill-concealed agitation at the breakfast table and letters of the greatest importance. Of course it's a bachelor's room, and my wife and I are at the other end of the house. But we saw the comedy three days ago—the day after we got here. A young fellow had been put there—I forget his name—the house was so full—and the usual consequence followed. Letters at breakfast — an awfully queer face—an urgent call to town—so very sorry his visit was cut short. Ashmore and his wife looked at each other, and off the poor devil went."

"Ah, that wouldn't suit me; I must paint my picture," said Lyon. "But do they mind your speaking of it? Some people who have a good ghost are very proud of it, you know."

What answer Colonel Capadose was on the point of making to this inquiry our hero was not to learn, for at that moment their host had walked into the room accompanied by three or four gentlemen. Lyon was conscious that he was partly answered by the Colonel's not going on with the subject. This, however, on the other hand, was rendered natural by the fact that one of the gentlemen appealed to him for an opinion on a point under discussion, something to do with the everlasting history of the day's run. To Lyon himself Mr. Ashmore began to talk, expressing his regret at having had so little direct conversation with him as yet. The topic that suggested itself was naturally that most closely connected with the motive of the artist's visit. Lyon remarked that it was a great disadvantage to him not to have had some preliminary acquaintance with Sir David—in most cases he found that so important. But the present sitter was so far advanced in life that there was doubtless no time to lose. "Oh, I can tell you all about him," said Mr. Ashmore; and for half an hour he told him a good deal. It was very interesting as well as very eulogistic, and Lyon could see that he was a very nice old man, to have endeared himself so to a son who was evidently not a gusher. At last he got up— he said he must go to bed if he wished to be fresh for his work in the morning. To which his host replied, "Then you must take your candle; the lights are out; I don't keep my servants up."

In a moment Lyon had his glimmering taper in hand, and as he was leaving the room (he did not disturb the others with a good-night; they were absorbed in the lemon-squeezer and the soda-water cork) he remembered other occasions on which he had made his way to bed alone through a darkened country house; such occasions had not been rare, for he was almost always the first to leave the smoking-room. If he had not stayed in houses conspicuously haunted, he had, none the less (having the artistic temperament), sometimes found the great black halls and staircases rather "creepy": there had been often a sinister effect, to his imagination, in the sound of his tread in the long passages or the way the winter moon peeped into tall windows on landings. It occurred to him that if houses without supernatural pretensions could look so wicked at night, the old corridors of Stayes would certainly give him a sensation. He didn't know whether the proprietors were sensitive; very often, as he had said to Colonel Capadose, people enjoyed the impeachment. What determined him to speak, with a certain sense of the risk, was the impression that the Colonel told queer stories. As he had his hand on the door he said to Arthur Ashmore, "I hope I shan't meet any ghosts."

"Any ghosts?"

"You ought to have some—in this fine old part."

"We do our best, but *que voulez-vous?*" said Mr. Ashmore. "I don't think they like the hot-water pipes."

"They remind them too much of their own climate?

But haven't you a haunted room—at the end of my passage?"

"Oh, there are stories—we try to keep them up."

"I should like very much to sleep there," Lyon said.

"Well, you can move there to-morrow if you like."

"Perhaps I had better wait till I have done my work."

"Very good; but you won't work there, you know. My father will sit to you in his own apartments."

"Oh, it isn't that; it's the fear of running away, like that gentleman three days ago."

"Three days ago? What gentleman?" Mr. Ashmore asked.

"The one who got urgent letters at breakfast and fled by the 10.20. Did he stand more than one night?"

"I don't know what you are talking about. There was no such gentleman—three days ago."

"Ah, so much the better," said Lyon, nodding good-night and departing. He took his course, as he remembered it, with his wavering candle, and, though he encountered a great many grewsome objects, safely reached the passage out of which his room opened. In the complete darkness it seemed to stretch away still further, but he followed it, for the curiosity of the thing, to the end. He passed several doors with the name of the room painted upon them, but he found nothing else. He was tempted to try the last door—to look into the room of evil fame; but he reflected that this would be indiscreet, since Colonel Capadose handled the brush—as a raconteur—with such freedom.   There might be a ghost and there might not; but the Colonel himself, he inclined to think, was the most mystifying figure in the house.

II

Lyon found Sir David Ashmore a capital subject and a very comfortable sitter into the bargain. Moreover he was a very agreeable old man, tremendously puckered, but not in the least dim; and he wore exactly the furred dressing-gown that Lyon would have chosen. He was proud of his age, but ashamed of his infirmities, which, however, he greatly exaggerated and which did not prevent him from sitting there as submissive as if portraiture in oils had been a branch of surgery. He demolished the legend of his having feared the operation would be fatal, giving an explanation which pleased our friend much better. He held that a gentleman should be painted but once in his life—that it was eager and fatuous to be hung up all over the place. That was good for women, who made a pretty wall-pattern; but the male face didn't lend itself to decorative repetition. The proper time for the likeness was at the last, when the whole man was there—you got the totality of his experience. Lyon could not reply that that period was not a real compendium—you had to allow so for leakage; for there had been no crack in Sir David's crystallization. He spoke of his portrait as a plain map of the country, to be consulted by his children in a case of uncertainty.

A proper map could be drawn up only when the country had been traveled. He gave Lyon his mornings till luncheon, and they talked of many things, not neglecting, as a stimulus to gossip, the people in the house.

Now that he did not "go out," as he said, he saw much less of the visitors at Stayes: people came and went whom he knew nothing about, and he liked to hear Lyon describe them. The artist sketched with a fine point and did not caricature, and it usually befell that when Sir David did not know the sons and daughters he had known the fathers and mothers. He was one of those terrible old gentlemen who are a repository of antecedents. But in the case of the Capadose family, at whom they arrived by an easy stage, his knowledge embraced two, or even three, generations. General Capadose was an old crony, and he remembered his father before him. The general was rather a smart soldier, but in private life of too speculative a turn—always sneaking into the City to put his money into some rotten thing. He married a girl who brought him something and they had half a dozen children. He scarcely knew what had become of the rest of them, except that one was in the Church and had found preferment—wasn't he Dean of Rockingham? Clement, the fellow who was at Stayes, had some military talent; he had served in the East, he had married a pretty girl. He had been at Eton with his son, and he used to come to Stayes in his holidays. Lately, coming back to England, he had turned up with his wife again; that was before he—the old

man—had been put to grass. He was a taking dog,
but he had a monstrous foible.

"A monstrous foible?" said Lyon.

"He's a thumping liar."

Lyon's brush stopped short, while he repeated, for
somehow the formula startled him, "A thumping liar?"

"You are very lucky not to have found it out."

"Well, I confess I have noticed a romantic tinge—"

"Oh, it isn't always romantic. He'll lie about the
time of day, about the name of his hatter. It appears
there are people like that."

"Well, they are precious scoundrels," Lyon declared, his voice trembling a little with the thought
of what Everina Brant had done with herself.

"Oh, not always," said the old man. "This fellow
isn't in the least a scoundrel. There is no harm in
him and no bad intention; he doesn't steal nor cheat
nor gamble nor drink; he's very kind—he sticks to
his wife, is fond of his children. He simply can't
give you a straight answer."

"Then everything he told me last night, I suppose,
was mendacious: he delivered himself of a series of
the stiffest statements. They stuck, when I tried to
swallow them, but I never thought of so simple an
explanation."

"No doubt he was in the vein," Sir David went on.
"It's a natural peculiarity—as you might limp or
stutter or be left-handed. I believe it comes and goes,
like intermittent fever. My son tells me that his
friends usually understand it and don't haul him up—
for the sake of his wife."

"Oh, his wife—his wife!" Lyon murmured, painting fast.

"I daresay she's used to it."

"Never in the world, Sir David. How can she be used to it?"

"Why, my dear sir, when a woman's fond!—And don't they mostly handle the long bow themselves? They are connoisseurs—they have a sympathy for a fellow-performer."

Lyon was silent a moment; he had no ground for denying that Mrs. Capadose was attached to her husband. But after a little he rejoined: "Oh, not this one! I knew her years ago—before her marriage; knew her well and admired her. She was as clear as a bell."

"I like her very much," Sir David said, "but I have seen her back him up."

Lyon considered Sir David for a moment, not in the light of a model. "Are you very sure?"

The old man hesitated; then he answered, smiling, "You're in love with her."

"Very likely. God knows I used to be!"

"She must help him out—she can't expose him."

"She can hold her tongue," Lyon remarked.

"Well, before you probably she will."

"That's what I am curious to see." And Lyon added, privately, "Mercy on us, what he must have made of her!" He kept this reflection to himself, for he considered that he had sufficiently betrayed his state of mind with regard to Mrs. Capadose. None the less it occupied him now immensely, the question

of how such a woman would arrange herself in such
a predicament.   He watched her with an interest
deeply quickened when he mingled with the company;
he had had his own troubles in life, but he had rarely
been so anxious about anything as he was now to see
what the loyalty of a wife and the infection of an example would have made of an absolutely truthful
mind.   Oh, he held it as immutably established that,
whatever other women might be prone to do, she, of
old, had been perfectly incapable of a deviation.   Even
if she had not been too simple to deceive she would
have been too proud; and if she had not had too much
conscience she would have had too little eagerness.
It was the last thing she would have endured or condoned—the particular thing she would not have forgiven.   Did she sit in torment while her husband
turned his somersaults, or was she now too so per-
verse that she thought it a fine thing to be striking
at the expense of one's honor?   It would have taken
a wondrous alchemy—working backward, as it were
—to produce this latter result.   Besides these two al-
ternatives (that she suffered tortures in silence and
that she was so much in love that her husband's hu-
miliating idiosyncrasy seemed to her only an added
richness—a proof of life and talent), there was still
the possibility that she had not found him out, that she
took his false pieces at his own valuation.   A little reflection rendered this hypothesis untenable; it was too
evident that the account he gave of things must
repeatedly have contradicted her own knowledge.
Within an hour or two of his meeting them Lyon had

seen her confronted with that perfectly gratuitous invention about the profit they had made off his early picture. Even then indeed she had not, so far as he could see, smarted, and—but for the present he could only contemplate the case.

Even if it had not been interfused, through his uneradicated tenderness for Mrs. Capadose, with an element of suspense, the question would still have presented itself to him as a very curious problem, for he had not painted portraits during so many years without becoming something of a psychologist. His inquiry was limited for the moment to the opportunity that the following three days might yield, as the Colonel and his wife were going on to another house. It fixed itself largely, of course, upon the Colonel too—this gentleman was such a rare anomaly. Moreover it had to go on very quickly. Lyon was too scrupulous to ask other people what they thought of the business—he was too afraid of exposing the woman he once loved. It was probable also that light would come to him from the talk of the rest of the company: the Colonel's queer habit, both as it affected his own situation and as it affected his wife, would be a familiar theme in any house in which he was in the habit of staying. Lyon had not observed in the circles in which he visited any marked abstention from comment on the singularities of their members. It interfered with his progress that the Colonel hunted all day, while he plied his brushes and chatted with Sir David; but a Sunday intervened and that partly made it up. Mrs Capadose fortunately did not hunt, and

when his work was over she was not inaccessible. He
took a couple of longish walks with her (she was fond
of that), and beguiled her at tea into a friendly nook
in the hall. Regard her as he might, he could not
make out to himself that she was consumed by a hidden shame; the sense of being married to a man whose
word had no worth was not, in her spirit, so far as he
could guess, the canker within the rose. Her mind
appeared to have nothing on it but its own placid frankness, and when he looked into her eyes (deeply, as he
occasionally permitted himself to do), they had no uncomfortable consciousness. He talked to her again
and still again of the dear old days—reminded her of
things that he had not (before this reunion) the least
idea that he remembered. Then he spoke to her of
her husband, praised his appearance, his talent for
conversation, professed to have felt a quick friendship for him and asked (with an inward audacity at
which he trembled a little) what manner of man he
was. "What manner?" said Mrs. Capadose. "Dear
me, how can one describe one's husband? I like him
very much."

"Ah, you have told me that already!" Lyon exclaimed, with exaggerated ruefulness.

"Then why do you ask me again?" She added
in a moment, as if she were so happy that she could
afford to take pity on him, "He is everything that's
good and kind. He's a soldier—and a gentleman—
and a dear! He hasn't a fault—he has great ability."

"Yes; he strikes one as having great ability. But
of course I can't think him a dear."

"I don't care what you think him!" said Mrs.
Capadose, looking, it seemed to him, as she smiled,
handsomer than he had ever seen her. She was
either deeply cynical or still more deeply impenetrable, and he had little prospect of winning from her
the intimation that he longed for—some hint that
it had come over her that after all she had better
have married a man who was not a by-word for the
most contemptible, the least heroic, of vices. Had
she not seen—had she not felt—the smile go round
when her husband executed some especially characteristic conversational caper? How could a woman of
her quality endure that day after day, year after year,
except by her quality's altering? But he would believe in the alteration only when he should have heard
her lie. He was fascinated by his problem and yet
half exasperated, and he asked himself all kinds of
questions. Did she not lie, after all, when she let
his falsehoods pass without a protest? Was not her
life a perpetual complicity, and did she not aid and
abet him by the simple fact that she was not disgusted
with him? Then again perhaps she *was* disgusted,
and it was the mere desperation of her pride that had
given her an inscrutable mask. Perhaps she protested
in private, passionately; perhaps every night, in their
own apartments, after the day's hideous performance,
she made him the most scorching scene. But if such
scenes were of no avail and he took no more trouble
to cure himself, how could she regard him, and after
so many years of marriage too, with the perfectly art-
less complacency that Lyon had surprised in her in

the course of the first day's dinner? If our friend had not been in love with her he could have taken the diverting view of the Colonel's delinquencies; but as it was they turned to the tragical in his mind, even while he had a sense that his solicitude might also have been laughed at.

The observation of these three days showed him that if Capadose was an abundant he was not a malignant liar, and that his fine faculty exercised itself mainly on subjects of small direct importance. "He is the liar platonic," he said to himself; "he is disinterested, he doesn't operate with a hope of gain or with a desire to injure. It is art for art and he is prompted by the love of beauty. He has an inner vision of what might have been, of what ought to be, and he helps on the good cause by the simple substitution of a *nuance*. He paints, as it were, and so do I!" His manifestations had a considerable variety, but a family likeness ran through them, which consisted mainly of their singular futility. It was this that made them offensive; they incumbered the field of conversation, took up valuable space, converted it into a sort of brilliant sun-shot fog. For a fib told under pressure a convenient place can usually be found, as for a person who presents himself with an author's order at the first night of a play. But the supererogatory lie is the gentleman without a voucher or a ticket who accommodates himself with a stool in the passage.

In one particular Lyon acquitted his successful rival; it had puzzled him that irrepressible as he was he had not got into a mess in the service. But he perceived

that he respected the service—that august institution
was sacred from his depredations. Moreover, though
there was a great deal of swagger in his talk, it was,
oddly enough, rarely swagger about his military ex-
ploits. He had a passion for the chase, he had followed it in far countries, and some of his finest flowers
were reminiscences of lonely danger and escape. The
more solitary the scene the bigger of course the flower.
A new acquaintance, with the Colonel, always received
the tribute of a bouquet: that generalization Lyon
very promptly made. And this extraordinary man had
inconsistencies and unexpected lapses—lapses into flat
veracity. Lyon recognized what Sir David had told
him, that his aberrations came in fits or periods—that
he would sometimes keep the truce of God for a month
at a time. The muse breathed upon him at her pleasure; she often left him alone. He would neglect the
finest openings and then set sail in the teeth of the
breeze. As a general thing he affirmed the false rather
than denied the true; yet this proportion was sometimes strikingly reversed. Very often he joined in the
laugh against himself—he admitted that he was trying it on and that a good many of his anecdotes had
an experimental character. Still he never completely
retracted nor retreated—he dived and came up in another place. Lyon divined that he was capable at intervals of defending his position with violence, but
only when it was a very bad one. Then he might
easily be dangerous—then he would hit out and become calumnious. Such occasions would test his wife's
equanimity—Lyon would have liked to see her there.

In the smoking-room and elsewhere the company, so far as it was composed of his familiars, had a hilarious protest always at hand; but among the men who had known him long his rich tone was an old story, so old that they had ceased to talk about it, and Lyon did not care, as I have said, to elicit the judgment of those who might have shared his own surprise.

The oddest thing of all was that neither surprise nor familiarity prevented the Colonel's being liked; his largest drafts on a sceptical attention passed for an overflow of life and gayety—almost of good looks. He was fond of portraying his bravery and used a very big brush, and yet he was unmistakably grave. He was a capital rider and shot, in spite of his fund of anecdote illustrating these accomplishments: in short, he was very nearly as clever and his career had been very nearly as wonderful as he pretended. His best quality, however, remained that indiscriminate sociability which took interest and credulity for granted and about which he bragged least. It made him cheap, it made him even in a manner vulgar; but it was so contagious that his listener was more or less on his side as against the probabilities. It was a private reflection of Oliver Lyon's that he not only lied, but made one feel one's self a bit of a liar, even (or especially) if one contradicted him. In the evening, at dinner and afterward, our friend watched his wife's face to see if some faint shade or spasm never passed over it. But she showed nothing, and the wonder was that when he spoke she almost always listened. That was her pride: she wished not to be even suspected of not facing the music. Lyon had none the less an importunate vision of a veiled figure coming the next day in the dusk to certain places to repair the Colonel's ravages, as the relatives of kleptomaniacs punctually call at the shops that have suffered from their pilferings.

"I must apologize, of course it wasn't true, I hope no harm is done, it is only his incorrigible—" Oh, to hear that woman's voice in that deep abasement! Lyon had no nefarious plan, no conscious wish to practice upon her shame or her loyalty; but he did say to himself that he should like to bring her round to feel that there would have been more dignity in a union with a certain other person. He even dreamed of the hour when, with a burning face, she would ask *him* not to take it up. Then he should be almost consoled—he would be magnanimous.

Lyon finished his picture and took his departure, after having worked in a glow of interest which made him believe in his success, until he found he had pleased every one, especially Mr. and Mrs. Ashmore, when he began to be sceptical. The party at any rate changed: Colonel and Mrs. Capadose went their way. He was able to say to himself, however, that his separation from the lady was not so much an end as a beginning, and he called on her soon after his return to town. She had told him the hours she was at home—she seemed to like him. If she liked him, why had she not married him, or at any rate why was she not sorry she had not? If she was sorry she concealed it too well. Lyon's curiosity on this point may strike the reader as fatuous, but something must be allowed to a disappointed man. He did not ask much after all; not that she should love him to-day or that she should allow him to tell her that he loved her, but only that she should give him some sign she was sorry. Instead of this, for the present, she contented herself with exhibiting her little daughter to him. The child was beautiful and had the prettiest eyes of innocence he had ever seen: which did not prevent him from wondering whether she told horrid fibs. This idea gave him much entertainment—the picture of the anxiety with which her mother would watch as she grew older for the symptoms of heredity. That was a nice occupation for Everina Brant! Did she lie to the child herself about her father—was that necessary, when she pressed her daughter to her bosom, to cover up his tracks? Did he control himself before the little girl —so that she might not hear him say things she knew to be other than he said? Lyon doubted this: his genius would be too strong for him, and the only safety for the child would be in her being too stupid to analyze. One couldn't judge yet—she was too young. If she should grow up clever she would be sure to tread in his steps—a delightful improvement in her mother's situation! Her little face was not shifty, but neither was her father's big one: so that proved nothing.

Lyon reminded his friends more than once of their promise that Amy should sit to him, and it was only a question of his leisure. The desire grew in him to paint the Colonel also—an operation from which he promised himself a rich private satisfaction. He

would draw him out, he would set him up in that
totality about which he had talked with Sir David,
and none but the initiated would know. They, however, would rank the picture high, and it would be indeed six rows deep—a masterpiece of subtle character-
ization, of legitimate treachery. He had dreamed for
years of producing something which should bear the
stamp of the psychologist as well as of the painter,
and here at last was his subject. It was a pity it was
not better, but that was not his fault. It was his impression that already no one drew the Colonel out more
than he, and he did it not only by instinct but on a
plan. There were moments when he was almost
frightened at the success of his plan—the poor gentleman went so terribly far. He would pull up some day,
look at Lyon between the eyes—guess he was being
played upon—which would lead to his wife's guessing
it also. Not that Lyon cared much for that, however,
so long as she failed to suppose (as she must) that
she was a part of his joke. He formed such a habit
now of going to see her of a Sunday afternoon that
he was angry when she went out of town. This occurred often, as the couple were great visitors and the
Colonel was always looking for sport, which he liked
best when it could be had at other people's expense.
Lyon would have supposed that this sort of life was
particularly little to her taste, for he had an idea
that it was in country-houses that her husband came
out strongest. To let him go off without her, not to
see him expose himself—that ought properly to have
been a relief and a luxury to her. She told Lyon in

fact that she preferred staying at home; but she neglected to say. it was because in other people's houses
she was on the rack: the reason she gave was that she
liked so to be with the child. It was not perhaps criminal to draw such a bow, but it was vulgar: poor Lyon
was delighted when he arrived at that formula. Certainly some day too he would cross the line—he would
become a noxious animal. Yes, in the meantime he
was vulgar, in spite of his talents, his fine person, his
impunity. Twice, by exception, toward the end of the
winter, when he left town for a few days' hunting, his
wife remained at home. Lyon had not yet reached the
point of asking himself whether the desire not to miss
two of his visits had something to do with her immobility. That inquiry would perhaps have been more in
place later, when he began to paint the child and she
always came with her. But it was not in her to give
the wrong name, to pretend, and Lyon could see that
she had the maternal passion, in spite of the bad blood
in the little girl's veins.

She came inveterately, though Lyon multiplied the
sittings: Amy was never intrusted to the governess or
the maid. He had knocked off poor old Sir David in
ten days, but the portrait of the simple-faced child bade
fair to stretch over into the following year. He asked
for sitting after sitting, and it would have struck any
one who might have witnessed the affair that he was
wearing the little girl out. He knew better, however,
and Mrs. Capadose also knew: they were present together at the long intermissions he gave her, when she
left her pose and roamed about the great studio, amus-

ing herself with its curiosities, playing with the old
draperies and costumes, having unlimited leave to handle. Then her mother and Mr. Lyon sat and talked;
he laid aside his brushes and leaned back in his chair;
he always gave her tea. What Mrs. Capadose did not
know was the way that during these weeks he neglected other orders: women have no faculty of imagination with regard to a man's work beyond a vague
idea that it doesn't matter. In fact Lyon put off everything and made several celebrities wait. There were
half-hours of silence, when he plied his brushes, during which he was mainly conscious that Everina was
sitting there. She easily fell into that if he did not
insist on talking, and she was not embarrassed nor
bored by it. Sometimes she took up a book—there
were plenty of them about; sometimes, a little way off,
in her chair, she watched his progress (though without in the least advising or correcting), as if she cared
for every stroke that represented her daughter. These
strokes were occasionally a little wild; he was thinking
so much more of his heart than of his hand. He was
not more embarrassed than she was, but he was agitated: it was as if in the sittings (for the child, too,
was beautifully quiet) something was growing between them or had already grown—a tacit confidence,
an inexpressible secret. He felt it that way; but after
all he could not be sure that she did. What he wanted
her to do for him was very little; it was not even to
confess that she was unhappy. He would be super-
abundantly gratified if she should simply let him know,
even by a silent sign, that she recognized that with him

her life would have been finer. Sometimes he guessed
—his presumption went so far—that he might see this
sign in her contentedly sitting there.

III

At last he broached the question of painting the
Colonel: it was now very late in the season—there
would be little time before the general dispersal. He
said they must make the most of it; the great thing
was to begin; then in the autumn, with the resumption
of their London life, they could go forward. Mrs.
Capadose objected to this that she really could not
consent to accept another present of such value. Lyon
had given her the portrait of herself of old and he had
seen what they had had the indelicacy to do with it.
Now he had offered her this beautiful memorial of the
child—beautiful it would evidently be when it was finished, if he could ever satisfy himself; a precious possession which they would cherish forever. But his
generosity must stop there—they couldn't be so tremendously "beholden" to him. They couldn't order
the picture—of course he would understand that, without her explaining: it was a luxury beyond their reach,
for they knew the great prices he received. Besides,
what had they ever done—what above all had she ever
done—that he should overload them with benefits? No,
he was too dreadfully good; it was really impossible
that Clement should sit. Lyon listened to her without
protest, without interruption, while he bent forward at
his work, and at last he said: "Well, if you won't take
it, why not let him sit for me for my own pleasure and

profit? Let it be a favor, a service I ask of him. It will do me a lot of good to paint him and the picture will remain in my hands."

"How will it do you a lot of good?" Mrs. Capadose asked.

"Why, he's such a rare model—such an interesting subject. He has such an expressive face. It will teach me no end of things."

"Expressive of what?" said Mrs. Capadose.

"Why, of his nature."

"And do you want to paint his nature?"

"Of course I do. That's what a great portrait gives you, and I shall make the Colonel's a great one. It will put me up high. So you see my request is eminently interested."

"How can you be higher than you are?"

"Oh, I'm insatiable! Do consent," said Lyon.

"Well, his nature is very noble," Mrs. Capadose remarked.

"Ah, trust me, I shall bring it out!" Lyon exclaimed, feeling a little ashamed of himself.

Mrs. Capadose said before she went away that her husband would probably comply with his invitation, but she added, "Nothing would induce me to let you pry into *me* that way!"

"Oh, you," Lyon laughed—"I could do you in the dark!"

The Colonel shortly afterward placed his leisure at the painter's disposal and by the end of July had paid him several visits. Lyon was disappointed neither in the quality of his sitter nor in the degree to which he

himself rose to the occasion; he felt really confident
that he should produce a fine thing. He was in the
humor; he was charmed with his *motif* and deeply interested in his problem. The only point that troubled
him was the idea that when he should send his picture
to the Academy he should not be able to give the title,
for the catalogue, simply as "The Liar." However,
it little mattered, for he had now determined that this
character should be perceptible even to the meanest intelligence—as overtopping as it had become to his own
sense in the living man. As he saw nothing else in
the Colonel to-day, so he gave himself up to the joy
of painting nothing else. How he did it he could not
have told you, but it seemed to him that the mystery
of how to do it was revealed to him afresh every time
he sat down to his work. It was in the eyes and it
was in the mouth, it was in every line of the face and
every fact of the attitude, in the indentation of the
chin, in the way the hair was planted, the mustache
was twisted, the smile came and went, the breath rose
and fell. It was in the way he looked out at a bam-
boozled world in short—the way he would look out
forever. There were half a dozen portraits in Europe
that Lyon rated as supreme; he regarded them as immortal, for they were as perfectly preserved as they
were consummately painted. It was to this small ex-
emplary group that he aspired to annex the canvas on
which he was now engaged. One of the productions
that helped to compose it was the magnificent Moroni
of the National Gallery—the young tailor, in the white
jacket, at his board with his shears. The Colonel was

not a tailor, nor was Moroni's model, unlike many
tailors, a liar; but as regards the masterly clearness
with which the individual should be rendered his work
should be on the same line as that. He had to a degree in which he had rarely had it before the satisfaction of feeling life grow and grow under his brush.
The Colonel, as it turned out, liked to sit and he liked
to talk while he was sitting: which was very fortu-
nate, as his talk largely constituted Lyon's inspiration.
Lyon put into practice that idea of drawing him out
which he had been nursing for so many weeks: he
could not possibly have been in a better relation to
him for the purpose. He encouraged, beguiled, excited him, manifested an unfathomable credulity, and
his only interruptions were when the Colonel did not
respond to it. He had his intermissions, his hours of
sterility, and then Lyon felt that the picture also lan-
guished. The higher his companion soared, the more
gyrations he executed, in the blue, the better he painted;
he couldn't make his flights long enough. He lashed
him on when he flagged; his apprehension became great
at moments that the Colonel would discover his game.
But he never did, apparently; he basked and expanded
in the fine steady light of the painter's attention. In
this way the picture grew very fast; it was astonishing
what a short business it was, compared with the little
girl's. By the fifth of August it was pretty well finished: that was the date of the last sitting the Colonel
was for the present able to give, as he was leaving
town the next day with his wife. Lyon was amply
content—he saw his way so clear: he should be able

to do at his convenience what remained, with or without his friend's attendance. At any rate, as there was
no hurry, he would let the thing stand over till his own
return to London, in November, when he would come
back to it with a fresh eye. On the Colonel's asking
him if his wife might come and see it the next day, if
she should find a minute—this was so greatly her desire—Lyon begged as a special favor that she would
wait: he was so far from satisfied as yet. This was the
repetition of a proposal Mrs. Capadose had made on
the occasion of his last visit to her, and he had then
asked for a delay—declared that he was by no means
content. He was really delighted, and he was again a
little ashamed of himself.

By the fifth of August the weather was very warm,
and on that day, while the Colonel sat straight and
gossiped, Lyon opened for the sake of ventilation a little subsidiary door which led directly from his studio
into the garden and sometimes served as an entrance
and as an exit for models and for visitors of the hum-
bler sort, and as a passage for canvases, frames, pack-
ing-boxes and other professional gear. The main entrance was through the house and his own apartments,
and this approach had the charming effect of admitting
you first to a high gallery, from which a crooked picturesque staircase enabled you to descend to the wide,
decorated, incumbered room. The view of this room,
beneath them, with all its artistic ingenuities and the
objects of value that Lyon had collected, never failed
to elicit exclamations of delight from persons stepping
into the gallery. The way from the garden was

plainer and at once more practicable and more private.
Lyon's domain, in St. John's Wood, was not vast, but
when the door stood open of a summer's day it offered
a glimpse of flowers and trees, you smelled something
sweet and you heard the birds. On this particular
morning the side-door had been found convenient by
an unannounced visitor, a youngish woman who stood
in the room before the Colonel perceived her and whom
he perceived before she was noticed by his friend.
She was very quiet, and she looked from one of the
men to the other. "Oh, dear, here's another!" Lyon
exclaimed, as soon as his eyes rested on her. She
belonged, in fact, to a somewhat importunate class—
the model in search of employment—and she explained
that she had ventured to come straight in, that way,
because very often when she went to call upon gentlemen the servants played her tricks, turned her off and
wouldn't take in her name.

"But how did you get into the garden?" Lyon
asked.

"The gate was open, sir—the servants' gate. The
butcher's cart was there."

"The butcher ought to have closed it," said Lyon.

"Then you don't require me, sir?" the lady continued.

Lyon went on with his painting; he had given her
a sharp look at first, but now his eyes lighted on her no
more. The Colonel, however, examined her with interest. She was a person of whom you could scarcely
say whether being young she looked old or old she
looked young; she had at any rate evidently rounded

several of the corners of life and had a face that was
rosy, but that somehow failed to suggest freshness.
Nevertheless she was pretty and even looked as if at
one time she might have sat for the complexion. She
wore a hat with many feathers, a dress with many
bugles, long black gloves, encircled with silver brace-
lets, and very bad shoes. There was something about
her that was not exactly of the governess out of place
nor completely of the actress seeking an engagement,
but that savored of an interrupted profession or even
of a blighted career. She was rather soiled and
tarnished, and after she had been in the room a few
moments the air, or at any rate the nostril, became
acquainted with a certain alcoholic waft. She was un-
practiced in the *h,* and when Lyon at last thanked her
and said he didn't want her—he was doing nothing
for which she could be useful—she replied with rather
a wounded manner, "Well, you know you 'ave 'ad
me!"

"I don't remember you," Lyon answered.

"Well, I daresay the people that saw your pictures
do! I haven't much time, but I thought I would
look in."

"I am much obliged to you."

"If ever you should require me, if you just send
me a postcard—"

"I never send postcards," said Lyon.

"Oh, well, I should value a private letter! Anything to Miss Geraldine, Mortimer Terrace Mews,
Notting 'ill—"

"Very good; I'll remember," said Lyon.

Miss Geraldine lingered. "I thought I'd just stop, on the chance."

"I'm afraid I can't hold out hopes, I'm so busy with portraits," Lyon continued.

"Yes; I see you are. I wish I was in the gentleman's place."

"I'm afraid in that case it wouldn't look like me," said the Colonel, laughing.

"Oh, of course it couldn't compare—it wouldn't be so 'andsome! But I do hate them portraits!" Miss Geraldine declared. "It's so much bread out of our mouths."

"Well, there are many who can't paint them," Lyon suggested comfortingly.

"Oh, I've sat to the very first—and only to the first! There's many that couldn't do anything without me."

"I'm glad you're in such demand." Lyon was beginning to be bored and he added that he wouldn't detain her—he would send for her in case of need.

"Very well; remember it's the Mews—more's the pity! You don't sit so well as us!" Miss Geraldine pursued, looking at the Colonel. "If you should require me, sir—"

"You put him out; you embarrass him," said Lyon.

"Embarrass him, oh gracious!" the visitor cried, with a laugh which diffused a fragrance. "Perhaps you send postcards, eh?" she went on to the Colonel; and then she retreated with a wavering step. She passed out into the garden as she had come.

"How very dreadful—she's drunk!" said Lyon. He was painting hard, but he looked up, checking himself:

Miss Geraldine, in the open doorway, had thrust back her head.

"Yes, I do hate it—that sort of thing!" she cried with an explosion of mirth which confirmed Lyon's declaration. And then she disappeared.

"What sort of thing—what does she mean?" the Colonel asked.

"Oh, my painting you, when I might be painting her."

"And have you ever painted her?"

"Never in the world; I have never seen her. She is quite mistaken."

The Colonel was silent a moment; then he remarked, "She was very pretty—ten years ago."

"I daresay, but she's quite ruined. For me the least drop too much spoils them; I shouldn't care for her at all."

"My dear fellow, she's not a model," said the Colonel, laughing.

"To-day, no doubt, she's not worthy of the name; but she has been one."

"*Jamais de la vie!* That's all a pretext."

"A pretext?" Lyon pricked up his ears—he began to wonder what was coming now.

"She didn't want you—she wanted me."

"I noticed she paid you some attention. What does she want of you?"

"Oh, to do me an ill turn. She hates me—lots of women do. She's watching me—she follows me."

Lyon leaned back in his chair—he didn't believe a

word of this. He was all the more delighted with it and with the Colonel's bright candid manner. The story had bloomed, fragrant, on the spot. "My dear Colonel!" he murmured, with friendly interest and commiseration.

"I was annoyed when she came in—but I wasn't startled," his sitter continued.

"You concealed it very well, if you were."

"Ah, when one has been through what I have! To-day, however, I confess I was half prepared. I have seen her hanging about—she knows my movements. She was near my house this morning—she must have followed me."

"But who is she then—with such a *toupet?*"

"Yes, she has that," said the Colonel, "but, as you observe, she was primed. Still, there was a cheek, as they say, in her coming in. Oh, she's a bad one! She isn't a model and she never was; no doubt she has known some of those women and picked up their form. She had hold of a friend of mine ten years ago—a stupid young gander who might have been left to be plucked, but whom I was obliged to take an interest in for family reasons. It's a long story—I had really forgotten all about it. She's thirty-seven if she's a day. I cut in and made him get rid of her—I sent her about her business. She knew it was me she had to thank. She has never forgiven me—I think she's off her head. Her name isn't Geraldine at all and I doubt very much if that's her address."

"Ah, what is her name?" Lyon asked, most attentive. The details always began to multiply, to

abound, when once his companion was well launched
—they flowed forth in battalions.

"It's Pearson—Harriet Pearson; but she used to
call herself Grenadine—wasn't that a rum appella-
tion?   Grenadine—Geraldine—the jump was easy."
Lyon was charmed with the promptitude of this response, and his interlocutor went on: "I hadn't
thought of her for years—I had quite lost sight of
her.   I don't know what her idea is, but practically
she's harmless.   As I came in I thought I saw her
a little way up the road.   She must have found out
I come here and have arrived before me.   I daresay
—or rather I'm sure—she's waiting for me there
now."

"Hadn't you better have protection?" Lyon asked,
laughing.

"The best protection is five shillings—I'm willing to
go that length.   Unless indeed she has a bottle of
vitriol.   But they only throw vitriol on the men who
have deceived them, and I never deceived her—I
told her the first time I saw her that it wouldn't do.
Oh, if she's there we'll walk a little way together and
talk it over, and, as I say, I'll go as far as five
shillings."

"Well," said Lyon, "I'll contribute another five."
He felt that this was little to pay for his entertainment.

That entertainment was interrupted, however, for
the time by the Colonel's departure.   Lyon hoped for
a letter recounting the fictive sequel; but apparently
his brilliant sitter did not operate with the pen.   At

any rate, he left town without writing; they had taken
a rendezvous for three months later. Oliver Lyon
always passed the holidays in the same way; during
the first weeks he paid a visit to his elder brother, the
happy possessor, in the south of England, of a rambling old house with formal gardens, in which he delighted, and then he went abroad—usually to Italy or
Spain. This year he carried out his custom after taking a last look at his all but finished work and feeling
as nearly pleased with it as he ever felt with the trans-
lation of the idea by the hand—always, as it seemed
to him, a pitiful compromise. One yellow afternoon,
in the country, as he was smoking his pipe on one
of the old terraces, he was seized with the desire to
see it again and do two or three things more to it: he
had thought of it so often while he lounged there.
The impulse was too strong to be dismissed, and
though he expected to return to town in the course of
another week, he was unable to face the delay. To
look at the picture for five minutes would be enough—
it would clear up certain questions which hummed in
his brain; so that the next morning, to give himself
this luxury, he took the train for London. He sent
no word in advance; he would lunch at his club and
probably return into Sussex by the 5.45.

In St. John's Wood the tide of human life flows at
no time very fast, and in the first days of September
Lyon found unmitigated emptiness in the straight
sunny roads where the little plastered garden-walls,
with their incommunicative doors, looked slightly
Oriental. There was definite stillness in his own

house, to which he admitted himself by his pass-key, having a theory that it was well sometimes to take servants unprepared. The good woman who was mainly in charge and who cumulated the functions of cook and housekeeper was, however, quickly summoned by his step, and (he cultivated frankness of intercourse with his domestics) received him without the confusion of surprise. He told her that she needn't mind the place being not quite straight, he had only come up for a few hours—he should be busy in the studio. To this she replied that he was just in time to see a lady and a gentleman who were there at the moment—they had arrived five minutes before. She had told them he was away from home; but they said it was all right; they only wanted to look at a picture and would be very careful of everything. "I hope it is all right, sir?" the housekeeper concluded. "The gentleman says he's a sitter and he gave me his name—rather an odd name; I think it's military. The lady's a very fine lady, sir; at any rate, there they are."

"Oh, it's all right," Lyon said, the identity of his visitors being clear. The good woman couldn't know, for she usually had little to do with the comings and goings; his man, who showed people in and out, had accompanied him to the country. He was a good deal surprised at Mrs. Capadose's having come to see her husband's portrait when she knew that the artist himself wished her to forbear; but it was a familiar truth to him that she was a woman of a high spirit. Besides, perhaps the lady was not Mrs. Capadose; the

Colonel might have brought some inquisitive friend, a person who wanted a portrait of *her* husband. What were they doing in town, at any rate, at that moment. Lyon made his way to the studio with a certain curiosity; he wondered vaguely what his friends were "up to." He pushed aside the curtain that hung in the door of communication—the door opening upon the gallery which it had been found convenient to construct at the time the studio was added to the house. When I say he pushed it aside I should amend my phrase; he laid his hand upon it, but at that moment he was arrested by a singular sound. It came from the floor of the room beneath him and it startled him extremely, consisting apparently as it did of a passionate wail—a sort of smothered shriek—accompanied by a violent burst of tears. Oliver Lyon listened intently a moment, and then he passed out upon the balcony, which was covered with an old thick Moorish rug. His step was noiseless, though he had not endeavored to make it so, and after that first instant he found himself profiting irresistibly by the accident of his not having attracted the attention of the two persons in the studio, who were some twenty feet below him. In truth, they were so deeply and so strangely engaged that their unconsciousness of observation was explained. The scene that took place before Lyon's eyes was one of the most extraordinary they had ever rested upon. Delicacy and the failure to comprehend kept him at first from interrupting it—for what he saw was a woman who had thrown herself in a flood of tears on her companion's

bosom—and these influences were succeeded after a
minute (the minutes were very few and very short)
by a definite motive which presently had the force to
make him step back behind the curtain. I may add
that it also had the force to make him avail himself
for further contemplation of a crevice formed by his
gathering together the two halves of the *portière*. He
was perfectly aware of what he was about—he was
for the moment an eavesdropper, a spy; but he was
also aware that a very odd business, in which his confidence had been trifled with, was going forward, and
that if in a measure it didn't concern him, in a measure it very definitely did. His observation, his reflections, accomplished themselves in a flash.

His visitors were in the middle of the room; Mrs.
Capadose clung to her husband, weeping, sobbing as
if her heart would break. Her distress was horrible to
Oliver Lyon, but his astonishment was greater than his
horror when he heard the Colonel respond to it by the
words, vehemently uttered, "Damn him, damn him,
damn him!" What in the world had happened? why
was she sobbing and whom was he damning? What
had happened, Lyon saw the next instant, was that the
Colonel had finally rummaged out his unfinished portrait (he knew the corner where the artist usually
placed it, out of the way, with its face to the wall) and
had set it up before his wife on an empty easel. She
had looked at it a few moments and then—apparently
—what she saw in it had produced an explosion of
dismay and resentment. She was too busy sobbing
and the Colonel was too busy holding her and reiterat-

ing his objurgation to look round or look up. The scene was so unexpected to Lyon that he could not take it, on the spot, as a proof of the triumph of his hand—of a tremendous hit: he could only wonder what on earth was the matter. The idea of the triumph came a little later. Yet he could see the portrait from where he stood; he was startled with its look of life—he had not thought it so masterly. Mrs. Capadose flung herself away from her husband—she dropped into the nearest chair, buried her face in her arms, leaning on a table. Her weeping suddenly ceased to be audible, but she shuddered there as if she were overwhelmed with anguish and shame. Her husband remained a moment staring at the picture; then he went to her, bent over her, took hold of her again, soothed her. "What is it, darling, what the devil is it?" he demanded.

Lyon heard her answer. "It's cruel—oh, it's too cruel!"

"Damn him—damn him—damn him!" the Colonel repeated.

"It's all there—it's all there!" Mrs. Capadose went on.

"Hang it, what's all there?"

"Everything there oughtn't to be—everything he has seen—it's too dreadful!"

"Everything he has seen? Why, ain't I a good-looking fellow? He has made me rather handsome."

Mrs. Capadose had sprung up again; she had darted another glance at the painted betrayal. "Handsome? Hideous, hideous! Not that—never, never!"

"Not *what*, in heaven's name?" the Colonel almost shouted. Lyon could see his flushed, bewildered face.

"What he has made of you—what you know! *He* knows—he has seen. Every one will know—every one will see. Fancy that thing in the Academy!"

"You're going wild, darling; but if you hate it so it needn't go."

"Oh, he'll send it—it's so good! Come away— come away!" Mrs. Capadose wailed, seizing her husband.

"It's so good?" the poor man cried.

"Come away—come way," she only repeated; and she turned toward the staircase that ascended to the gallery.

"Not that way—not through the house, in the state you're in," Lyon heard the Colonel object. "This way—we can pass," he added; and he drew his wife to the small door that opened into the garden. It was bolted, but he pushed the bolt and opened the door.

She passed out quickly, but he stood there looking back into the room. "Wait for me a moment!" he cried out to her; and with an excited stride he re-entered the studio. He came up to the picture again, and again he stood looking at it. "Damn him—damn him—damn him!" he broke out once more. It was not clear to Lyon whether this malediction had for its object the original or the painter of the portrait. The Colonel turned away and moved rapidly about the room, as if he were looking for something; Lyon was

unable for the instant to guess his intention. Then
the artist said to himself, below his breath, "He's going to do it a harm!" His first impulse was to rush
down and stop him; but he paused, with the sound of
Everina Brant's sobs still in his ears. The Colonel
found what he was looking for—found it among some
odds and ends on a small table and rushed back with
it to the easel. At one and the same moment Lyon
perceived that the object he had seized was a small
Eastern dagger and that he had plunged it into the
canvas. He seemed animated by a sudden fury, for
with extreme vigor of hand he dragged the instru-
ment down (Lyon knew it to have no very fine edge),
making a long, abominable gash. Then he plucked it
out and dashed it again several times into the face of
the likeness, exactly as if he were stabbing a human
victim: it had the oddest effect—that of a sort of fig-
urative suicide. In a few seconds more the Colonel
had tossed the dagger away—he looked at it as he did
so, as if he expected it to reek with blood—and hurried out of the place, closing the door after him.

The strangest part of all was—as will doubtless appear—that Oliver Lyon made no movement to save
his picture. But he did not feel as if he were losing
it or cared not if he were, so much more did he feel
that he was gaining a certitude. His old friend *was*
ashamed of her husband, and he had made her so, and
he had scored a great success, even though the picture
had been reduced to rags. The revelation excited him
so—as indeed the whole scene did—that when he
came down the steps after the Colonel had gone he

trembled with his happy agitation; he was dizzy and
had to sit down a moment. The portrait had a dozen
jagged wounds—the Colonel literally had hacked it
to death. Lyon left it where it was, never touched it,
scarcely looked at it; he only walked up and down his
studio, still excited, for an hour. At the end of this
time his good woman came to recommend that he
should have some luncheon; there was a passage under
the staircase from the offices.

"Ah, the lady and gentleman have gone, sir? I
didn't hear them."

"Yes; they went by the garden."

But she had stopped, staring at the picture on the
easel. "Gracious, how you 'ave served it, sir!"

Lyon imitated the Colonel. "Yes, I cut it up—in
a fit of disgust."

"Mercy, after all your trouble! Because they
weren't pleased, sir?"

"Yes; they weren't pleased."

"Well, they must be very grand! Blessed if I
would!"

"Have it chopped up; it will do to light fires," Lyon
said.

He returned to the country by the 3.30 and a few
days later passed over to France. During the two
months that he was absent from England he expected
something—he could hardly have said what; a manifestation of some sort on the Colonel's part. Wouldn't
he write, wouldn't he explain, wouldn't he take for
granted Lyon had discovered the way he had, as the
cook said, served him and deem it only decent to take

pity in some fashion or other on his mystification?
Would he plead guilty or would he repudiate suspicion? The latter course *would* be difficult and make
a considerable draft upon his genius, in view of the
certain testimony of Lyon's housekeeper, who had admitted the visitors and would establish the connection
between their presence and the violence wrought.
Would the Colonel proffer some apology or some
amends, or would any word from him be only a further
expression of that destructive petulance which our
friend had seen his wife so suddenly and so potently
communicate to him? He would have either to de-
clare that he had not touched the picture or to admit
that he had, and in either case he would have to tell
a fine story. Lyon was impatient for the story and, as
no letter came, disappointed that it was not produced.
His impatience, however, was much greater in respect
to Mrs. Capadose's version, if version there was to be;
for certainly that would be the real test, would show
how far she would go for her husband, on the one side,
or for him, Oliver Lyon, on the other. He could
scarcely wait to see what line she would take; whether
she would simply adopt the Colonel's, whatever it
might be. He wanted to draw her out without waiting to get an idea in advance. He wrote to her, to this
end, from Venice, in the tone of their established
friendship, asking for news, narrating his wanderings,
hoping they should soon meet in town and not saying
a word about the picture. Day followed day, after the
time, and he received no answer; upon which he reflected that she couldn't trust herself to write—was

still too much under the influence of the emotion produced by his "betrayal." Her husband had espoused
that emotion and she had espoused the action he had
taken in consequence of it, and it was a complete rupture and everything was at an end. Lyon considered
this prospect rather ruefully, at the same time that he
thought it deplorable that such charming people should
have put themselves so grossly in the wrong. He was
at last cheered, though little further enlightened, by the
arrival of a letter, brief, but breathing good-humor
and hinting neither at a grievance nor at a bad conscience. The most interesting part of it to Lyon was
the postscript, which consisted of these words: "I have
a confession to make to you. We were in town for a
couple of days, the 1st of September, and I took the
occasion to defy authority—it was very bad of me,
but I couldn't help it. I made Clement take me to
your studio—I wanted so dreadfully to see what you
had done with him, your wishes to the contrary notwithstanding. We made your servants let us in and I
took a good look at the picture. It is really wonderful!" "Wonderful" was non-committal, but at least
with this letter there was no rupture.

The third day after Lyon's return to London was
a Sunday, so that he could go and ask Mrs. Capadose
for luncheon. She had given him in the spring a general invitation to do so and he had availed himself of
it several times. These had been the occasions (before
he sat to him) when he saw the Colonel most famil-
iarly. Directly after the meal his host disappeared (he
went out, as he said, to call on *his* women) and the

second half-hour was the best, even when there were
other people. Now, in the first days of December,
Lyon had the luck to find the pair alone, without even
Amy, who appeared but little in public. They were
in the drawing-room, waiting for the repast to be announced, and as soon as he came in the Colonel broke
out, "My dear fellow, I'm delighted to see you! I'm
so keen to begin again."

"Oh, do go on, it's so beautiful," Mrs. Capadose
said, as she gave him her hand.

Lyon looked from one to the other; he didn't know
what he had expected, but he had not expected this.
"Ah, then, you think I've got something?"

"You've got everything," said Mrs. Capadose, smiling from her golden-brown eyes.

"She wrote you of our little crime?" her husband
asked. "She dragged me there—I had to go!" Lyon
wondered for a moment whether he meant by their
little crime the assault on the canvas; but the Colonel's
next words didn't confirm this interpretation. "You
know I like to sit—it gives such a chance to my *bavar-
dise*. And just now I have time."

"You must remember I had almost finished," Lyon
remarked.

"So you had. More's the pity. I should like you
to begin again."

"My dear fellow, I shall have to begin again!" said
Oliver Lyon with a laugh, looking at Mrs. Capadose.
She did not meet his eyes—she had got up to ring
for luncheon. "The picture has been smashed," Lyon
continued.

"Smashed? Ah, what did you do that for?" Mrs. Capadose asked, standing there before him in all her clear, rich beauty. Now that she looked at him she was impenetrable.

"I didn't—I found it so—with a dozen holes punched in it!"

"I say!" cried the Colonel.

Lyon turned his eyes to him, smiling. "I hope *you* didn't do it?"

"Is it ruined?" the Colonel inquired. He was as brightly true as his wife and he looked simply as if Lyon's question could not be serious. "For the love of sitting to you? My dear fellow, if I had thought of it, I would!"

"Nor you either?" the painter demanded of Mrs. Capadose.

Before she had time to reply her husband had seized her arm, as if a highly suggestive idea had come to him. "I say, my dear, that woman—that woman!"

"That woman?" Mrs. Capadose repeated; and Lyon, too, wondered what woman he meant.

"Don't you remember when we came out, she was at the door—or a little way from it? I spoke to you of her—I told you about her. Geraldine—Grenadine —the one who burst in that day," he explained to Lyon. "We saw her hanging about—I called Everina's attention to her."

"Do you mean she got at my picture?"

"Ah, yes, I remember," said Mrs. Capadose, with a sigh.

"She burst in again—she had learned the way—

she was waiting for her chance," the Colonel continued. "Ah, the little brute!"

Lyon looked down; he felt himself coloring. This was what he had been waiting for—the day the Colonel should wantonly sacrifice some innocent person. And could his wife be a party to that final atrocity? Lyon had reminded himself repeatedly during the previous weeks that when the Colonel perpetrated his misdeed she had already quitted the room; but he had argued none the less—it was a virtual certainty—that he had on rejoining her immediately made his achievement plain to her. He was in the flush of performance; and even if he had not mentioned what he had done she would have guessed it. He did not for an instant believe that poor Miss Geraldine had been hovering about his door, nor had the account given by the Colonel the summer before of his relations with this lady deceived him in the slightest degree. Lyon had never seen her before the day she planted herself in his studio; but he knew her and classified her as if he had made her. He was acquainted with the London female model and all her varieties—in every phase of her development and every step of her decay. When he entered his house that September morning, just after the arrival of his two friends, there had been no symptoms whatever, up and down the road, of Miss Geraldine's reappearance. That fact had been fixed in his mind by his recollecting the vacancy of the prospect when his cook told him that a lady and a gentleman were in his studio: he had wondered there was not a carriage nor a cab at his door. Then he re-

flected that they would have come by the underground
railway; he was close to the Marlborough Road station, and he knew the Colonel, coming to his sittings, more than once had availed himself of that
convenience. "How in the world did she get in?"
He addressed the question to his companions in-
differently.

"Let us go down to luncheon," said Mrs. Capadose,
passing out of the room.

"We went by the garden—without troubling your
servant—I wanted to show my wife."   Lyon followed his hostess with her husband, and the Colonel
stopped him at the top of the stairs.   "My dear fellow,
I *can't* have been guilty of the folly of not fastening
the door?"

"I am sure I don't know, Colonel," Lyon said as
they went down.   "It was a very determined hand
—a perfect wild-cat."

"Well, she *is* a wild-cat—confound her! That's
why I wanted to get him away from her."

"But I don't understand her motive."

"She's off her head—and she hates me; that was
her motive."

"But she doesn't hate me, my dear fellow!" Lyon
said, laughing.

"She hated the picture—don't you remember she
said so? The more portraits there are the less employment for such as her."

"Yes; but if she is not really the model she pre-
tends to be, how can that hurt her?" Lyon asked.

The inquiry baffled the Colonel an instant—but only

an instant. "Ah, she was in a vicious muddle! As I say, she's off her head."

They went into the dining-room, where Mrs. Capadose was taking her place. "It's too bad, it's too horrid!" she said. "You see the fates are against you. Providence won't let you be so disinterested—painting masterpieces for nothing."

"Did *you* see the woman?" Lyon demanded, with something like a sternness that he could not mitigate.

Mrs. Capadose appeared not to perceive it, or not to heed it if she did. "There was a person, not far from your door, whom Clement called my attention to. He told me something about her, but we were going the other way."

"And do you think she did it?"

"How can I tell? If she did she was mad, poor wretch."

"I should like very much to get hold of her," said Lyon. This was a false statement, for he had no desire for any further conversation with Miss Geraldine. He had exposed his friends to himself, but he had no desire to expose them to any one else, least of all to themselves.

"Oh, depend upon it she will never show again. You're safe!" the Colonel exclaimed.

"But I remember her address—Mortimer Terrace Mews, Notting Hill."

"Oh, that's pure humbug; there isn't any such place."

"Lord, what a deceiver!" said Lyon.

"Is there any one else you suspect?" the Colonel went on.

"Not a creature."

"And what do your servants say?"

"They say it wasn't *them,* and I reply that I never said it was. That's about the substance of our conferences."

"And when did they discover the havoc?"

"They never discovered it at all. I noticed it first —when I came back."

"Well, she could easily have stepped in," said the Colonel. "Don't you remember how she turned up that day, like the clown in the ring?"

"Yes, yes; she could have done the job in three seconds, except that the picture wasn't out."

"My dear fellow, don't curse me!—but of course I dragged it out."

"You didn't put it back?" Lyon asked tragically.

"Ah, Clement, Clement, didn't I tell you to?" Mrs. Capadose exclaimed in a tone of exquisite reproach.

The Colonel groaned, dramatically; he covered his face with his hands. His wife's words were for Lyon the finishing touch; they made his whole vision crumble—his theory that she had secretly kept herself true. Even to her old lover she wouldn't be so! He was sick: he couldn't eat; he knew that he looked very strange. He murmured something about it being useless to cry over spilled milk—he tried to turn the conversation to other things. But it was a horrid effort, and he wondered whether they felt it as much as he. He wondered all sorts of things: whether they guessed he disbelieved them (that he had seen them of course they would never guess) ; whether they had arranged their story in advance or it was only on inspiration of the moment; whether she had resisted, protested, when the Colonel proposed it to her, and then had been borne down by him; whether, in short, she didn't loathe herself as she sat there. The cruelty, the cowardice of fastening their unholy act upon the wretched woman struck him as monstrous—no less monstrous indeed than the levity that could make them run the risk of her giving them, in her righteous indignation, the lie. Of course, that risk could only exculpate her and not inculpate them—the probabilities protected them so perfectly; and what the Colonel counted on (what he would have counted upon the day he delivered himself, after first seeing her, at the studio, if he had thought about the matter then at all and not spoken from the pure spontaneity of his genius) was simply that Miss Geraldine had really vanished forever into her native unknown. Lyon wanted so much to quit the subject that when after a little Mrs. Capadose said to him, "But can nothing be done, can't the picture be repaired? You know they do such wonders in that way now," he only replied, "I don't know, I don't care, it's all over, *n'en parlons plus!*" Her hypocrisy revolted him. And yet, by way of plucking off the last veil of her shame, he broke out to her again, shortly afterward, "And you *did* like it, really?" To which she returned, looking him straight in his face, without a blush, a pallor, an evasion, "Oh, I loved it!" Truly her husband had trained her well. After that Lyon said no more, and his companions forbore temporarily to insist, like people of tact and sympathy, aware that the odious incident had made him sore.

When they quitted the table the Colonel went away without coming upstairs; but Lyon returned to the drawing-room with his hostess, remarking to her, however, on the way that he could remain but a moment. He spent that moment—it prolonged itself a little—standing with her before the chimney-piece. She neither sat down nor asked him to; her manner denoted that she intended to go out. Yes, her husband had trained her well; yet Lyon dreamed for a moment that now he was alone with her she would perhaps break down, retract, apologize, confide, say to him, "My dear old friend, forgive this hideous comedy—you understand!" And then how he would have loved her and pitied her, guarded her, helped her always! If she were not ready to do something of that sort, why had she treated him as if he were a dear old friend; why had she let him for months suppose certain things —or almost; why had she come to his studio day after day to sit near him on the pretext of her child's portrait, as if she liked to think what might have been? Why had she come so near a tacit confession, in a word, if she was not willing to go an inch further? And she was not willing—she was not; he could see that as he lingered there. She moved about the room a little, rearranging two or three objects on the tables, but she did nothing more. Suddenly he said to her: "Which way was she going when you came out?"

"She—the woman we saw?"

"Yes, your husband's strange friend. It's a clew worth following." He had no desire to frighten her; he only wanted to communicate the impulse which would make her say, "Ah, spare me—and spare *him!* There was no such person."

Instead of this Mrs. Capadose replied, "She was going away from us—she crossed the road. We were coming toward the station."

"And did she appear to recognize the Colonel—did she look round?"

"Yes; she looked round, but I didn't notice much. A hansom came along and we got into it. It was not till then that Clement told me who she was: I remember he said that she was there for no good. I suppose we ought to have gone back."

"Yes; you would have saved the picture."

For a moment she said nothing; then she smiled. "For you, I am very sorry. But you must remember that I possess the original!"

At this Lyon turned away. "Well, I must go," he said; and he left her without any other farewell and made his way out of the house. As he went slowly up the street the sense came back to him of that first glimpse of her he had had at Stayes—the way he had seen her gaze across the table at her husband. Lyon stopped at the corner, looking vaguely up and down. He would never go back—he couldn't. She was still in love with the Colonel—he had trained her too well.

AGAINST HIS JUDGMENT

BY ROBERT GRANT

Judge Robert Grant (born in Boston, January 24, 1852) began flirting with literature in his court-room about twenty-five years ago, producing several volumes of juvenile stories and trivial verse. Later he took up authorship more seriously, and gradually won his way to the front of all our social philosophers. "Unleavened Bread," his best novel (published in 1900), is a powerful study of character, dealing with three successive matrimonial ventures of an energetic and ambitious but essentially commonplace woman. The present story sets forth an interesting psychological problem, in the solution of which there is shown a wide difference between theory and practice.

AGAINST HIS JUDGMENT

BY ROBERT GRANT

THREE days had passed, and the excitement
in the neighborhood was nearly at an end.
The apothecary's shop at the corner into
which John Baker's body and the living four-year-
old child had been carried together immediately after
the catastrophe had lost most of its interest for the
curious, although the noses of a few idlers were still
pressed against the large pane in apparent search of
something beyond the brilliant colored bottles or the
soda-water fountains. Now that the funeral was
over, the womenkind whose windows commanded a
view of the house where the dead man had been lying
had taken their heads in and resumed their sweeping
and washing, and knots of their husbands and fathers
no longer stood in gaping conclave close to the very
door-sill, rehearsing again and again the details of
the distressing incident. Even the little child that
had been so miraculously saved from the jaws of
death, although still decked in the dirty finery which
its mother deemed appropriate to its having suddenly become a public character, was beginning to
fall into obscurity and to cease to be the recipient of
the dimes of the tender-hearted. Curiously enough,
such is the capriciousness of the human temperament

at times of emotional excitement, the plan of a subscription for the victim's family had not been mooted
until what was to its parents a small fortune had been
bestowed on the rescued child; but the scale of justice
had gradually righted itself, and contributions were
now pouring in, especially since it was known that the
mayor and several other well-known persons had
headed the list with subscriptions of fifty dollars each;
and there was reason to believe that a lump sum of
from fifteen hundred to two thousand dollars would
be collected for the benefit of the widow and seven
children before the public generosity was exhausted.

Local interest was on the wane; but, thanks to the
telegraph and the press, the facts were being dissemi-
nated through the country, and every leading newspaper in the land was chronicling, with more or less
periphrasis according to the character of its patrons,
the item that John Baker, the gatekeeper at a railroad crossing in a Pennsylvania city, had snatched
a toddling child from the pathway of a swiftly moving
locomotive and been crushed to death.

A few days later a dinner company of eight was
gathered at a country-house several hundred miles
distant from the scene of the calamity. The host
and hostess were people of wealth and leisure, who
enjoyed inviting congenial parties from their social
acquaintance in the neighboring city to share with
them for two or three days at a time the charms of
nature. The dinner was appetizing and the wine good,
and all present were engaged in that gracious unbend-
ing of self which ordinarily follows the action of re-

freshment and light on minds under the influence of pleasant impressions.

In a tavern the best result is joviality; at the dinner-table of intelligent gentlefolk—and of such we are speaking—the texture of the most agreeable conversation, though smooth as the choicest Lafitte and sparkling as champagne, has ever a thread of seriousness in the woof.

They had talked on a variety of topics: of the climate and landscape of Florida, where two of the party had sojourned during the winter months; of amateur photography, in which the hostess was proficient; of the very general use in common parlance of "don't" for "doesn't" and "but what" for "but that"; of Mrs. Langtry's beauty before she became an actress, concerning which one of the gentlemen who had met her in London was very eloquent; of some recent pictures and publications; of the impropriety and the increasing custom of feeing employees to do their duty; and of certain breaches of trust by bank officers and treasurers that, happening within a short time of one another, had startled the sensibilities of the community. This last subject begot a somewhat doleful train of commentary from two or three of the company, complaints of a too easy-going standard of morality, of a willingness not to be severe on anybody and to pass over lightly faults that our forefathers never would have condoned, of the decay of ideal considerations, and of the lack of enthusiasm for all but money-spinning among the rank and file of the people.

"The gist is here," reiterated in substance one of
the speakers : "we insist upon tangible proof of everything, of being able to see and feel it—to get our dollar's worth, in short. We weigh and measure and
scrutinize, and discard as fusty and outworn, conduct
and guides to conduct that do not promise six per cent
per annum in full sight."

"What have you to say to John Baker?" said mine
host, breaking the pause that followed these remarks.
"I take it for granted that you are all familiar with his
story : the newspapers have been full of it. *There* was
a man who did not stop to measure or scrutinize."

A murmur of approbation followed, which was interrupted by Mrs. Caspar Green, a stout and rather
languid lady, inquiring to whom he referred. "You
know I never read the newspapers," she added, with a
decidedly superior air, putting up her eyeglass.

"Except the deaths and marriages," exclaimed her
husband, a lynx-eyed little stock-broker, who was per-
petually poking what he called fun at his more ponderous half.

"Well, this was a death : so there was no excuse
for her not seeing it," said Henry Lawford, the host.
"No, seriously, Mrs. Green, it was a splendid instance
of personal heroism : a gatekeeper at a railway crossing in Pennsylvania, perceiving a child of four on the
track just in front of the fast express, rushed forward
and managed to snatch up the little creature and deposit it on one side before—poor fellow!—he was
struck and killed. There was no suggestion of count-
ing upon six per cent there, was there?"

"Unless in another sphere," interjected Caspar Green.

"Don't be sacrilegious, Caspar," pleaded his wife, though she added her mite to the ripple of laughter that greeted the sally.

"It was superb!—superb!" exclaimed Miss Ann Newbury, a young woman not far from thirty, with a long neck and a high-bred, pale, intellectual face. "He is one of the men who make us proud of being men and women." She spoke with sentamious earnestness and looked across the table appealingly at George Gorham.

"He left seven children, I believe?" said he, with precision.

"Yes, seven, Mr. Gorham—the eldest eleven," answered Mrs. Lawford, who was herself the mother of five. "Poor little things!"

"I think he made a great mistake," remarked George, laconically.

For an instant there was a hiatus. The company was evidently making sure that it had understood his speech correctly. Then Miss Newbury gave a gasp, and Henry Lawford, with a certain stern dignity that he knew how to assume, said:

"A mistake? How so, pray?"

"In doing what he did—sacrificing his life to save the child."

"Why, Mr. Gorham!" exclaimed the hostess, while everybody turned toward him. He was a young man between thirty and thirty-five, a lawyer beginning to be well thought of in his profession, with a thoughtful, pleasant expression and a vigorous physique.

"It seems to me," he continued, slowly, seeking his words, "if John Baker had stopped to think, he would have acted differently. To be sure, he saved the life of an innocent child; but, on the other hand, he robbed of their sole means of support seven other no less innocent children and their mother. He was a brave man, I agree; but I, for one, should have admired him more if he had stopped to think."

"And let the child be killed?" exclaimed Mr. Carter, the gentleman who had deplored so earnestly the decay of ideal considerations. He was a young mill-treasurer, with aristocratic tendencies and a strong interest in church affairs.

"Yes, if needs be. It was in danger through no fault of his. Its natural guardians had neglected it."

"What a frightful view to take!" murmured Mrs. Green; and, although she was very well acquainted with George Gorham's physiognomy, she examined him disapprovingly through her glass, as if there must be something compromising about it that had hitherto escaped detection.

"Well, I don't agree with you at all," said the host, emphatically.

"Nor I," said Mr. Carter.

"Nor I, Mr. Gorham," said Mrs. Lawford, so plaintively as to convey the impression that if a woman as ready as she to accept new points of view abandoned him there could be no chance of his being right.

"No, you're all wrong, my dear fellow," said Caspar Green. "Such ideas may go down among your long-haired artistic and literary friends at the Argonaut Club, but you can't expect civilized Christians to accept them. Why, man, it's monstrous—monstrous, by Jove!—to depreciate that noble fellow's action—a man that we all ought to be proud of, as Miss Newbury says. If we don't encourage such people, how can we expect them to be willing to risk their lives?" Thereupon the little broker, as a relief to his outraged feelings, emptied his champagne glass at a draught and scowled irascibly. His jesting equanimity was rarely disturbed; consequently, everybody felt the importance of his testimony.

"I'm sorry to be so completely in the minority," said Gorham, "but that's the way the matter strikes me. I don't think you quite catch my point, though, Caspar," he added, glancing at Mr. Green. At a less heated moment the company, with the possible exception of Mrs. Green, might have tacitly agreed that this was extremely probable; but now Miss Newbury, who had hitherto refrained from comment in order to digest the problem thoroughly before speaking, came to the broker's aid.

"It seems to me, Mr. Gorham," she said, "that your proposition is a very plain one: you claim simply that John Baker had better not have saved the child if in order to do so it was necessary to lose his own life."

"Precisely," exclaimed Mr. Green, in a tone of some contempt.

"Was not Mr. Gorham's meaning that, though it

required very great courage to do what Baker did, a man who stopped to think of his own wife and children would have shown even greater courage in restraining his impulse to save the child?" asked Miss Emily Vincent. She was the youngest of the party, a beautiful girl, of fine presence, with a round face, dark eyes, and brilliant pink-and-white coloring. She had been invited to stay by the Lawfords because George Gorham was attentive to her; or, more properly speaking, George Gorham had been asked because he was attentive to her.

"Thank you, Miss Vincent: you have expressed my meaning perfectly," said Gorham; and his face gladdened. He was dead in love with her, and this was the first civil word, so to speak, that she had said to him during the visit.

"Do you agree with him?" inquired Miss Newbury, with intellectual sternness.

"And do you agree with Mr. Gorham?" asked Mrs. Lawford, at the same moment, caressingly.

All eyes were turned on Emily Vincent, and she let hers fall confusedly. She felt that she would have given worlds not to have spoken. Why had she spoken?

"I understand what he means; but I don't believe a man in John Baker's place could help himself," she said, quietly.

"Of course he couldn't!" cried Mrs. Lawford. "There, Mr. Gorham, you have lost your champion. What have you to say now?" A murmur of approval went round the table.

"I appreciate my loss, but I fear I have nothing to add to what has been said already," he replied, with smiling firmness. "Although in a pitiful minority, I shall have to stand or fall by that."

"Ah, but when it came to action we know that under all circumstances Mr. Gorham would be his father's son," said Mrs. Lawford, with less than her usual tact, though she intended to be very ingratiating. Gorham's father had been killed in the Civil War, after having become conspicuous for gallantry.

Gorham bowed a little stiffly, feeling that there was nothing for him to say. There was a pause, evincing that the topic was getting threadbare, which prompted the host to anticipate Mr. Carter, who, having caught Miss Newbury's eye, was about to philosophize further on the same lines, by calling his wife's attention to the fact that one of the candles was flaring. This turned the current of conversation, and the subject was not alluded to again.

During the twelve months following his visit at the Lawfords' the attentions of George Gorham to Emily began to be noticeable. He had loved her for three years in secret; but the consciousness that he was not able to support a wife had hindered him from devoting himself pronouncedly to her. He knew that she, or rather her father, had considerable property; but Gorham was not willing to take this into consideration; he would never offer himself until his own income was sufficient for both their needs. But, on the other hand, his ideas of a sufficient income were not extravagant. He looked forward to building a

comfortable little house in the suburbs in the midst of
a few acres of garden and lawn, so that his neighbors' windows need not overlook his domesticity. He
would have a horse and buggy wherewith to drive his
wife through the country on summer afternoons, and
later, if his bank-account warranted it, a saddle-horse
for Emily and one for himself. He would keep open
house in the sense of encouraging his friends to visit
him; and, that they might like to come, he would have
a thoroughly good plain cook—thereby eschewing
French kickshaws—and his parlor and his own snug-
gery should afford the best new books, and on the
walls etchings and sketches winsome to the eye, done
by men who were rising rather than men who had
risen. There should be no formality; his guests
should do what they pleased and wear what they
pleased, and, above all, they should become intimate
with his wife, instead of merely tolerating her after
the manner of the bachelor friends of so many other
men.

Thus he had been in the habit of depicting to himself the future as he would have it be, and at last, by
dint of strict undeviating attention to his business, he
had got to the point where he could afford to realize
his project if his lady-love were willing. His practice was increasing steadily, and he had laid by a few
thousand dollars to meet any unexpected emergency.
His life was insured for fifty thousand dollars, and the
policy was now ten years old. He had every reason
to expect that in course of time as the older lawyers
died off he would either succeed to the lucrative con-

duct of large suits or be made a judge of one of the
higher tribunals. In this manner his ambition would
be amply satisfied. His aim was to progress slowly
but solidly, without splurge or notoriety, until every
one came to regard him tacitly as a man of sound
dispassionate judgment, keen understanding, and
simple, earnest life. His especial antipathy was for
so-called cranks, people who went off at half-cock, who
thought nothing out, but were governed by the impulse of the moment, shilly-shally and controlled by
unmasculine sentimentality.

It was with hope and yet with his heart in his mouth
that he set out one afternoon determined to ask Emily
Vincent to become his wife. She lived in the suburbs,
within fifteen miles by the train, or an hour's walk
from town. Gorham took the cars. It was a beautiful day, almost the counterpart of that which they had
passed together at the Lawfords' just a year before.
As he sat in the train he analyzed the situation once
more for the hundredth time, taking care not to give
himself the advantage of any ambiguous symptoms.
Certainly she was not indifferent to him; she accepted
his attentions without demur, and seemed interested
in his interests. But was that love? Was it any more
than esteem or cordial liking that would turn to pity
at the first hint of affection on his part? But surely
she could not plead ignorance of his intentions; she
must long ere this have realized that he was seriously
attentive to her. Still, girls were strange creatures.
He could not help feeling nervous, because so very
much was involved for him in the result. Should she

refuse him, he would be and remain for a long time excessively unhappy. He obliged himself to regard that alternative, and his heart sank before the possibility of its coming to pass. Not that the idea of dying or doing anything desperate presented itself to him. Such extravagance would have seemed out of keeping with respect either for her or for himself. Doubtless he might recover some day, but the interim would be terribly hard to endure. Rejection meant a dark, dreary bachelorhood; success, the crowning of his dearest hopes.

He found his sweetheart at home, and she came down to greet him with roses that he had sent her in her bosom. It was not easy for him to do or say anything extravagant, and Emily Vincent, while she might have pardoned unseemly effusiveness to his exceeding love for her, was well content with the deeply earnest though unriotous expression of his passion. When finally he had folded her in his arms she felt that the greatest happiness existence can give was hers, and he knew himself to be an utterly blissful lover. He had won the prize for which he had striven with a pertinacity like Jacob's, and life looked very roseate.

The news was broken to her family that evening, and received delightedly, though without the surprise the lovers had expected. They were left alone for a little while before the hour of parting, and in the sweet kisses given and taken Gorham redeemed himself in his mistress's estimation for any lack of folly he had been guilty of when he had asked her to be his wife.

There was riot now in his eyes and in his embraces,
revealing that he had needed only to be sure of her
encouragement to become as ridiculous as she could
desire.   He stood disclosed to himself in a new light;
and when he had kissed her once more for the last
time he went tripping down the lawn radiantly happy,
turning now and again to throw back with his fingers
a message from his lips to the one being in all
the world for him who stood on the threshold,
adding poetry and symmetry to the beautiful June
evening.

When out of sight of the house, Gorham sped
fleetly along the road.   He intended to walk to town,
for he felt like glorying in his happiness under the
full moon which was shedding her silver light from a
clear heaven.   The air was not oppressive, and it was
scented with the perfume of the lilacs and apple-
blossoms, so that Gorham was fain every now and
then to draw a deep breath in order to inhale their
fragrance.   There was no dust, and nature looked
spruce and trig, without a taint of the frowziness that
is observable in the foliage a month later.

Gorham took very little notice of the details; his
eyes were busy rather with mind-problems than with
the particular beauties of the night; yet his rapt gaze
swept the brilliant heaven as though he felt its lustre
to be in harmony with the radiance in his own soul.
He was imagining the future—his hearth forever
blessed by her sweet presence, their mutual joys
and sorrows sweetened and alleviated through being
shared, his efforts to live a life in accord with the

highest intimations of his being, fortified by her example and counsel. How the pleasures of walking and riding and reading and traveling—of everything, in fact—would be a hundredfold enhanced by being able to interchange impressions with each other! He pictured to himself the cosey evenings they would pass at home beside the lamp when the day's work was done, and the jolly trips they would take together when vacation time arrived. How he would watch over her, and how he would guard her and tend her and comfort her if misfortune came or ill health assailed her! There would be little ones, perhaps, to claim their joint devotion and bid him redouble his energies; he smiled at the thought of baby fingers about his neck, and there arose to his mind's eyes a sweet vision of Emily sitting, pale but triumphant, rocking her new-born child upon her breast.

He walked swiftly on the wings of transport. It was almost as light as day, yet he met but few travelers along the country road. An occasional vehicle passed him, breaking the silvery stillness with its rumble that subsided at last into the distance. A pair of whispering lovers, arm in arm, who slunk into the shadow as he came abreast of them, won from him a glance of sympathy, and just after he had left them behind the shrill whistle of a locomotive jarring upon the silence seemed to bring him a message from the woman he adored. Had he not preferred to walk, that was the train he would have taken, and it must have stopped not many hundred yards from her door. He breathed a prayer of blessing on her rest as he listened to it thundering past almost parallel to him in the cut below.

A little beyond this point the road curved and ran with gradual incline so as to cross the railroad track at grade about half a mile further on. This stretch of road was lined on each side by horse-chestnut trees set near to one another, the spreading foliage of which darkened the graveled footpath, so that Gorham, who was enjoying the moonlight, preferred to keep in the middle of the road, which, by way of contrast, gleamed almost like a river. He was pursuing his way with elastic steps, when of a sudden his attention was arrested about a hundred and fifty yards from the crossing by something lying at the foot of one of the trees on the right-hand side. At a second glance he saw that it was a woman's figure. Probably she was asleep: but she might be ill or injured. It was a lonely spot: so it occurred to him that it was proper for him to ascertain which. Accordingly he stepped to her side and bent over her. From her calico dress, which was her only covering, she evidently belonged to the laboring class. She was a large, coarse-looking woman, and was lying, in what appeared to Gorham to be drunken slumber, on her bonnet, the draggled strings of which protruded. He hesitated a moment, and then shook her by the arm. She groaned boozily, but after he had shaken her again two or three times she rolled over and raised herself on her elbow, rubbing her eyes and staring at him glassily.

"Are you hurt, woman?" he asked.

She made a guttural response which might have

meant anything, but she proved that she was uninjured by getting on her feet.   She stared at her
disturber bewilderedly, then, perceiving her bonnet,
stooped to pick it up, and stood for a moment trying
sleepily to poke it into shape and readjust its tawdry
plumage.   But all of a sudden she gave a start and
began looking around her with recovered energy.
She missed something, evidently.   Gorham followed
the direction of her gaze as it shifted, and as his
glance met the line of the road he perceived a little
figure standing in the middle of the railway crossing.
It was a child—her child, without doubt—and as he
said so to himself the roar of an approaching train,
coupled with the sound of the whistle, made him start
with horror.   The late express from town was due.
Gorham remembered that there was a considerable
curve in the railroad at this point.   The woman had
not perceived the situation—she was too far in the
shade—but Gorham from where he stood commanded
a clear view of the track.

Without an instant's hesitation, he sprang forward
and ran at full speed.   His first thought was that the
train was very near.   He ran with all his might and
main, his eyes fixed on the little white figure and
shouting to warn it of its danger.   Suddenly there
flashed before his mind with vividness the remembrance of John Baker, and he recalled his argument at
the Lawfords'.   But he did not abate his speed.   The
child had plumped itself down on one of the sleepers,
and was apparently playing with some pebbles.   It
was on the further track, and, startled by his cries and

by the clang of the approaching train, looked up at him. He saw a pale, besmeared little countenance; he heard behind him the agonizing screams of the mother, who had realized her baby's peril; in his ears rang the shrill warning of the engineer as the engine rounded the curve. Would he be in time?

As he reached the edge of the tracks, thought of Emily and a terrible consciousness of the sorrow she would feel if anything were to happen to him compressed his heart. But he did not falter. He was aware of the jangle of a fiercely rung bell, the hiss of steam, and a blinding glare; he could feel on his cheek the breath of the iron monster. With set teeth he threw himself forward, stooped, and reached out over the rail: in another instant he had tossed the child from the pathway of danger, and he himself had been mangled to death by the powerful engine.

A MICHIGAN MAN

BY ELIA W. PEATTIE

Elia Wilkinson (born at Kalamazoo, Mich., January 15, 1862) married in 1883 Robert Burns Peattie, a Chicago newspaper man and soon after achieved a reputation in journalism for herself. She has written many short stories, through all of which runs a line of distinct individuality; a strong cord, as it were interlinked of ruddy heart-strings and the vivid tendrils of wintry. "A Michigan Man" is a typical story of the author's, presenting in simple yet powerful fashion the spell which the forest exerts over its destroyer the lumberman.

A MICHIGAN MAN

BY ELIA W. PEATTIE

Elia Wilkinson (born at Kalamazoo, Mich., January 15, 1862) married in 1883 Robert Burns Peattie, a Chicago newspaper man, and soon after achieved a reputation in journalism for herself. She has written many short stories, through all of which runs a line of distinct individuality, a strong cord, as it were, intertwisted of ruddy heart-strings and the virid tendrils of nature. "A Michigan Man" is a typical story of the author's, presenting in simple yet powerful fashion the spell which the forest exerts over its destroyer, the lumberman.

A MICHIGAN MAN

BY ELIA W. PEATTIE

A PINE forest is nature's expression of solemnity and solitude. Sunlight, rivers, cascades, people, music, laughter, or dancing could not make it gay. With its unceasing reverberations and its eternal shadows, it is as awful and as holy as a cathedral.

Thirty good fellows working together by day and drinking together by night can keep up but a moody imitation of jollity. Spend twenty-five of your forty years, as Luther Dallas did, in this perennial gloom, and your soul—that which enjoys, aspires, competes—will be drugged as deep as if you had quaffed the cup of oblivion. Luther Dallas was counted one of the most experienced axe-men in the northern camps. He could fell a tree with the swift surety of an executioner, and in revenge for his many arboral murders the woodland had taken captive his mind, captured and chained it as Prospero did Ariel. The resounding footsteps of Progress driven on so mercilessly in this mad age could not reach his fastness. It did not concern him that men were thinking, investigating, inventing. His senses responded only to the sonorous music of the woods: a steadfast wind ringing metallic melody from the pine-tops contented him, as the sound of the

Copyright 1897 by J. B. Lippincott & Co.

A MICHIGAN MAN

BY ELIA W PEATTIE

A PINE forest is nature's expression of solemnity and solitude. Sunlight, rivers, cascades, people, music, laughter, or dancing could not make it gay. With its unceasing reverberations and its eternal shadows, it is as awful and as holy as a cathedral.

Thirty good fellows working together by day and drinking together by night can keep up but a moody imitation of jollity. Spend twenty-five of your forty years, as Luther Dallas did, in this perennial gloom, and your soul—that which enjoys, aspires, competes— will be drugged as deep as if you had quaffed the cup of oblivion. Luther Dallas was counted one of the most experienced axe-men in the northern camps. He could fell a tree with the swift surety of an executioner, and in revenge for his many arboral murders the woodland had taken captive his mind, captured and chained it as Prospero did Ariel. The resounding footsteps of Progress driven on so mercilessly in this mad age could not reach his fastness. It did not concern him that men were thinking, investigating, inventing. His senses responded only to the sonorous music of the woods; a steadfast wind ringing metallic melody from the pine-tops contented him as the sound of the sea does the sailor; and dear as the odors of the ocean to the mariner were the resinous scents of the forest to him. Like a sailor, too, he had his superstitions. He had a presentiment that he was to die by one of these trees—that some day, in chopping, the tree would fall upon and crush him as it did his father the day they brought him back to the camp on a litter of pine boughs.

One day the gang boss noticed a tree that Dallas had left standing in a most unwoodmanlike manner in the section which was allotted to him.

"What in thunder is that standing there for?" he asked.

Dallas raised his eyes to the pine, towering in stern dignity a hundred feet above them.

"Well," he said, feebly, "I noticed it, but kind-a left it t' the last."

"Cut it down to-morrow," was the response.

The wind was rising, and the tree muttered savagely. Luther thought it sounded like a menace, and turned pale. No trouble has yet been found that will keep a man awake in the keen air of the pineries after he has been swinging his axe all day, but the sleep of the chopper was so broken with disturbing dreams that night that the beads gathered on his brow, and twice he cried aloud. He ate his coarse flap-jacks in the morning and escaped from the smoky shanty as soon as he could.

"It'll bring bad luck, I'm afraid," he muttered as he went to get his axe from the rack. He was as fond of his axe as a soldier of his musket, but to-day

he shouldered it with reluctance. He felt like a man
with his destiny before him. The tree stood like a
sentinel. He raised his axe, once, twice, a dozen
times, but could not bring himself to make a cut in the
bark. He walked backward a few steps and looked
up. The funereal green seemed to grow darker and
darker till it became black. It was the embodiment
of sorrow. Was it not shaking giant arms at him?
Did it not cry out in angry challenge? Luther did
not try to laugh at his fears; he had never seen any
humor in life. A gust of wind had someway crept
through the dense barricade of foliage that flanked the
clearing, and struck him with an icy chill. He looked
at the sky: the day was advancing rapidly. He went
at his work with an energy as determined as despair.
The axe in his practiced hand made clean straight cuts
in the trunk, now on this side, now on that. His task
was not an easy one, but he finished it with wonderful
expedition. After the chopping was finished, the tree
stood firm a moment; then, as the tensely strained
fibres began a weird moaning, he sprang aside, and
stood waiting. In the distance he saw two men hew-
ing a log. The axe-man sent them a shout and threw
up his arms for them to look. The tree stood out clear
and beautiful against the gray sky; the men ceased
their work and watched it. The vibrations became
more violent, and the sounds they produced grew
louder and louder till they reached a shrill wild cry.
There came a pause; then a deep shuddering groan.
The topmost branches began to move slowly, the
whole stately bulk swayed, and then shot toward the

ground. The gigantic trunk bounded from the stump, recoiled like a cannon, crashed down, and lay conquered, with a roar as of an earthquake, in a cloud of flying twigs and chips.

When the dust had cleared away, the men at the log on the outside of the clearing could not see Luther. They ran to the spot, and found him lying on the ground with his chest crushed in. His fearful eyes had not rightly calculated the distance from the stump to the top of the pine, nor rightly weighed the power of the massed branches, and so, standing spell-bound, watching the descending trunk as one might watch his Nemesis, the rebound came and left him lying worse than dead.

Three months later, when the logs, lopped of their branches, drifted down the streams, the woodman, a human log lopped of his strength, drifted to a great city. A change, the doctor said, might prolong his life. The lumbermen made up a purse, and he started out, not very definitely knowing his destination. He had a sister, much younger than himself, who at the age of sixteen had married and gone, he believed, to Chicago. That was years ago, but he had an idea that he might find her. He was not troubled by his lack of resources: he did not believe that any man would want for a meal unless he were "shiftless." He had always been able to turn his hand to something.

He felt too ill from the jostling of the cars to notice much of anything on the journey. The dizzy scenes whirling past made him faint, and he was glad to lie with closed eyes. He imagined that his little sister in her pink calico frock and bare feet (as he remembered her) would be at the station to meet him. "Oh, Lu!" she would call from some hiding-place, and he would go and find her.

The conductor stopped by Luther's seat and said that they were in the city at last; but it seemed to the sick man as if they went miles after that, with a multitude of twinkling lights on one side and a blank darkness that they told him was the lake on the other. The conductor again stopped by his seat.

"Well, my man," said he, "how are you feeling?"

Luther, the possessor of the toughest muscles in the gang, felt a sick man's irritation at the tone of pity.

"Oh, I'm all right!" he said, gruffly, and shook off the assistance the conductor tried to offer with his overcoat. "I'm going to my sister's," he explained, in answer to the inquiry as to where he was going. The man, somewhat piqued at the spirit in which his overtures were met, left him, and Luther stepped on to the platform. There was a long vista of semi-light, down which crowds of people walked and baggage-men rushed. The building, if it deserved the name, seemed a ruin, and through the arched doors Luther could see men—hackmen—dancing and howling like dervishes. Trains were coming and going, and the whistles and bells kept up a ceaseless clangor. Luther, with his small satchel and uncouth dress, slouched by the crowd unnoticed, and reached the street. He walked amid such an illumination as he had never dreamed of, and paused half blinded in the glare of a broad sheet of electric light that filled a pillared entrance into which many people passed. He looked about him. Above on every side rose great, many-windowed buildings; on the street the cars and carriages thronged, and jostling crowds dashed headlong among the vehicles. After a time he turned down a street that seemed to him a pandemonium filled with madmen. It went to his head like wine, and hardly left him the presence of mind to sustain a quiet exterior. The wind was laden with a penetrating moisture that chilled him as the dry icy breezes from Huron never had done, and the pain in his lungs made him faint and dizzy. He wondered if his red-cheeked little sister could live in one of those vast, impregnable buildings. He thought of stopping some of those serious-looking men and asking them if they knew her, but he could not muster up the courage. The distressing experience that comes to almost every one some time in life, of losing all identity in the universal humanity, was becoming his. The tears began to roll down his wasted face from loneliness and exhaustion. He grew hungry with longing for the dirty but familiar cabins of the camp, and staggered along with eyes half closed, conjuring visions of the warm interiors, the leaping fires, the groups of laughing men seen dimly through clouds of tobacco smoke.

A delicious scent of coffee met his hungry sense and made him really think he was taking the savory black draught from his familiar tin cup; but the muddy streets, the blinding lights, the cruel, rushing people, were still there. The buildings, however, now became different. They were lower and meaner, with dirty windows. Women laughing loudly crowded about the doors, and the establishments seemed to be equally divided between saloon-keepers, pawnbrokers, and dealers in second-hand clothes. Luther wondered where they all drew their support from. Upon one signboard he read, "Lodgings 10 cents to 50 cents. A Square Meal for 15 cents," and, thankful for some haven, entered. Here he spent his first night and other nights, while his purse dwindled and his strength waned. At last he got a man in a drug store to search the directory for his sister's residence. They found a name he took to be his brother-in-law's. It was two days later when he found the address—a great, many-storied mansion on one of the southern boulevards—and found also that his search had been in vain. Sore and faint, he staggered back to his miserable shelter, only to arise feverish and ill in the morning. He frequented the great shop doors, thronged with brilliantly dressed ladies, and watched to see if his little sister might not dash up in one of those satin-lined coaches and take him were he would be warm and safe and would sleep undisturbed by drunken, ribald songs and loathsome surroundings. There were days when he almost forgot his name, and, striving to remember, would lose his senses for a moment and drift back to the harmonious solitudes of the North and breathe the resin-scented frosty atmosphere. He grew terrified at the blood he coughed from his lacerated lungs, and wondered bitterly why the boys did not come to take him home.

One day, as he painfully dragged himself down a

residence street, he tried to collect his thoughts and form some plan for the future. He had no trade, understood no handiwork: he could fell trees! He looked at the gaunt, scrawny, transplanted specimens that met his eye, and gave himself up to the homesickness that filled his soul. He slept that night in the shelter of a stable, and spent his last money in the morning for a biscuit.

He traveled many miles that afternoon looking for something to which he might turn his hand. Once he got permission to carry a hod for half an hour. At the end of that time he fainted. When he recovered, the foreman paid him twenty-five cents. "For God's sake, man, go home," he said. Luther stared at him with a white face and went on.

There came days when he so forgot his native dignity as to beg. He seldom received anything; he was referred to various charitable institutions whose existence he had never heard of.

One morning, when a pall of smoke enveloped the city and the odors of coal-gas refused to lift their nauseating poison through the heavy air, Luther, chilled with dew and famished, awoke to a happier life. The loneliness at his heart was gone. The feeling of hopeless imprisonment that the miles and miles of streets had terrified him with gave place to one of freedom and exaltation. Above him he heard the rasping of pine boughs; his feet trod on a rebounding mat of decay; the sky was as coldly blue as the bosom of Huron. He walked as if on ether, singing a senseless jargon the woodmen had aroused the echoes with:

"Hi yi halloo!
The owl sees you!
Look what you do!
Hi yi halloo!"

Swung over his shoulder was a stick he had used to assist his limping gait, but now transformed into the beloved axe. He would reach the clearing soon, he thought, and strode on like a giant, while people hurried from his path. Suddenly a smooth trunk, stripped of its bark and bleached by weather, arose before him.

"Hi yi halloo!" High went the wasted arm—crash! —a broken staff, a jingle of wires, a maddened, shouting man the centre of a group of amused spectators! A few moments later, four broad-shouldered men in blue had him in their grasp, pinioned and guarded, clattering over the noisy streets behind two spirited horses. They drew after them a troop of noisy, jeering boys, who danced about the wagon like a swirl of autumn leaves. Then came a halt, and Luther was dragged up the steps of a square brick building with a belfry on the top. They entered a large bare room with benches ranged about the walls, and brought him before a man at a desk.

"What is your name?" asked the man at the desk.

"Hi yi halloo!" said Luther.

"He's drunk, sergeant," said one of the men in blue, and the axe-man was led into the basement. He was conscious of an involuntary resistance, a short struggle, and a final shock of pain—then oblivion.

The chopper awoke to the realization of three stone walls and an iron grating in front. Through this he looked out upon a stone flooring across which was a row of similar apartments. He neither knew nor cared where he was. The feeling of imprisonment was no greater than he had felt on the endless, cheerless streets. He laid himself on the bench that ran along a side wall, and, closing his eyes, listened to the babble of the clear stream and the thunder of the "drive" on its journey. How the logs hurried and jostled! crushing, whirling, ducking, with the merry lads leaping about them with shouts and laughter. Suddenly he was recalled by a voice. Some one handed a narrow tin cup full of coffee and a thick slice of bread through the grating. Across the way he dimly saw a man eating a similar slice of bread. Men in other compartments were swearing and singing. He knew these now for the voices he had heard in his dreams. He tried to force some of the bread down his parched and swollen throat, but failed; the coffee strangled him, and he threw himself upon the bench.

The forest again, the night-wind, the whistle of the axe through the air! Once when he opened his eyes he found it dark. It would soon be time to go to work. He fancied there would be hoar-frost on the trees in the morning. How close the cabin seemed! Ha!—here came his little sister. Her voice sounded like the wind on a spring morning. How loud it swelled now! "Lu! Lu!" she cried.

The next morning the lock-up keeper opened the

cell door.   Luther lay with his head in a pool of
blood.   His soul had escaped from the thrall of the
forest.

"Well, well!" said the little fat police justice, when
he was told of it.   "We ought to have a doctor around
to look after such cases."

MY TERMINAL MORAINE

BY FRANK R. STOCKTON

*Of Francis Richard Stockton (born in
Philadelphia, April 5, 1834; died in 1902)
Mr. W. D. Howells wrote: "He is of the
few, of the little group sparely increased by
the fastidious ages, whom we call masters.
. . . The means in all [his stories] have been
the same: the quiet confidence that every intelligent person enjoys an absurdity reduced
from the most logical argument, and pre-
fers the wildest capers of the fancy performed
with a countenance of the gravest sobriety."
Of Stockton's style Mr. Henry C. Vedder
said: "It is very plain, simple, flowing English, the sort of writing that appears to
the inexperienced the easiest thing in the
world to do—until they have tried." "My
Terminal Moraine" is a typical Stockton
story which was written specially for
COLLIER'S "Once a Week Library."*

MY TERMINAL MORAINE

BY FRANK R. STOCKTON

A MAN'S birth is generally considered the most important event of his existence; but I truly think that what I am about to relate was more important to me than my entrance into this world; because, had not these things happened, I am of the opinion that my life would have been of no value to me and my birth a misfortune.

My father, Joshua Cuthbert, died soon after I came to my majority, leaving me what he had considered a comfortable property. This consisted of a large house and some forty acres of land, nearly the whole of which lay upon a bluff, which upon three sides descended to a little valley, through which ran a gentle stream. I had no brothers or sisters. My mother died when I was a boy, and I, Walter Cuthbert, was left the sole representative of my immediate family.

My estate had been a comfortable one to my father, because his income from the practice of his profession as a physician enabled him to keep it up and provide satisfactorily for himself and me. I had his profession and but a very small income, the result of a few investments my father had made. Left to myself, I felt no inducement to take up any profession or business. My wants were simple, and for a few years I

MY TERMINAL MORAINE

BY FRANK R. STOCKTON

A MAN'S birth is generally considered the most important event of his existence, but I truly think that what I am about to relate was more important to me than my entrance into this world; because, had not these things happened, I am of the opinion that my life would have been of no value to me and my birth a misfortune.

My father, Joshua Cuthbert, died soon after I came to my majority, leaving me what he had considered a comfortable property. This consisted of a large house and some forty acres of land, nearly the whole of which lay upon a bluff, which upon three sides descended to a little valley, through which ran a gentle stream. I had no brothers or sisters. My mother died when I was a boy, and I, Walter Cuthbert, was left the sole representative of my immediate family.

My estate had been a comfortable one to my father, because his income from the practice of his profession as a physician enabled him to keep it up and provide satisfactorily for himself and me. I had no profession and but a very small income, the result of a few investments my father had made. Left to myself, I felt no inducement to take up any profession or business. My wants were simple, and for a few years I

lived without experiencing any inconvenience from
the economies which I was obliged to practice.
My books, my dog, my gun and my rod made
life pass very pleasantly to me, and the subject of an
increase of income never disturbed my mind.

But as time passed on the paternal home began to
present an air of neglect and even dilapidation, which
occasionally attracted my attention and caused, as I
incidentally discovered, a great deal of unfavorable
comment among my neighbors, who thought that I
should go to work and at least earn money enough to
put the house and grounds in a condition which should
not be unworthy the memory of the good Dr. Cuthbert. In fact, I began to be looked upon as a shiftless
young man; and, now and then, I found a person old
enough and bold enough to tell me so.

But, instead of endeavoring to find some suitable
occupation by which I might better my condition and
improve my estate, I fell in love, which, in the opinion
of my neighbors, was the very worst thing that could
have happened to me at this time. I lived in a thrifty
region, and for a man who could not support himself
to think of taking upon him the support of a wife,
especially such a wife as Agnes Havelot would be,
was considered more than folly and looked upon as
a crime. Everybody knew that I was in love with
Miss Havelot, for I went to court her as boldly as I
went to fish or shoot. There was a good deal of talk
about it, and this finally came to the ears of Mr.
Havelot, my lady's father, who, thereupon, promptly
ordered her to have no more to do with me.

The Havelot estate, which adjoined mine, was a very large one, containing hundreds and hundreds of acres; and the Havelots were rich, rich enough to frighten any poor young man of marrying intent. But I did not appreciate the fact that I was a poor young man. I had never troubled my head about money as it regarded myself, and I now did not trouble my head about it as it regarded Agnes. I loved her, I hoped she loved me, and all other considerations were thrown aside. Mr. Havelot, however, was a man of a different way of thinking.

It was a little time before I became convinced that the decision of Agnes's father, that there should be no communication between that dear girl and myself, really meant anything. I had never been subjected to restrictions, and I did not understand how people of spirit could submit to them; but I was made to understand it when Mr. Havelot, finding me wandering about his grounds, very forcibly assured me that if I should make my appearance there again, or if he discovered any attempt on my part to communicate with his daughter in any way, he would send her from home. He concluded the very brief interview by stating that if I had any real regard for his daughter's happiness I would cease attentions which would meet with the most decided disapprobation from her only surviving parent and which would result in exiling her from home. I begged for one more interview with Miss Havelot, and if it had been granted I should have assured her of the state of my affections, no matter if there were reasons to suppose that

I would never see her again; but her father very sternly forbade anything of the kind, and I went away crushed.

It was a very hard case, for if I played the part of a bold lover and tried to see Agnes without regard to the wicked orders of her father, I should certainly be discovered; and then it would be not only myself, but the poor girl, who would suffer. So I determined that I would submit to the Havelot decree. No matter if I never saw her again, never heard the sound of her voice, it would be better to have her near me, to have her breathe the same air, cast up her eyes at the same sky, listen to the same birds, that I breathed, looked at and listened to, than to have her far away, probably in Kentucky, where I knew she had relatives, and where the grass was blue and the sky probably green, or at any rate would appear so to her if in the least degree she felt as I did in regard to the ties of home and the affinities between the sexes.

I now found myself in a most doleful and even desperate condition of mind. There was nothing in the world which I could have for which I cared. Hunting, fishing, and the rambles through woods and fields that had once been so delightful to me now became tasks which I seldom undertook. The only occupation in which I felt the slightest interest was that of sitting in a tower of my house with a telescope, endeavoring to see my Agnes on some portion of her father's grounds; but, although I diligently directed my glass at the slightest stretch of lawn or bit of path which I could discern through openings in the foliage, I never caught sight of her. I knew, however, by means of daily questions addressed to my cook, whose daughter was a servant in the Havelot house, that Agnes was yet at home. For that reason I remained at home. Otherwise, I should have become a wanderer.

About a month after I had fallen into this most unhappy state an old friend came to see me. We had been school-fellows, but he differed from me in almost every respect. He was full of ambition and energy, and, although he was but a few years older than myself, he had already made a name in the world. He was a geologist, earnest and enthusiastic in his studies and his investigations. He told me frankly that the object of his visit was twofold. In the first place, he wanted to see me, and, secondly, he wanted to make some geological examinations on my grounds, which were situated, as he informed me, upon a terminal moraine, a formation which he had not yet had an opportunity of practically investigating.

I had not known that I lived on a moraine, and now that I knew it, I did not care. But Tom Burton glowed with high spirits and lively zeal as he told me how the great bluff on which my house stood, together with the other hills and wooded terraces which stretched away from it along the side of the valley, had been formed by the minute fragments of rock and soil, which, during ages and ages, had been gradually pushed down from the mountains by a great glacier which once occupied the country to the northeast of my house. "Why, Walter, my boy," he cried, "if I had not read it all in the books I should have known for myself, as soon as I came here, that there had once been a glacier up there, and as it gradually moved to the southwest it had made this country what it is. Have you a stream down there in that dell which I see lies at right angles with the valley and opens into it?"

"No," said I; "I wish there were one. The only stream we have flows along the valley and not on my property."

Without waiting for me Tom ran down into my dell, pushed his way through the underbrush to its upper end, and before long came back flushed with heat and enthusiasm.

"Well, sir," he said, "that dell was once the bed of a glacial stream, and you may as well clear it out and plant corn there if you want to, for there never will be another stream flowing through it until there is another glacier out in the country beyond. And now I want you to let me dig about here. I want to find out what sort of stuff the glacier brought down from the mountains. I will hire a man and will promise you to fill up all the holes I make."

I had no objection to my friend's digging as much as he pleased, and for three days he busied himself in getting samples of the soil of my estate. Sometimes I went out and looked at him, and gradually a little of his earnest ardor infused itself into me, and with some show of interest I looked into the holes he had made and glanced over the mineral specimens he showed me.

"Well, Walter," said he, when he took leave of me,

"I am very sorry that I did not discover that the glacier had raked out the bed of a gold mine from the mountains up there and brought it down to you, or at any rate, some valuable iron ore. But I am obliged to say it did not do anything of the sort. But I can tell you one thing it brought you, and, although it is not of any great commercial value, I should think you could make good use of it here on your place. You have one of the finest deposits of gravel on this bluff that I have met with, and if you were to take out a lot of it and spread it over your driveways and paths, it would make it a great deal pleasanter for you to go about here in bad weather and would wonderfully improve your property. Good roads always give an idea of thrift and prosperity." And then he went away with a valise nearly full of mineral specimens which he assured me were very interesting.

My interest in geological formations died away as soon as Tom Burton had departed, but what he said about making gravel roads giving the place an air of thrift and prosperity had its effect upon my mind. It struck me that it would be a very good thing if people in the neighborhood, especially the Havelots, were to perceive on my place some evidences of thrift and prosperity. Most palpable evidences of unthrift and impecuniosity had cut me off from Agnes, and why might it not be that some signs of improved circumstances would remove, to a degree at least, the restrictions which had been placed between us? This was but a very little thing upon which to build hopes;

but ever since men and women have loved they have built grand hopes upon very slight foundations. I determined to put my roadways in order.

My efforts in this direction were really evidence of anything but thriftiness, for I could not in the least afford to make my drives and walks resemble the smooth and beautiful roads which wound over the Havelot estate, although to do this was my intention, and I set about the work without loss of time. I took up this occupation with so much earnestness that it seriously interfered with my observations from the tower.

I hired two men and set them to work to dig a gravel-pit. They made excavations at several places, and very soon found what they declared to be a very fine quality of road-gravel. I ordered them to dig on until they had taken out what they believed to be enough to cover all my roads. When this had been done, I would have it properly spread and rolled. As this promised to be a very good job, the men went to work in fine spirits and evidently made up their minds that the improvements I desired would require a vast deal of gravel.

When they had dug a hole so deep that it became difficult to throw up the gravel from the bottom, I suggested that they should dig at some other place. But to this they objected, declaring that the gravel was getting better and better, and it would be well to go on down as long as the quality continued to be so good. So, at last, they put a ladder into the pit, one man carrying the gravel up in a hod, while the other dug it; and when they had gone down so deep that this was no longer practicable, they rigged up a derrick and windlass and drew up the gravel in a bucket.

Had I been of a more practical turn of mind I might have perceived that this method of working made the job a very long and, consequently, to the laborers, a profitable one; but no such idea entered into my head, and not noticing whether they were bringing up sand or gravel I allowed them to proceed.

One morning I went out to the spot where the excavation was being made and found that the men had built a fire on the ground near the opening of the pit, and that one of them was bending over it warming imself. As the month was July this naturally surprised me, and I inquired the reason for so strange a performance.

"Upon my soul," said the man, who was rubbing his hands over the blaze, "I do not wonder you are surprised, but it's so cold down at the bottom of that pit that me fingers is almost frosted; and we haven't struck any wather neither, which couldn't be expected, of course, a-diggin' down into the hill like this."

I looked into the hole and found it was very deep. "I think it would be better to stop digging here," said I, "and try some other place."

"I wouldn't do that just now," said the other man, who was preparing to go down in the bucket; "to be sure, it's a good deal more like a well than a gravel-pit, but it's bigger at the top than at the bottom, and there's no danger of its cavin' in, and now that we've got everything rigged up all right, it would be a pity to make a change yet awhile."

So I let them go on; but the next day when I went out again I found that they had come to the conclusion that it was time to give up digging in that hole. They both declared that it almost froze their feet to stand on the ground where they worked at the bottom of the excavation. The slow business of drawing up the gravel by means of a bucket and windlass was, therefore, reluctantly given up. The men now went to work to dig outward from this pit toward the edge of the bluff which overlooked my little dell, and gradually made a wide trench, which they deepened until —and I am afraid to say how long they worked before this was done—they could walk to the original pit from the level of the dell. They then deepened the inner end of the trench, wheeling out the gravel in barrows, until they had made an inclined pathway from the dell to the bottom of the pit. The wheeling now became difficult, and the men soon declared that they were sure that they had quite gravel enough.

When they made this announcement, and I had gone into some financial calculations, I found that I would be obliged to put an end to my operations, at least for the present, for my available funds were gone, or would be when I had paid what I owed for the work. The men were very much disappointed by the sudden ending of this good job, but they departed, and I was left to gaze upon a vast amount of gravel, of which, for the present at least, I could not afford to make the slightest use.

The mental despondency which had been somewhat lightened during my excavating operations now returned, and I became rather more gloomy and downcast than before. My cook declared that it was of no use to prepare meals which I never ate, and suggested that it would save money if I discharged her. As I had not paid her anything for a long time, I did not see how this would benefit me.

Wandering about one day with my hat pulled down over my eyes and my hands thrust deep into my pockets, I strolled into the dell and stood before the wide trench which led to the pit in which I had foolishly sunk the money which should have supported me for months. I entered this dismal passage and walked slowly and carefully down the incline until I reached the bottom of the original pit, where I had never been before. I stood here looking up and around me and wondering how men could bring themselves to dig down into such dreary depths simply for the sake of a few dollars a week, when I involuntarily began to stamp my feet. They were very cold, although I had not been there more than a minute. I wondered at this and took up some of the loose gravel in my hand. It was quite dry, but it chilled my fingers. I did not understand it, and I did not try to, but walked up the trench and around into the dell, thinking of Agnes.

I was very fond of milk, which, indeed, was almost the only food I now cared for, and I was consequently much disappointed at my noonday meal when I found that the milk had soured and was not fit to drink.

"You see, sir," said Susan, "ice is very scarce and
dear, and we can not afford to buy much of it. There
was no freezin' weather last winter, and the price has
gone up as high as the thermometer, sir, and so,
between the two of 'em, I can't keep things from
spoilin'."

The idea now came to me that if Susan would take
the milk, and anything else she wished to keep cool
in this hot weather, to the bottom of the gravel-pit,
she would find the temperature there cold enough to
preserve them without ice, and I told her so.

The next morning Susan came to me with a pleased
countenance and said, "I put the butter and the milk
in that pit last night, and the butter's just as hard
and the milk's as sweet as if it had been kept in an
ice-house. But the place is as cold as an ice-house,
sir, and unless I am mistaken, there's ice in it. Anyway, what do you call that?" And she took from a
little basket a piece of grayish ice as large as my fist.
"When I found it was so cold down there, sir," she
said, "I thought I would dig a little myself and see
what made it so; and I took a fire-shovel and hatchet,
and, when I had scraped away some of the gravel, I
came to something hard and chopped off this piece of
it, which is real ice, sir, or I know nothing about it.
Perhaps there used to be an ice-house there, and you
might get some of it if you dug, though why anybody should put it down so deep and then cover it up,
I'm sure I don't know. But as long as there's any
there, I think we should get it out, even if there's only
a little of it; for I can not take everything down to

that pit, and we might as well have it in the refrigerator."

This seemed to me like very good sense, and if I had had a man I should have ordered him to go down to the pit and dig up any lumps of ice he might find and bring them to the house. But I had no man, and I therefore became impressed with the opinion that if I did not want to drink sour milk for the rest of the summer, it might be a good thing for me to go down there and dig out some of the ice myself. So with pickaxe and shovel I went to the bottom of the pit and set myself to work.

A few inches below the surface I found that my shovel struck something hard, and, clearing away the gravel from this for two or three square feet, I looked down upon a solid mass of ice. It was dirty and begrimed, but it was truly ice. With my pick I detached some large pieces of it. These, with some discomfort, I carried out into the dell where Susan might come with her basket and get them.

For several days Susan and I took out ice from the pit, and then I thought that perhaps Tom Burton might feel some interest in this frozen deposit in my terminal moraine, and so I wrote to him about it. He did not answer my letter, but instead arrived himself the next afternoon.

"Ice at the bottom of a gravel-pit," said he, "is a thing I never heard of. Will you lend me a spade and a pickaxe?"

When Tom came out of that pit—it was too cold a place for me to go with him and watch his proceedings—I saw him come running toward the house.

"Walter," he shouted, "we must hire all the men we can find and dig, dig, dig. If I am not mistaken something has happened on your place that is wonderful almost beyond belief. But we must not stop to talk. We must dig, dig, dig; dig all day and dig all night. Don't think of the cost. I'll attend to that. I'll get the money. What we must do is to find men and set them to work."

"What's the matter?" said I. "What has happened?"

"I haven't time to talk about it now; besides I don't want to, for fear that I should find that I am mistaken. But get on your hat, my dear fellow, and let's go over to the town for men."

The next day there were eight men working under the direction of my friend Burton, and although they did not work at night as he wished them to do, they labored steadfastly for ten days or more before Tom was ready to announce what it was he had hoped to discover, and whether or not he had found it. For a day or two I watched the workmen from time to time, but after that I kept away, preferring to await the result of my friend's operations. He evidently expected to find something worth having, and whether he was successful or not, it suited me better to know the truth all at once and not by degrees.

On the morning of the eleventh day Tom came into the room where I was reading and sat down near me. His face was pale, his eyes glittering. "Old friend,"

said he, and as he spoke I noticed that his voice was a
little husky, although it was plain enough that his
emotion was not occasioned by bad fortune—"my
good old friend, I have found out what made the bottom of your gravel-pit so uncomfortably cold. You
need not doubt what I am going to tell you, for my
excavations have been complete and thorough enough
to make me sure of what I say. Don't you remember
that I told you that ages ago there was a vast glacier
in the country which stretches from here to the mountains? Well, sir, the foot of that glacier must have
reached further this way than is generally supposed.
At any rate a portion of it did extend in this direction
as far as this bit of the world which is now yours.
This end or spur of the glacier, nearly a quarter of a
mile in width, I should say, and pushing before it a
portion of the terminal moraine on which you live,
came slowly toward the valley until suddenly it detached itself from the main glacier and disappeared
from sight. That is to say, my boy"—and as he spoke
Tom sprang to his feet, too excited to sit any longer—
"it descended to the bowels of the earth, at least for a
considerable distance in that direction. Now you
want to know how this happened. Well, I'll tell you.
In this part of the country there are scattered about
here and there great caves. Geologists know one or
two of them, and it is certain that there are others un-
discovered. Well, sir, your glacier spur discovered one
of them, and when it had lain over the top of it for an
age or two, and had grown bigger and bigger, and
heavier and heavier, it at last burst through the rock

roof of the cave, snapping itself from the rest of the glacier and falling in one vast mass to the bottom of the subterranean abyss. Walter, it is there now. The rest of the glacier came steadily down; the moraines were forced before it; they covered up this glacier spur, this broken fragment, and by the time the climate changed and the average of temperature rose above that of the glacial period, this vast sunken mass of ice was packed away below the surface of the earth, out of the reach of the action of friction, or heat, or moisture, or anything else which might destroy it. And through all the long procession of centuries that broken end of the glacier has been lying in your terminal moraine. It is there now. It is yours, Walter Cuthbert. It is an ice-mine. It is wealth, and so far as I can make out, it is nearly all upon your land. To you is the possession, but to me is the glory of the discovery. A bit of the glacial period kept in a cave for us! It is too wonderful to believe! Walter, have you any brandy?"

It may well be supposed that by this time I was thoroughly awakened to the importance and the amazing character of my friend's discovery, and I hurried with him to the scene of operations. There he explained everything and showed me how, by digging away a portion of the face of the bluff, he had found that this vast fragment of the glacier, which had been so miraculously preserved, ended in an irregularly perpendicular wall, which extended downward he knew not how far, and the edge of it on its upper side had been touched by my workmen in digging their pit.

"It was the gradual melting of the upper end of this glacier," said Tom, "probably more elevated than the lower end, that made your dell. I wondered why the depression did not extend further up toward the spot where the foot of the glacier was supposed to have been. This end of the fragment, being sunk in deeper and afterward covered up more completely, probably never melted at all."

"It is amazing—astounding," said I; "but what of it, now that we have found it?"

"What of it?" cried Tom, and his whole form trembled as he spoke. "You have here a source of wealth, of opulence which shall endure for the rest of your days. Here at your very door, where it can be taken out and transported with the least possible trouble, is ice enough to supply the town, the county, yes, I might say, the State, for hundreds of years. No, sir, I can not go in to supper. I can not eat. I leave to you the business and practical part of this affair. I go to report upon its scientific features."

"Agnes," I exclaimed, as I walked to the house with my hands clasped and my eyes raised to the sky, "the glacial period has given thee to me!"

This did not immediately follow, although I went that very night to Mr. Havelot and declared to him that I was now rich enough to marry his daughter. He laughed at me in a manner which was very annoying, and made certain remarks which indicated that he thought it probable that it was not the roof of the cave, but my mind, which had given way under the influence of undue pressure.

The contemptuous manner in which I had been received aroused within me a very unusual state of mind.
While talking to Mr. Havelot I heard not far away
in some part of the house a voice singing. It was the
voice of Agnes, and I believed she sang so that I
could hear her.   But as her sweet tones reached my
ear there came to me at the same time the harsh, contemptuous words of her father.   I left the house determined to crush that man to the earth beneath a
superincumbent mass of ice—or the evidence of the
results of the ownership of such a mass—which would
make him groan and weep as he apologized to me for
his scornful and disrespectful utterances and at the
same time offered me the hand of his daughter.

When the discovery of the ice-mine, as it grew to be
called, became generally known, my grounds were
crowded by sightseers, and reporters of newspapers
were more plentiful than squirrels.   But the latter
were referred to Burton, who would gladly talk to
them as long as they could afford to listen, and I felt
myself at last compelled to shut my gates to the first.

I had offers of capital to develop this novel source
of wealth, and I accepted enough of this assistance
to enable me to begin operations on a moderate scale.
It was considered wise not to uncover any portion of
the glacier spur, but to construct an inclined shaft down
to its wall-like end and from this tunnel into the great
mass.   Immediately the leading ice company of the
neighboring town contracted with me for all the ice
I could furnish, and the flood-gates of affluence began
slowly to rise.

The earliest, and certainly one of the greatest, benefits which came to me from this bequest from the unhistoric past was the new energy and vigor with which my mind and body were now infused. My old, careless method of life and my recent melancholy, despairing mood were gone, and I now began to employ myself upon the main object of my life with an energy and enthusiasm almost equal to that of my friend, Tom Burton. This present object of my life was to prepare my home for Agnes.

The great piles of gravel which my men had dug from the well-like pit were spread upon the roadways and rolled smooth and hard; my lawn was mowed; my flower-beds and borders put in order; useless bushes and undergrowth cut out and cleared away; my outbuildings were repaired and the grounds around my house rapidly assumed their old appearance of neatness and beauty.

Ice was very scarce that summer, and, as the wagons wound away from the opening of the shaft which led down to the glacier, carrying their loads to the nearest railway station, so money came to me; not in large sums at first, for preparations had not yet been perfected for taking out the ice in great quantities, but enough to enable me to go on with my work as rapidly as I could plan it. I set about renovating and brightening and newly furnishing my house. Whatever I thought that Agnes would like I bought and put into it. I tried to put myself in her place as I selected the paper-hangings and the materials with which to cover the furniture.

Sometimes, while thus employed selecting ornaments or useful articles for my house, and using as far as was possible the taste and judgment of another instead of my own, the idea came to me that perhaps Agnes had never heard of my miraculous good fortune. Certainly her father would not be likely to inform her, and perhaps she still thought of me, if she thought at all, as the poor young man from whom she had been obliged to part because he was poor.

But whether she knew that I was growing rich, or whether she thought I was becoming poorer and poorer, I thought only of the day when I could go to her father and tell him that I was able to take his daughter and place her in a home as beautiful as that in which she now lived, and maintain her with all the comforts and luxuries which he could give her.

One day I asked my faithful cook, who also acted as my housekeeper and general supervisor, to assist me in making out a list of china which I intended to purchase.

"Are you thinking of buying china, sir?" she asked. "We have now quite as much as we really need."

"Oh, yes," said I, "I shall get complete sets of everything that can be required for a properly furnished household."

Susan gave a little sigh. "You are spendin' a lot of money, sir, and some of it for things that a single gentleman would be likely not to care very much about; and if you was to take it into your head to travel and stay away for a year or two, there's a good many things you've bought that would look shabby when you come back, no matter how careful I might be in dustin' 'em and keepin' 'em covered."

"But I have no idea of traveling," said I. "There's no place so pleasant as this to me."

Susan was silent for a few moments, and then she said: "I know very well why you are doing all this, and I feel it my bounden duty to say to you that there's a chance of its bein' no use. I do not speak without good reason, and I would not do it if I didn't think that it might make trouble lighter to you when it comes."

"What are you talking about, Susan; what do you mean?"

"Well, sir, this is what I mean: It was only last night that my daughter Jane was in Mr. Havelot's dining-room after dinner was over, and Mr. Havelot and a friend of his were sitting there, smoking their cigars and drinking their coffee. She went in and come out again as she was busy takin' away the dishes, and they paid no attention to her, but went on talkin' without knowing, most likely, she was there. Mr. Havelot and the gentleman were talkin' about you, and Jane she heard Mr. Havelot say as plain as anything, and she said she couldn't be mistaken, that even if your nonsensical ice-mine proved to be worth anything, he would never let his daughter marry an ice-man. He spoke most disrespectful of ice-men, sir, and said that it would make him sick to have a son-in-law whose business it was to sell ice to butchers, and hotels, and grog-shops, and pork-packers, and all that sort of people, and that he would as soon have his daughter

marry the man who supplied a hotel with sausages as
the one who supplied it with ice to keep those sausages from spoiling. You see, sir, Mr. Havelot lives
on his property as his father did before him, and he is
a very proud man, with a heart as hard and cold as
that ice down under your land; and it's borne in on
me very strong, sir, that it would be a bad thing for
you to keep on thinkin' that you are gettin' this house
all ready to bring Miss Havelot to when you have
married her. For if Mr. Havelot keeps on livin', which
there's every chance of his doin', it may be many a
weary year before you get Miss Agnes, if you ever
get her. And havin' said that, sir, I say no more, and
I would not have said this much if I hadn't felt it my
bounden duty to your father's son to warn him that
most likely he was workin' for what he might never
get, and so keep him from breakin' his heart when he
found out the truth all of a sudden."

With that Susan left me, without offering any assistance in making out a list of china. This was a
terrible story; but, after all, it was founded only upon
servants' gossip. In this country, even proud, rich
men like Mr. Havelot did not have such absurd ideas
regarding the source of wealth. Money is money,
and whether it is derived from the ordinary products
of the earth, from which came much of Mr. Havelot's
revenue, or from an extraordinary project such as my
glacier spur, it truly could not matter so far as concerned the standing in society of its possessor. What
utter absurdity was this which Susan had told me!
If I were to go to Mr. Havelot and tell him that I

would not marry his daughter because he supplied
brewers and bakers with the products of his fields,
would he not consider me an idiot? I determined to
pay no attention to the idle tale. But alas! deter-
minations of that sort are often of little avail. I did
pay attention to it, and my spirits drooped.

The tunnel into the glacier spur had now attained
considerable length, and the ice in the interior was
found to be of a much finer quality than that first met
with, which was of a grayish hue and somewhat inclined to crumble. When the workmen reached a
grade of ice as good as they could expect, they began
to enlarge the tunnel into a chamber, and from this
they proposed to extend tunnels in various directions
after the fashion of a coal-mine. The ice was hauled
out on sledges through the tunnel and then carried up
a wooden railway to the mouth of the shaft.

It was comparatively easy to walk down the shaft
and enter the tunnel, and when it happened that the
men were not at work I allowed visitors to go down
and view this wonderful ice-cavern. The walls of the
chamber appeared semi-transparent, and the light of
the candles or lanterns gave the whole scene a weird
and beautiful aspect. It was almost possible to imagine
one's self surrounded by limpid waters, which might
at any moment rush upon him and ingulf him.

Every day or two Tom Burton came with a party
of scientific visitors, and had I chosen to stop the work
of taking out ice, admitted the public and charged a
price for admission, I might have made almost as
much money as I at that time derived from the sale

of the ice. But such a method of profit was repugnant to me.

For several days after Susan's communication to me I worked on in my various operations, endeavoring to banish from my mind the idle nonsense she had spoken of; but one of its effects upon me was to make me feel that I ought not to allow hopes so important to rest upon uncertainties. So I determined that as soon as my house and grounds should be in a condition with which I should for the time be satisfied, I would go boldly to Mr. Havelot, and, casting out of my recollection everything that Susan had said, invite him to visit me and see for himself the results of the discovery of which he had spoken with such derisive contempt. This would be a straightforward and business-like answer to his foolish objections to me, and I believed that in his heart the old gentleman would properly appreciate my action.

About this time there came to my place Aaron Boyce, an elderly farmer of the neighborhood, and, finding me outside, he seized the opportunity to have a chat with me.

"I tell you what it is, Mr. Cuthbert," said he, "the people in this neighborhood hasn't give you credit for what's in you. The way you have fixed up this place, and the short time you have took to do it, is enough to show us now what sort of a man you are; and I tell you, sir, we're proud of you for a neighbor. I don't believe there's another gentleman in this county of your age that could have done what you have done in so short a time. I expect now you will be thinking

of getting married and startin' housekeepin' in a regular fashion.   That comes just as natural as to set
hens in the spring.   By the way, have you heard that
old Mr. Havelot's thinkin' of goin' abroad?   I didn't
believe he would ever do that again, because he's gettin' pretty well on in years, but old men will do queer
things as well as young ones."

"Going abroad!" I cried.   "Does he intend to take
his daughter with him?"

Mr. Aaron Boyce smiled grimly.   He was a great
old gossip, and he had already obtained the information he wanted.   "Yes," he said, "I've heard it was on
her account he's going.   She's been kind of weakly
lately, they tell me, and hasn't took to her food, and
the doctors has said that what she wants is a sea
voyage and a change to foreign parts."

Going abroad!   Foreign parts!   This was more terrible than anything I had imagined.   I would go to
Mr. Havelot that very evening, the only time which
I would be certain to find him at home, and talk to
him in a way which would be sure to bring him to his
senses, if he had any.   And if I should find that he
had no sense of propriety or justice, no sense of his
duty to his fellow-man and to his offspring, then I
would begin a bold fight for Agnes, a fight which I
would not give up until, with her own lips, she told
me that it would be useless.   I would follow her to
Kentucky, to Europe, to the uttermost ends of the
earth.   I could do it now.   The frozen deposits in
my terminal moraine would furnish me with the
means.   I walked away and left the old farmer stand-

ing grinning. No doubt my improvements and reno-
vations had been the subject of gossip in the neighborhood, and he had come over to see if he could
find out anything definite in regard to the object of
them. He had succeeded, but he had done more: he
had nerved me to instantly begin the conquest of
Agnes, whether by diplomacy or war.

I was so anxious to begin this conquest that I could
scarcely wait for the evening to come. At the noon
hour, when the ice-works were deserted, I walked
down the shaft and into the ice-chamber to see what
had been done since my last visit. I decided to insist
that operations upon a larger scale should be immediately begun, in order that I might have plenty of
money with which to carry on my contemplated campaign. Whether it was one of peace or war, I should
want all the money I could get.

I took with me a lantern and went around the chamber, which was now twenty-five or thirty feet in diameter, examining the new inroads which had been made
upon its walls. There was a tunnel commenced opposite the one by which the chamber was entered, but
it had not been opened more than a dozen feet, and it
seemed to me that the men had not been working with
any very great energy. I wanted to see a continuous
stream of ice-blocks from that chamber to the mouth
of the shaft.

While grumbling thus I heard behind me a sudden
noise like thunder and the crashing of walls, and,
turning quickly, I saw that a portion of the roof of
the chamber had fallen in. Nor had it ceased to fall.

As I gazed, several great masses of ice came down from above and piled themselves upon that which had already fallen.

Startled and frightened, I sprang toward the opening of the entrance tunnel; but, alas! I found that that was the point where the roof had given way, and between me and the outer world was a wall of solid ice through which it would be as impossible for me to break as if it were a barrier of rock. With the quick instinct which comes to men in danger I glanced about to see if the workmen had left their tools; but there were none. They had been taken outside. Then I stood and gazed stupidly at the mass of fallen ice, which, even as I looked upon it, was cracking and snapping, pressed down by the weight above it, and forming itself into an impervious barrier without crevice or open seam.

Then I madly shouted. But of what avail were shouts down there in the depths of the earth? I soon ceased this useless expenditure of strength, and, with my lantern in my hand, began to walk around the chamber, throwing the light upon the walls and the roof. I became impressed with the fear that the whole cavity might cave in at once and bury me here in a tomb of ice. But I saw no cracks, nor any sign of further disaster. But why think of anything more? Was not this enough? For, before that ice-barrier could be cleared away, would I not freeze to death?

I now continued to walk, not because I expected to find anything or do anything, but simply to keep myself warm by action. As long as I could move about I believed that there was no immediate danger of succumbing to the intense cold; for, when a young man, traveling in Switzerland, I had been in the cave of a glacier, and it was not cold enough to prevent some old women from sitting there to play the zither for the sake of a few coppers from visitors. I could not expect to be able to continue walking until I should be rescued, and if I sat down, or by chance slept from exhaustion, I must perish.

The more I thought of it, the more sure I became that in any case I must perish. A man in a block of ice could have no chance of life. And Agnes! Oh, Heavens! what demon of the ice had leagued with old Havelot to shut me up in this frozen prison? For a long time I continued to walk, beat my body with my arms and stamp my feet. The instinct of life was strong within me. I would live as long as I could, and think of Agnes. When I should be frozen I could not think of her.

Sometimes I stopped and listened. I was sure I could hear noises, but I could not tell whether they were above me or not. In the centre of the ice-barrier, about four feet from the ground, was a vast block of the frozen substance which was unusually clear and seemed to have nothing on the other side of it; for through it I could see flickers of light, as though people were going about with lanterns. It was quite certain that the accident had been discovered; for, had not the thundering noise been heard by persons outside, the workmen would have seen what had hap-

pened as soon as they came into the tunnel to begin
their afternoon operations.

At first I wondered why they did not set to work
with a will and cut away this barrier and let me out.
But there suddenly came to my mind a reason for this
lack of energy which was more chilling than the glis-
tening walls around me : Why should they suppose that
I was in the ice-chamber? I was not in the habit of
coming here very often, but I was in the habit of wandering off by myself at all hours of the day. This
thought made me feel that I might as well lie down
on the floor of this awful cave and die at once. The
workmen might think it unsafe to mine any further
in this part of the glacier, and begin operations at some
other point. I did sit down for a moment, and then I
rose involuntarily and began my weary round. Suddenly I thought of looking at my watch. It was nearly
five o'clock. I had been more than four hours in that
dreadful place, and I did not believe that I could continue to exercise my limbs very much longer. The
lights I had seen had ceased. It was quite plain that
the workmen had no idea that any one was imprisoned
in the cave.

But soon after I had come to this conclusion I saw
through the clear block of ice a speck of light, and it
became stronger and stronger, until I believed it to be
close to the other side of the block. There it remained stationary; but there seemed to be other points
of light which moved about in a strange way, and
near it. Now I stood by the block watching. When
my feet became very cold, I stamped them; but there

I stood fascinated, for what I saw was truly surprising. A large coal of fire appeared on the other side of the block; then it suddenly vanished and was succeeded by another coal. This disappeared, and another took its place, each one seeming to come nearer and nearer to me. Again and again did these coals appear. They reached the centre of the block; they approached my side of it. At last one was so near to me that I thought it was about to break through, but it vanished. Then there came a few quick thuds and the end of a piece of iron protruded from the block. This was withdrawn, and through the aperture there came a voice which said: "Mr. Cuthbert, are you in there?" It was the voice of Agnes!

Weak and cold as I was, fire and energy rushed through me at these words. "Yes," I exclaimed, my mouth to the hole; "Agnes, is that you?"

"Wait a minute," came from the other side of the aperture. "I must make it bigger. I must keep it from closing up."

Again came the coals of fire, running backward and forward through the long hole in the block of ice. I could see now what they were. They were irons used by plumbers for melting solder and that sort of thing, and Agnes was probably heating them in a little furnace outside, and withdrawing them as fast as they cooled. It was not long before the aperture was very much enlarged; and then there came grating through it a long tin tube nearly two inches in diameter, which almost, but not quite, reached my side of the block.

Now came again the voice of Agnes: "Oh, Mr.

Cuthbert, are you truly there? Are you crushed? Are you wounded? Are you nearly frozen? Are you starved? Tell me quickly if you are yet safe."

Had I stood in a palace padded with the softest silk and filled with spicy odors from a thousand rose gardens, I could not have been better satisfied with my surroundings than I was at that moment. Agnes was not two feet away! She was telling me that she cared for me! In a very few words I assured her that I was uninjured. Then I was on the point of telling her I loved her, for I believed that not a moment should be lost in making this avowal. I could not die without her knowing that. But the appearance of a mass of paper at the other end of the tube prevented the expression of my sentiments. This was slowly pushed on until I could reach it. Then there came the words: "Mr. Cuthbert, these are sandwiches. Eat them immediately and walk about while you are doing it. You must keep yourself warm until the men get to you."

Obedient to the slightest wish of this dear creature, I went twice around the cave, devouring the sandwiches as I walked. They were the most delicious food that I had ever tasted. They were given to me by Agnes. I came back to the opening. I could not immediately begin my avowal. I must ask a question first. "Can they get to me?" I inquired. "Is anybody trying to do that? Are they working there by you? I do not hear them at all."

"Oh, no," she answered; "they are not working here. They are on top of the bluff, trying to dig down to you. They were afraid to meddle with the ice here for fear that more of it might come down and crush you and the men, too. Oh, there has been a dreadful excitement since it was found that you were in there!"

"How could they know I was here?" I asked.

"It was your old Susan who first thought of it. She saw you walking toward the shaft about noon, and then she remembered that she had not seen you again; and when they came into the tunnel here they found one of the lanterns gone and the big stick you generally carry lying where the lantern had been. Then it was known that you must be inside. Oh, then there was an awful time! The foreman of the ice-men examined everything, and said they must dig down to you from above. He put his men to work; but they could do very little, for they had hardly any spades. Then they sent into town for help and over to the new park for the Italians working there. From the way these men set to work you might have thought that they would dig away the whole bluff in about five minutes; but they didn't. Nobody seemed to know what to do, or how to get to work; and the hole they made when they did begin was filled up with men almost as fast as they threw out the stones and gravel. I don't believe anything would have been done properly if your friend, Mr. Burton, hadn't happened to come with two scientific gentlemen, and since that he has been directing everything. You can't think what a splendid fellow he is! I fairly adored him when I saw him giving his orders and making everybody skip around in the right way."

"Tom is a very good man," said I; "but it is his business to direct that sort of work, and it is not surprising that he knows how to do it. But, Agnes, they may never get down to me, and we do not know that this roof may not cave in upon me at any moment; and before this or anything else happens I want to tell you—"

"Mr. Cuthbert," said Agnes, "is there plenty of oil in your lantern? It would be dreadful if it were to go out and leave you there in the dark. I thought of that and brought you a little bottle of kerosene so that you can fill it. I am going to push the bottle through now, if you please." And with this a large phial, cork end foremost, came slowly through the tube, propelled by one of the soldering irons. Then came Agnes's voice: "Please fill your lantern immediately, because if it goes out you can not find it in the dark; and then walk several times around the cave, for you have been standing still too long already."

I obeyed these injunctions, but in two or three minues was again at the end of the tube. "Agnes," said I, "how did you happen to come here? Did you contrive in your own mind this method of communicating with me?"

"Oh, yes; I did," she said. "Everybody said that this mass of ice must not be meddled with, but I knew very well it would not hurt it to make a hole through it."

"But how did you happen to be here?" I asked.

"Oh, I ran over as soon as I heard of the accident.

Everybody ran here. The whole neighborhood is on top of the bluff; but nobody wanted to come into the tunnel, because they were afraid that more of it might fall in. So I was able to work here all by myself, and I am very glad of it. I saw the soldering iron and the little furnace outside of your house where the plumbers had been using them, and I brought them here myself. Then I thought that a simple hole through the ice might soon freeze up again, and if you were alive inside I could not do anything to help you; and so I ran home and got my diploma case, that had had one end melted out of it, and I brought that to stick in the hole. I'm so glad that it is long enough, or almost."

"Oh, Agnes," I cried, "you thought of all this for me?"

"Why, of course, Mr. Cuthbert," she answered, before I had a chance to say anything more. "You were in great danger of perishing before the men got to you, and nobody seemed to think of any way to give you immediate relief. And don't you think that a collegiate education is a good thing for girls—at least, that it was for me?"

"Agnes," I exclaimed, "please let me speak. I want to tell you, I must tell you—"

But the voice of Agnes was clearer than mine and it overpowered my words. "Mr. Cuthbert," she said, "we can not both speak through this tube at the same time in opposite directions. I have here a bottle of water for you, but I am very much afraid it will not go through the diploma case."

'Oh, I don't want any water," I said. "I can eat ice if I am thirsty. What I want is to tell you—"

"Mr. Cuthbert," said she, "you must not eat that ice. Water that was frozen countless ages ago may be very different from the water of modern times, and might not agree with you. Don't touch it, please. I am going to push the bottle through if I can. I tried to think of everything that you might need and brought them all at once; because, if I could not keep the hole open, I wanted to get them to you without losing a minute."

Now the bottle came slowly through. It was a small beer-bottle, I think, and several times I was afraid it was going to stick fast and cut off communication between me and the outer world—that is to say, between me and Agnes. But at last the cork and the neck appeared, and I pulled it through. I did not drink any of it, but immediately applied my mouth to the tube.

"Agnes," I said, "my dear Agnes, really you must not prevent me from speaking. I can not delay another minute. This is an awful position for me to be in, and as you don't seem to realize—"

"But I do realize, Mr. Cuthbert, that if you don't walk about you will certainly freeze before you can be rescued. Between every two or three words you want to take at least one turn around that place. How dreadful it would be if you were suddenly to become benumbed and stiff! Everybody is thinking of that. The best diggers that Mr. Burton had were three col-

ored men; but after they had gone down nothing like
as deep as a well, they came up frightened and said
they would not dig another shovelful for the whole
world. Perhaps you don't know it, but there's a story
about the neighborhood that the negro hell is under
your property. You know many of the colored people
expect to be everlastingly punished with ice and not
with fire—"

"Agnes," I interrupted, "I am punished with ice and
fire both. Please let me tell you—"

"I was going on to say, Mr. Cuthbert," she interrupted, "that when the Italians heard why the colored
men had come out of the hole they would not go in
either, for they are just as afraid of everlasting ice
as the negroes are, and were sure that if the bottom
came out of that hole they would fall into a frozen
lower world. So there was nothing to do but to send
for paupers, and they are working now. You know
paupers have to do what they are told without regard
to their beliefs. They got a dozen of them from the
poorhouse. Somebody said they just threw them into
the hole. Now I must stop talking, for it is time for
you to walk around again. Would you like another
sandwich?"

"Agnes," said I, endeavoring to speak calmly, "all
I want it to be able to tell you—"

"And when you walk, Mr. Cuthbert, you had better
keep around the edge of the chamber, for there is no
knowing when they may come through. Mr. Burton
and the foreman of the ice-men measured the bluff so
that they say the hole they are making is exactly over

the middle of the chamber you are in, and if you walk around the edge the pieces may not fall on you."

"If you don't listen to me, Agnes," I said, "I'll go and sit anywhere, everywhere, where death may come to me quickest. Your coldness is worse than the coldness of the cave. I can not bear it."

"But, Mr. Cuthbert," said Agnes, speaking, I thought, with some agitation, "I have been listening to you, and what more can you possibly have to say? If there is anything you want, let me know. I will run and get it for you."

"There is no need that you should go away to get what I want," I said. "It is there with you. It is you."

"Mr. Cuthbert," said Agnes, in a very low voice, but so distinctly that I could hear every word, "don't you think it would be better for you to give your whole mind to keeping yourself warm and strong? For if you let yourself get benumbed you may sink down and freeze."

"Agnes," I said, "I will not move from this little hole until I have told you that I love you, that I have no reason to care for life or rescue unless you return my love, unless you are willing to be mine. Speak quickly to me, Agnes, because I may not be rescued and may never know whether my love for you is returned or not."

At this moment there was a tremendous crash behind me, and, turning, I saw a mass of broken ice upon the floor of the cave, with a cloud of dust and smaller fragments still falling. And then with a great scratching and scraping, and a howl loud enough to waken the echoes of all the lower regions, down came a red-headed, drunken shoemaker. I can not say that he was drunk at that moment, but I knew the man the moment I saw his carroty poll, and it was drink which had sent him to the poorhouse.

But the sprawling and howling cobbler did not reach the floor. A rope had been fastened around his waist to prevent a fall in case the bottom of the pit should suddenly give way, and he hung dangling in mid air with white face and distended eyes, cursing and swearing and vociferously entreating to be pulled up. But before he received any answer from above, or I could speak to him, there came through the hole in the roof of the cave a shower of stones and gravel, and with them a frantic Italian, his legs and arms outspread, his face wild with terror.

Just as he appeared in view he grasped the rope of the cobbler, and, though in a moment he came down heavily upon the floor of the chamber, this broke his fall, and he did not appear to be hurt. Instantly he crouched low and almost upon all fours, and began to run around the chamber, keeping close to the walls and screaming, I suppose to his saints, to preserve him from the torments of the frozen damned.

In the midst of this hubbub came the voice of Agnes through the hole: "Oh, Mr. Cuthbert, what has happened? Are you alive?"

I was so disappointed by the appearance of these wretched interlopers at the moment it was about to be decided whether my life—should it last for years, or

but for a few minutes—was to be black or bright, and
I was so shaken and startled by the manner of their
entry upon the scene, that I could not immediately
shape the words necessary to inform Agnes what had
happened.   But, collecting my faculties, I was about
to speak, when suddenly, with the force of the hind
leg of a mule, I was pushed away from the aperture,
and the demoniac Italian clapped his great mouth to
the end of the tube and roared through it a volume of
oaths and supplications.   I attempted to thrust aside
the wretched being, but I might as well have tried to
move the ice barrier itself.   He had perceived that
some one outside was talking to me, and in his frenzy
he was imploring that some one should let him out.

While still endeavoring to move the man, I was
seized by the arm, and turning, beheld the pallid face
of the shoemaker.   They had let him down so that he
reached the floor.   He tried to fall on his knees before
me, but the rope was so short that he was able to go
only part of the way down, and presented a most lu-
dicrous appearance, with his toes scraping the icy
floor and his arms thrown out as if he were paddling
like a tadpole.   "Oh, have mercy upon me, sir," he
said, "and help me get out of this dreadful place.   If
you go to the hole and call up it's you, they will pull
me up; but if they get you out first they will never
think of me.   I am a poor pauper, sir, but I never
did nothin' to be packed in ice before I am dead."

Noticing that the Italian had left the end of the
aperture in the block of ice, and that he was now
shouting up the open shaft, I ran to the channel of

communication which my Agnes had opened for me,
and called through it; but the dear girl had gone.

The end of a ladder now appeared at the opening
in the roof, and this was let down until it reached the
floor. I started toward it, but before I had gone half
the distance the frightened shoemaker and the maniac
Italian sprang upon it, and, with shrieks and oaths,
began a maddening fight for possession of the ladder.
They might quickly have gone up one after the other,
but each had no thought but to be first; and as one
seized the rounds he was pulled away by the other,
until I feared the ladder would be torn to pieces. The
shoemaker finally pushed his way up a little distance,
when the Italian sprang upon his back, endeavoring to
climb over him; and so on they went up the shaft, fighting, swearing, kicking, scratching, shaking and wrenching the ladder, which had been tied to another one in
order to increase its length, so that it was in danger of
breaking, and tearing at each other in a fashion which
made it wonderful that they did not both tumble headlong downward. They went on up, so completely filling the shaft with their struggling forms and their
wild cries that I could not see or hear anything, and
was afraid, in fact, to look up toward the outer air.

As I was afterward informed, the Italian, who had
slipped into the hole by accident, ran away like a
frightened hare the moment he got his feet on firm
ground, and the shoemaker sat down and swooned.
By this performance he obtained from a benevolent by-
stander a drink of whiskey, the first he had had since
he was committed to the poorhouse.

But a voice soon came down the shaft calling to me. I recognized it as that of Tom Burton, and replied that I was safe, and that I was coming up the ladder. But in my attempt to climb, I found that I was unable to do so. Chilled and stiffened by the cold and weakened by fatigue and excitement, I believe I never should have been able to leave that ice chamber if my faithful friend had not come down the ladder and vigorously assisted me to reach the outer air.

Seated on the ground, my back against a great oak tree, I was quickly surrounded by a crowd of my neighbors, the workmen and the people who had been drawn to the spot by the news of the strange accident, to gaze at me as if I were some unknown being excavated from the bowels of the earth. I was sipping some brandy and water which Burton had handed me, when Aaron Boyce pushed himself in front of me.

"Well, sir," he said, "I am mighty glad you got out of that scrape. I'm bound to say I didn't expect you would. I have been sure all along that it wasn't right to meddle with things that go agin Nature, and I haven't any doubt that you'll see that for yourself and fill up all them tunnels and shafts you've made. The ice that comes on ponds and rivers was good enough for our forefathers, and it ought to be good enough for us. And as for this cold stuff you find in your gravel-pit, I don't believe it's ice at all; and if it is, like as not it's made of some sort of pizen stuff that freezes easier than water. For everybody knows that water don't freeze in a well, and if it don't do that, why should it do it in any kind of a hole in the ground?

So perhaps it's just as well that you did git shut up there, sir, and find out for yourself what a dangerous thing it is to fool with Nature and try to git ice from the bottom of the ground instead of the top of the water."

This speech made me angry, for I knew that old Boyce was a man who was always glad to get hold of anything which had gone wrong and try to make it worse; but I was too weak to answer him.

This, however, would not have been necessary, for Tom Burton turned upon him. "Idiot," said he, "if that is your way of thinking you might as well say that if a well caves in you should never again dig for water, or that nobody should have a cellar under his house for fear that the house should fall into it. There's no more danger of the ice beneath us ever giving way again than there is that this bluff should crumble under our feet. That break in the roof of the ice tunnel was caused by my digging away the face of the bluff very near that spot. The high temperature of the outer air weakened the ice, and it fell. But down here, under this ground and secure from the influences of the heat of the outer air, the mass of ice is more solid than rock. We will build a brick arch over the place where the accident happened, and then there will not be a safer mine on this continent than this ice-mine will be."

This was a wise and diplomatic speech from Burton, and it proved to be of great service to me; for the men who had been taking out ice had been a good deal frightened by the fall of the tunnel, and when it was proved that what Burton had said in regard to the cause of the weakening of the ice was entirely correct, they became willing to go to work again.

I now began to feel stronger and better, and, rising to my feet, I glanced here and there into the crowd, hoping to catch a sight of Agnes. But I was not very much surprised at not seeing her, because she would naturally shrink from forcing herself into the midst of this motley company; but I felt that I must go and look for her without the loss of a minute, for if she should return to her father's house I might not be able to see her again.

On the outskirts of the crowd I met Susan, who was almost overpowered with joy at seeing me safe again. I shook her by the hand, but, without replying to her warm-hearted protestations of thankfulness and delight, I asked her if she had seen Miss Havelot.

"Miss Agnes!" she exclaimed. "Why, no, sir; I expect she's at home; and if she did come here with the rest of the neighbors I didn't see her; for when I found out what had happened, sir, I was so weak that I sat down in the kitchen all of a lump, and have just had strength enough to come out."

"Oh, I know she was here," I cried; "I am sure of that, and I do hope she's not gone home again."

"Know she was here!" exclaimed Susan. "Why, how on earth could you know that?"

I did not reply that it was not on the earth but under it, that I became aware of the fact, but hurried toward the Havelot house, hoping to overtake Agnes if she had gone that way. But I did not see her, and

suddenly a startling idea struck me, and I turned and
ran home as fast as I could go. When I reached my
grounds I went directly to the mouth of the shaft.
There was nobody there, for the crowd was collected
into a solid mass on the top of the bluff, listening to
a lecture from Tom Burton, who deemed it well to
promote the growth of interest and healthy opinion
in regard to his wonderful discovery and my valuable
possession. I hurried down the shaft, and near the end
of it, just before it joined the ice tunnel, I beheld
Agnes sitting upon the wooden track. She was not
unconscious, for as I approached she slightly turned
her head. I sprang toward her; I kneeled beside her;
I took her in my arms. "Oh, Agnes, dearest Agnes,"
I cried, "what is the matter? What has happened to
you? Has a piece of ice fallen upon you? Have you
slipped and hurt yourself?"

She turned her beautiful eyes up toward me and for
a moment did not speak. Then she said: "And they
got you out? And you are in your right mind?"

"Right mind!" I exclaimed. "I have never been
out of my mind. What are you thinking of?"

"Oh, you must have been," she said, "when you
screamed at me in that horrible way. I was so frightened that I fell back, and I must have fainted."

Tremulous as I was with love and anxiety, I could
not help laughing. "Oh, my dear Agnes, I did not
scream at you. That was a crazed Italian who fell
through the hole that they dug." Then I told her what
had happened.

She heaved a gentle sigh. "I am so glad to hear

that," she said. "There was one thing that I was thinking about just before you came and which gave me a little bit of comfort; the words and yells I heard were dreadfully oniony, and somehow or other I could not connect that sort of thing with you."

It now struck me that during this conversation I had been holding my dear girl in my arms, and she had not shown the slightest sign of resistance or disapprobation. This made my heart beat high. "Oh, Agnes," I said, "I truly believe you love me or you would not have been here, you would not have done for me all that you did. Why did you not answer me when I spoke to you through that wall of ice, through the hole your dear love had made in it? Why, when I was in such a terrible situation, not knowing whether I was to die or live, did you not comfort my heart with one sweet word?"

"Oh, Walter," she answered, "it wasn't at all necessary for you to say all that you did say, for I had suspected it before, and as soon as you began to call me Agnes I knew, of course, how you felt about it. And, besides, it really was necessary that you should move about to keep yourself from freezing. But the great reason for my not encouraging you to go on talking in that way was that I was afraid people might come into the tunnel, and as, of course, you would not know that they were there, you would go on making love to me through my diploma case, and you know I should have perished with shame if I had had to stand there with that old Mr. Boyce, and I don't know who else, listening to your words, which were very sweet to me,

Walter, but which would have sounded awfully funny to them."

When she said that my words had been sweet to her I dropped the consideration of all other subjects.

When, about ten minutes afterward, we came out of the shaft we were met by Susan.

"Bless my soul and body, Mr. Cuthbert!" she exclaimed. "Did you find that young lady down there in the centre of the earth? It seems to me as if everything that you want comes to you out of the ground. But I have been looking for you to tell you that Mr. Havelot has been here after his daughter, and I'm sure if he had known where she was, he would have been scared out of his wits."

"Father here!" exclaimed Agnes. "Where is he now?"

"I think he has gone home, miss. Indeed I'm sure of it; for my daughter Jennie, who was over here the same as all the other people in the county, I truly believe told him—and I was proud she had the spirit to speak up that way to him—that your heart was almost broke when you heard about Mr. Cuthbert being shut up in the ice, and that most likely you was in your own room a-cryin' your eyes out. When he heard that he stood lookin' all around the place, and he asked me if he might go in the house; and when I told him he was most welcome, he went in. I offered to show him about, which he said was no use, that he had been there often enough; and he went everywhere, I truly believe, except in the garret and the cellar.

And after he got through with that he went out to the barn and then walked home."

"I must go to him immediately," said Agnes.

"But not alone," said I.   And together we walked through the woods, over the little field and across the Havelot lawn to the house.   We were told that the old gentleman was in his library, and together we entered the room.

Mr. Havelot was sitting by a table on which were lying several open volumes of an encyclopedia.   When he turned and saw us, he closed his book, pushed back his chair and took off his spectacles.   "Upon my word, sir," he cried; "and so the first thing you do after they pull you out of the earth is to come here and break my commands."

"I came on the invitation of your daughter, sir."

"And what right has she to invite you, I'd like to know?"

"She has every right, for to her I owe my existence."

"What rabid nonsense!" exclaimed the old gentleman.   "People don't owe their existence to the silly creatures they fall in love with."

"I assure you I am correct, sir."   And then I related to him what his daughter had done, and how through her angelic agency my rescuers had found me a living being instead of a frozen corpse.

"Stuff!" said Mr. Havelot.   "People can live in a temperature of thirty-two degrees above zero all winter.   Out in Minnesota they think that's hot.   And you gave him victuals and drink through your diploma case! Well, miss, I told you that if you tried to roast chestnuts in that diploma case the bottom would come out."

"But you see, father," said Agnes, earnestly, "the reason I did that was because when I roasted them in anything shallow they popped into the fire, but they could not jump out of the diploma case."

"Well, something else seems to have jumped out of it," said the old gentleman, "and something with which I am not satisfied. I have been looking over these books, sir, and have read the articles on ice, glaciers and caves, and I find no record of anything in the whole history of the world which in the least resembles the cock-and-bull story I am told about the butt-end of a glacier which tumbled into a cave in your ground, and has been lying there through all the geological ages, and the eras of formation, and periods of animate existence down to the days of Noah, and Moses, and Methuselah, and Rameses II, and Alexander the Great, and Martin Luther, and John Wesley, to this day, for you to dig out and sell to the Williamstown Ice Company."

"But that's what happened, sir," said I.

"And besides, father," added Agnes, "the gold and silver that people take out of mines may have been in the ground as long as that ice has been."

"Bosh!" said Mr. Havelot. "The cases are not at all similar. It is simply impossible that a piece of a glacier should have fallen into a cave and been preserved in that way. The temperature of caves is always above the freezing-point, and that ice would have melted a million years before you were born."

"But, father," said Agnes, "the temperature of caves filled with ice must be very much lower than that of common caves."

"And apart from that," I added, "the ice is still there, sir."

"That doesn't make the slightest difference," he replied. "It's against all reason and common-sense that such a thing could have happened. Even if there ever was a glacier in this part of the country and if the lower portion of it did stick out over an immense hole in the ground, that protruding end would never have broken off and tumbled in. Glaciers are too thick and massive for that."

"But the glacier is there, sir," said I, "in spite of your own reasoning."

"And then again," continued the old gentleman, "if there had been a cave and a projecting spur the ice would have gradually melted and dripped into the cave, and we would have had a lake and not an ice-mine. It is a perfect absurdity."

"But it's there, notwithstanding," said I.

"And you can not subvert facts, you know, father," added Agnes.

"Confound facts!" he cried. "I base my arguments on sober, cool-headed reason; and there's nothing that can withstand reason. The thing's impossible and, therefore it has never happened. I went over to your place, sir, when I heard of the accident, for the misfortunes of my neighbors interest me, no matter what may be my opinion of them, and when I found that you had been extricated from your ridiculous predicament, I went through your house, and I was pleased to find it in as good or better condition than I had known it in the days of your respected father. I was glad to see the improvement in your circumstances; but when I am told, sir, that your apparent prosperity rests upon such an absurdity as a glacier in a gravel hill, I can but smile with contempt, sir."

I was getting a little tired of this. "But the glacier is there, sir," I said, "and I am taking out ice every day, and have reason to believe that I can continue to take it out for the rest of my life. With such facts as these before me, I am bound to say, sir, that I don't care in the least about reason."

"And I am here, father," said Agnes, coming close to me, "and here I want to continue for the rest of my days."

The old gentleman looked at her. "And, I suppose," he said, "that you, too, don't in the least care about reason?"

"Not a bit," said Agnes.

"Well," said Mr. Havelot, rising, "I have done all I can to make you two listen to reason, and I can do no more. I despair of making sensible human beings of you, and so you might as well go on acting like a couple of ninny-hammers."

"Do ninny-hammers marry and settle on the property adjoining yours, sir?" I asked.

"Yes, I suppose they do," he said "And when the aboriginal ice-house, or whatever the ridiculous thing is that they have discovered, gives out, I suppose that they can come to a reasonable man and ask him for a little money to buy bread and butter."

Two years have passed, and Agnes and the glacier are still mine; great blocks of ice now flow in almost a continuous stream from the mine to the railroad station, and in a smaller but quite as continuous stream an income flows in upon Agnes and me; and from one of the experimental excavations made by Tom Burton on the bluff comes a stream of ice-cold water running in a sparkling brook a-down my dell. On fine mornings before I am up, I am credibly informed that Aaron Boyce may generally be found, in season and out of season, endeavoring to catch the trout with which I am trying to stock that ice-cold stream. The diploma case, which I caused to be carefully removed from the ice-barrier which had imprisoned me, now hangs in my study and holds our marriage certificate.

Near the line-fence which separates his property from mine, Mr. Havelot has sunk a wide shaft. "If the glacier spur under your land was a quarter of a mile wide," he says to me, "it was probably at least a half a mile long; and if that were the case, the upper end of it extends into my place, and I may be able to strike it." He has a good deal of money, this worthy Mr. Havelot, but he would be very glad to increase his riches, whether they are based upon sound reason or ridiculous facts. As for Agnes and myself, no facts or any reason could make us happier than our ardent love and our frigid fortune.

THE INDIAN'S HAND

BY LORIMER STODDARD

Lorimer Stoddard, the gifted son of that gifted couple, Richard Henry and Elizabeth Stoddard, was born in New York City in 1863, and died in 1901. He was best known as a playwright. He wrote "Napoleon" for Richard Mansfield, and dramatized "Tess of the D'Urbervilles," Thomas Hardy's novel, for Mrs. Fiske, and "In the Palace of the King," F. Marion Crawford's novel, for Viola Allen. Mr. Stoddard also wrote a number of short stories remarkable for intense dramatic situation. Of these the present selection is thoroughly representative.

THE INDIAN'S HAND

BY LORIMER STODDARD

THE men had driven away. Their carts and horses disappeared behind the roll of the low hills. They appeared now and then, like boats on the crest of a wave, further each time. And their laughter and singing and shouts grew fainter as the bushes hid them from sight.

The women and children remained, with two old men to protect them. They might have gone too, the hunters said. "What harm could come in the broad daylight?—the bears and panthers were far away. They'd be back by night, with only two carts to fill."

Then Jim, the crack shot of the settlement, said, "We'll drive home the bears in the carts."

The children shouted and danced as they thought of the sport to come, of the hunters' return with their game, of the bonfires they always built.

One pale woman clung to her husband's arm. "But the Indians!" she said.

That made the men all laugh. "Indians!" they cried; "why, there've been none here for twenty years! We drove them away, down there"—pointing across the plain—"to a hotter place than this, where the sand burns their feet and they ride for days for water."

The pale woman murmured, "Ah, but they returned."

"Yes," cried her big husband, whose brown beard covered his chest, "and burned two cabins. Small harm they did, the curs!"

"Hush," said the pale woman, pressing her husband's arm; and the men around were quiet, pretending to fix their saddles, as they glanced at another woman, dressed in black, who turned and went into her house.

"I forgot her boy," said the bearded man, as he gravely picked up his gun.

They started off in the morning cool, toward the mountains where the trees grew. And the long shadows lessened as the sun crept up the sky.

The woman in black stood silent by her door. No one bade her good-by. The other women went back to their houses to work. The children played in the dust; clouds rose as they shouted and ran. A day's freedom lay before them.

But the woman in black still stood by her door, like a spectre in the sunshine, her thin hands clasped together as she gazed away over the plain toward Mexico.

Her face was parched and drawn, as if the sun from the sand had burned into the bone. Her eyes alone seemed to live; they were hard and bright.

Her house was a little away from the rest, on the crest of a hill facing the desert plain.

She had heard the words of the bearded man: "Small harm the Indians did." Had he forgotten her boy? How could he forget, while she was there to remind them of the dead? Near her house was a small rock roughly marked. The rude letters "Will, gone, '69," she had cut on it with her own hands. It marked the last place where her boy had played. She remembered how she went away softly—so he should not cry to follow her—without a word, without a kiss.

Here her hands beat the side of the house.

"Oh, to have that kiss now and die!" But she had gone, unthinking, up the road where the pale woman lived, then a rosy-cheeked happy bride, not a widow like herself. They laughed and discussed the newcomers at the settlement. It was a holiday, for the men were away over the hills, cutting down trees to build their houses with.

As they talked there idly, they heard what they thought was the shrill bark of dogs running up the hill. Startled, they went to the window. Round the curve of the road came horses wildly galloping, and upon their backs— Here the pale woman shrieked and fled. They were Indians, beating their horses with their bare legs, their black hair streaming in the wind.

Like a flash, she had bolted the door and barred the shutters as they galloped up. She turned then. Through the open back door she saw the women run screaming up the hill, their children in their arms.

Their children! Where was hers? She stopped as if turned to stone, then undid the door.

They dragged her out by the wrists, by the hair. She fought with them stronger than ten men. But there were twenty; she was alone. The little street was empty. They strangled her, beat down her face, dragged her upon a horse, and, with her crosswise on the saddle, galloped up and down, as they fired the cabins and the sheds. Her hands were shackled, and her eyes blind with blood, but she thought only of her child. "Where could he be?"

There were gunshots. Down the hills like mad came the white men for their wives and children.

Then the Indians turned back toward the plain. They rode past her house.

There, where she had left him, stood the child, dazed with surprise. She held out her arms tied together and called to him to come.

"Fool! fool!" Here the woman in black struck her temples with her hands. "Fool!" Why had she not galloped by and never noticed him?

But she begged, caught at the horse's head, struggled to get to him; and the Indian stopped for a moment in his flight and caught up the child and went on.

Then the thought came to her of the end of that ride —what was to come—after. And she tried to drop the boy, to let him slide gently to the ground; but the Indian held them fast.

Behind, nearer, came the following men, louder the guns. The horse she was on snorted, staggered under the weight of the three, and as they reached the plain the child was torn from her, she was pushed away. But she rose and staggered after them amid the blinding dust. They must take her too. Sobbing, she called to them as she stumbled on. Many times she fell. Then she could go no more.

That was all. Her story ended there, with the thundering of horses' hoofs and the taste of dust in her mouth. They found her there unconscious. Her friends tended her. When she came back to life she asked no questions but left her neighbor's house and came to her door, where she was standing now, and gazed away over the sand where *he* had gone, down toward Mexico.

The years went by, and she was still alone in the house where *two* should have been. And now far off she saw the dust blowing in a long, rolling, pinkish line. But the dust blew so often, and nothing came of it—not even the Indians.

The boy she knew was dead, but they—his murderers—remained, somewhere.

If she could have one now in her power!

The woman in black pondered, as she had so many times, how she should torture him. No pain could be too horrible. She looked at the fire in the stove, and piled on the logs—the logs that were brought with such trouble from the mountains where the trees grew. She could not make it hot enough. She dropped on her knees and watched the iron grow red. And the letters of the maker's name stamped on it grew distinct, and the word "Congress," half defaced, and the figures "64." Ah, those letters! she could have kissed the spot, for her child had touched it. Charmed by the glow, when left alone, he laid his baby hand flat on it, and burned deep into the palm where those letters, "S S, 64."

She would know him among a million by that mark.

But he was dead. The Indians remained.

The woman in black stood up. Why should she not go to them? There were pools in the plain where she could drink. That would be enough.

The men were away; the women were at work. Who could stop her?

She put on her bonnet and started off down the hill through the green bushes. The air was still crisp, though the sun was hot.

The desert must have an end. She would keep on to Mexico. She walked quickly, and her dress grew gray with dust, and the air scorching, as she reached the plain. But she kept on, and only looked back once at the house on the hill, and at the window where the pale woman sat.

The dust choked her, and she stumbled, and the sole of one shoe came half off, and slapped, and banged, and delayed her as she walked. She tore it off and went on, but the sand cut and burned her so that she sat down and wept, and wanted to go back for her other pair, the ones she wore on Sundays. The hill, though, looked so distant that she wearily got up and went on, on, till she could go no more, and crept under the shadow of a rock. There was no water near. Her throat was parched, and her temples beat wildly. She must go back and start again, strengthened, fortified. She would start to-morrow, or at night, when the cool would let her get too far to return.

By slow degrees she dragged herself up the hill. The pale woman came out of her house, and nodded, but the woman in black did not smile in return. She closed her door, and went up to her bed, and fell on it, and slept, amid the buzzing of the flies and the fitful flapping of the window-shade in the breeze.

The pale woman sighed and glanced across the plain. The roll of blowing dust was larger, and more reg- ular, and nearer. The woman shuddered as she watched it creep slowly along behind the sand mounds. "It always blows," she said to herself, "but not like that, so steadily, so even." She strained her eyes, but there was only dust to be seen. Then she thought of a telescope that belonged to the minister's wife, who came from a seaport town, and ran to fetch it. The two women came out with it together, the minister's wife laughing at her friend, she was such a timid thing!

But the pale woman was paler than ever, and trem- bled so she could not steady it. The laughing one looked through it, and laughed no more.

"I see a head over the mound there," she said.

The pale woman shrieked.

"They are miles away. We may have time."

"For what?"

"To get away."

"They may be friends—"

"They are Indians! White men would not live through that sand. We must go to the woods. Help me. Warn the women. Gather the children. Come."

She rushed into her house. The other still stood and looked.

The dust cloud was a little nearer. In a moment all was wild confusion, names were called, but not loudly, girls sobbed, some carried their little treasures, mothers held their children. All gathered together, hidden from the plain by a house.

The pale woman led out her father, then ran to her neighbor's door. She opened it, and called clearly, but softly, "Mary, Mary," There was no answer. The woman in black, on her bed, slept on. Her neighbor hesitated, then hurried after the others, as they ran up the low hills toward the mountains, where their men had gone.

The dust cloud grew nearer. Now and then a head could be seen. But all was as still as the grave. The woman in black slept heavily and dreamed that revenge had come at last—that in her hand she held an Indian's head.

The window-shade flapped loudly, and she woke with an apprehension crushing her. She went to the window and looked out. There was no blowing dust upon the plains, and the street was empty. The doors of the houses stood open; a shawl lay in the middle of the road. The woman leaned out and looked toward the woods.

She saw on the crest of a hill the white skirts of the flying women, and then, below, down the road, her ears sharpened, her heart tightening, she heard the soft, regular thumping of horses' feet.

Then she *knew*.

She sat on the edge of the bed. This was what she had waited for! Was it her turn now?—or theirs again?

She could kill *one*.

Where was her gun?

She had loaned it to the men.

But her axe—that was below.

As she started for it, there was a burst of war cries.

She ran down the narrow stairs, and took the axe from its place on the wall.

They were passing her door. The room grew lighter. She turned. One stood in the open doorway, black against the sunshine. She set her teeth hard, hid the axe behind her skirts, watched him motionless.

He stretched out his hand clawlike, and laughed, his eyes gleaming, as catlike he moved nearer. A terror seized her: with a hoarse cry, she sprang up the stairs, flinging down a chair as he followed panting.

Quickly she climbed up the ladder to the loft, threw down the trapdoor, fell on it, bolted it, waited. All was still. Outside she heard the distant yells. She stooped noiselessly and put her ear upon the floor. There was soft breathing underneath, and through a crack in the floor she saw an eye peering up at her.

She stood a long time, motionless, axe in hand, ready.

Her back was to the bolt, but suddenly she *felt* that there was something there. She turned softly. A slim brown hand was almost through a crevice in the floor.

She raised her axe. The slender fingers touched the bolt and gently drew it back.

Then with the force of all her hatred fell the axe

upon the wrist.   The hand sprang up at her.   With a
howl of agony the creature fell bumping beneath.

Then all again was still.

Her face was wet and warm with the spattered
blood.

Outside she heard the crackling of a burning house,
then gunshots far away, and distant shouts.   On tiptoe she went to the garret window, and peeped round
its edge.   Over the hills, quite near, she saw the men
returning.   One house was blazing—the minister's.
The Indians were retreating.   Near her door, grazing,
stood a riderless horse.   *She* knew its owner.   As
they rode past, they caught at it, but were stopped by
a shout from her door.   An Indian rushed out, handsome, young, holding aloft a bare right arm without
a hand.   In his language he shrieked to them for revenge, pointing up with his red wrist to the attic where
she stood.

The eyes of the woman shot fire.   She leaned far
out and shook her fist from the garret window.

"One Indian at least!"

She hurled the axe at them.   It fell far short.   They
fired as they passed, but none hit her.   Nearer came
the men.

The wounded man leaped to his horse and with a
curse rode on.   The woman laughed as he passed beneath, then sat down in the dusky loft with a red pool
at her feet.

Shortly the men returned.   Some went by down the
hill, after the Indians.   Others put out the fire.   All
was confusion, bustle, shouts.

Then the women and the children came and added
to the din, and the men who had followed returned.
But the woman in black sat alone in the loft, till she
heard the crowd at her door below, and the voice of
the pale woman say:

"Where is Mary?"

She rose and lifted the trap-door—it was unbolted—
and went down.

The pale woman came to her, but she pushed her
aside, and wiped her face with her sleeve.

"Are they killed? any of them?" she said.   Her
friend answered, "No, Mary, not one."   "No harm
this time," said the bearded man.   "Except my house,
it is burned," said the minister's wife.   "We'll soon
have another."

"I don't mean *you!*" cried the woman in black.   "I
mean them—red devils.   Have you got any?—killed
any?   *You*"—this to Jim, who never missed a shot—
"you"—this to the bearded man—"have *you* killed
any?"

And the men answered, "No."

And one man said, "Their horses were faster than
ours."

"Not one!"   The woman in black drew herself up
proudly.   "Yes, one; better than killed.   Wait."   The
women shrunk from her as she darted up the stair.
They looked at each other wonderingly.   The woman
returned with something in her grasp.   She flung it
on the table.   "It is an Indian's hand.   His arm will
shrivel to the bone.   They will leave him some day
to die in the sand."   The women shuddered and drew

back; the men crowded round, but they did not touch the hand.

"Are you afraid?" said the woman in black. "Afraid of that thing!"

She bent back the fingers and looked in it with a smile of contempt. Her face took an ashen hue: the hand struck the table edge and fell upon the floor. She seemed to be trying to think for a second, then she gave one awful cry, and leaned her face against the wall, with her hands hanging at her side.

The pale woman tried to go to her, but her husband drew her back, and, with a silent crowd around, slowly picked up the hand.

For a second he hesitated, then did as she had done, but gently. He bent back the fingers of the severed hand and read its history written there, "S S, 64," in white letters on the palm.

He remembered then how, twenty years ago, when she brought the child to him, he had tied its little hand in cooling salve.

It was larger now.

The whisper went around, "It is her boy's hand," and they crept toward the door.

The pale woman took a flower from her dress, one she had put there hours before, and placed it in the brown fingers on the table and went out.

The woman did not stir from the wall. "Leave the hand," she said.

"It is there," and the bearded man closed the door gently behind him.

The woman in black turned. Her hard eyes were dim now. She took the hand from the table and undid her dress and placed it in her breast, and went to the window, and watched, far off, a cloud of dust made golden by the sun, as it rolled away across the plain, down toward Mexico.

THE UPPER BERTH

BY F. MARION CRAWFORD

Mr. F. Marion Crawford (born in Italy, August 2, 1854), while the most prolific of novelists, has written few short stories. One of these, however, the present selection, is held by the critics to be a most successful tour de force *in the literature of brief terror. For about the space of the proverbial "bad quarter of an hour" the reader is gripped with a sense of mysterious dread—an effect which is produced by the author's mastery of narrative style rather than by any cleverness in central conception or ingenuity in complication and solution of situation. It will be interesting to compare this story with "The Horla," by Guy de Maupassant, and "The Damned Thing," by Ambrose Bierce.*

THE UPPER BERTH

BY F. MARION CRAWFORD

I

SOMEBODY asked for the cigars. We had talked long, and the conversation was beginning to languish; the tobacco smoke had got into the heavy curtains, the wine had got into those brains which were liable to become heavy, and it was already perfectly evident that, unless somebody did something to rouse our oppressed spirits, the meeting would soon come to its natural conclusion, and we, the guests, would speedily go home to bed, and most certainly to sleep. No one had said anything very remarkable; it may be that no one had anything very remarkable to say. Jones had given us every particular of his last hunting adventure in Yorkshire. Mr. Tompkins, of Boston, had explained at elaborate length those working principles by the due and careful maintenance of which the Atchison, Topeka, and Santa Fé Railroad not only extended its territory, increased its departmental influence, and transported live stock without starving them to death before the day of actual delivery, but, also, had for years succeeded in deceiving those passengers who bought its tickets into the fallacious belief that the corporation aforesaid was really able to transport human life without destroying it. Signor Tombola had endeavored to persuade us, by arguments which we took no trouble to oppose, that the unity of his country in no way resembled the average modern torpedo, carefully planned, constructed with all the skill of the greatest European arsenals, but, when constructed, destined to be directed by feeble hands into a region where it must undoubtedly explode, unseen, unfeared, and unheard, into the illimitable wastes of political chaos.

It is unnecessary to go into further details. The conversation had assumed proportions which would have bored Prometheus on his rock, which would have driven Tantalus to distraction, and which would have impelled Ixion to seek relaxation in the simple but instructive dialogues of Herr Ollendorff, rather than submit to the greater evil of listening to our talk. We had sat at table for hours; we were bored, we were tired, and nobody showed signs of moving.

Somebody called for cigars. We all instinctively looked toward the speaker. Brisbane was a man of five-and-thirty years of age, and remarkable for those gifts which chiefly attract the attention of men. He was a strong man. The external proportions of his figure presented nothing extraordinary to the common eye, though his size was above the average. He was a little over six feet in height, and moderately broad in the shoulder; he did not appear to be stout, but, on the other hand, he was certainly not thin; his small head was supported by a strong and sinewy neck; his broad, muscular hands appeared to possess a peculiar skill in breaking walnuts without the assistance of the ordinary cracker, and, seeing him in profile, one could not help remarking the extraordinary breadth of his sleeves and the unusual thickness of his chest. He was one of those men who are commonly spoken of among men as deceptive; that is to say that though he looked exceedingly strong he was in reality very much stronger than he looked. Of his features I need say little. His head is small, his hair is thin, his eyes are blue, his nose is large, he has a small mustache and a square jaw. Everybody knows Brisbane, and when he asked for a cigar everybody looked at him.

"It is a very singular thing," said Brisbane.

Everybody stopped talking. Brisbane's voice was not loud, but possessed a peculiar quality of penetrating general conversation and cutting it like a knife. Everybody listened. Brisbane, perceiving that he had attracted their general attention, lighted his cigar with great equanimity.

"It is very singular," he continued, "that thing about ghosts. People are always asking whether anybody has seen a ghost. I have."

"Bosh! What, you? You don't mean to say so, Brisbane? Well, for a man of his intelligence!"

A chorus of exclamations greeted Brisbane's remarkable statement. Everybody called for cigars, and Stubbs, the butler, suddenly appeared from the depths of nowhere with a fresh bottle of dry champagne. The situation was saved; Brisbane was going to tell a story.

"I am an old sailor," said Brisbane, "and as I have to cross the Atlantic pretty often, I have my favorites.

Most men have their favorites. I have seen a man
wait in a Broadway bar for three-quarters of an hour
for a particular car which he liked. I believe the
barkeeper made at least one-third of his living by
that man's preference. I have a habit of waiting for
certain ships when I am obliged to cross that duck-
pond. It may be a prejudice, but I was never cheated
out of a good passage but once in my life. I re-
memeber it very well; it was a warm morning in
June, and the custom house officials, who were hanging about waiting for a steamer already on her way
up from the quaratine, presented a peculiarly hazy and
thoughtful appearance. I had not much luggage—I
never have. I mingled with the crowd of passengers,
porters, and officious individuals in blue coats and
brass buttons, who seemed to spring up like mush-
rooms from the deck of a moored steamer to obtrude
their unnecessary services upon the independent passenger. I have often noticed with a certain interest
the spontaneous evolution of these fellows. They are
not there when you arrive; five minutes after the
pilot has called 'Go ahead!' they, or at least their blue
coats and brass buttons, have disappeared from deck
and gangway as completely as though they had been
consigned to that locker which tradition unanimously
ascribes to Davy Jones. But, at the moment of starting, they are there, clean-shaved, blue-coated, and
ravenous for fees. I hastened on board. The 'Kamtschatka' was one of my favorite ships. I say was,
because she emphatically no longer is. I can not con-
ceive of any inducement which could entice me to

make another voyage in her. Yes, I know what you are going to say. She is uncommonly clean in the run aft, she has enough bluffing off in the bows to keep her dry, and the lower berths are most of them double. She has a lot of advantages, but I won't cross in her again. Excuse the digression. I got on board. I hailed a steward, whose red nose and redder whiskers were equally familiar to me.

" 'One hundred and five, lower berth,' said I, in the business-like tone peculiar to men who think no more of crossing the Atlantic than taking a whiskey cocktail at downtown Delmonico's.

"The steward took my portmanteau, greatcoat, and rug. I shall never forget the expression of his face. Not that he turned pale. It is maintained by the most eminent divines that even miracles can not change the course of nature. I have no hesitation in saying that he did not turn pale; but, from his expression, I judged that he was either about to shed tears, to sneeze, or to drop my portmanteau. As the latter contained two bottles of particularly fine old sherry presented to me for my voyage by my old friend Snigginson van Pickyns, I felt extremely nervous. But the steward did none of these things.

" 'Well, I'm d——d!' said he in a low voice, and led the way.

"I supposed my Hermes, as he led me to the lower regions, had had a little grog, but I said nothing, and followed him. One hundred and five was on the port side, well aft. There was nothing remarkable about the stateroom. The lower berth, like most of those

upon the 'Kamtschatka,' was double. There was
plenty of room; there was the usual washing appara-
tus, calculated to convey an idea of luxury to the
mind of a North American Indian; there were the
usual inefficient racks of brown wood, in which it is
more easy to hang a large-sized umbrella than the
common tooth-brush of commerce. Upon the unin-
viting mattresses were carefully folded together those
blankets which a great modern humorist has aptly
compared to cold buckwheat cakes. The question of
towels was left entirely to the imagination. The glass
decanters were filled with a transparent liquid faintly
tinged with brown, but from which an odor less faint,
but not more pleasing, ascended to the nostrils, like a
far-off seasick reminiscence of oily machinery. Sad-
colored curtains half closed the upper berth. The
hazy June daylight shed a faint illumination upon the
desolate little scene. Ugh! how I hate that stateroom!

"The steward deposited my traps and looked at
me as though he wanted to get away—probably in
search of more passengers and more fees. It is
always a good plan to start in favor with those func-
tionaries, and I accordingly gave him certain coins
there and then.

" 'I'll try and make yer comfortable all I can,' he
remarked, as he put the coins in his pocket. Nevertheless, there was a doubtful intonation in his voice
which surprised me. Possibly his scale of fees had
gone up, and he was not satisfied; but on the whole
I was inclined to think that, as he himself would have

expressed it, he was 'the better for a glass.' I was wrong, however, and did the man injustice.

II

"Nothing especially worthy of mention occurred during that day. We left the pier punctually, and it was very pleasant to be fairly under way, for the weather was warm and sultry, and the motion of the steamer produced a refreshing breeze.

"Everybody knows what the first day at sea is like. People pace the decks and stare at each other, and occasionally meet acquaintances whom they did not know to be on board. There is the usual uncertainty as to whether the food will be good, bad, or indifferent, until the first two meals have put the matter beyond a doubt; there is the usual uncertainty about the weather, until the ship is fairly off Fire Island. The tables are crowded at first, and then suddenly thinned. Pale-faced people spring from their seats and precipitate themselves toward the door, and each old sailor breathes more freely as his seasick neighbor rushes from his side, leaving him plenty of elbow room and an unlimited command over the mustard.

"One passage across the Atlantic is very much like another, and we who cross very often do not make the voyage for the sake of novelty. Whales and icebergs are indeed always objects of interest, but, after all, one whale is very much like another whale, and one rarely sees an iceberg at close quarters. To the majority of us the most delightful moment of the day on board an ocean steamer is when we have

taken our last turn on deck, have smoked our last
cigar, and having succeeded in tiring ourselves, feel
at liberty to turn in with a clear conscience.   On
that first night of the voyage I felt particularly lazy,
and went to bed in one hundred and five rather earlier
than I usually do.   As I turned in, I was amazed to
see that I was to have a companion.   A portmanteau,
very like my own, lay in the opposite corner, and in
the upper berth had been deposited a neatly folded rug
with a stick and umbrella.   I had hoped to be alone,
and I was disappointed; but I wondered who my room-
mate was to be, and I determined to have a look at him.

"Before I had been long in bed he entered.   He
was, as far as I could see, a very tall man, very thin,
very pale, with sandy hair and whiskers and colorless gray eyes.   He had about him, I thought, an air
of rather dubious fashion; the sort of man you might
see in Wall Street, without being able precisely to say
what he was doing there—the sort of man who fre-
quents the Café Anglais, who always seems to be
alone and who drinks champagne; you might meet him
on a race-course, but he would never appear to be
doing anything there either.   A little overdressed—a
little odd.   There are three or four of his kind on every
ocean steamer.   I made up my mind that I did not
care to make his acquaintance, and I went to sleep
saying to myself that I would study his habits
in order to avoid him.   If he rose early, I would
rise late; if he went to bed late, I would go to bed
early.   I did not care to know him.   If you once know
people of that kind they are always turning up.   Poor

fellow! I need not have taken the trouble to come to
so many decisions about him, for I never saw him
again after that first night in one hundred and five.

"I was sleeping soundly when I was suddenly waked
by a loud noise. To judge from the sound, my room-
mate must have sprung with a single leap from the
upper berth to the floor. I heard him fumbling with
the latch and bolt of the door, which opened almost immediately, and then I heard his footsteps as he ran
at full speed down the passage, leaving the door open
behind him. The ship was rolling a little, and I expected to hear him stumble or fall, but he ran as though
he were running for his life. The door swung on its
hinges with the motion of the vessel, and the sound
annoyed me. I got up and shut it, and groped my
way back to my berth in the darkness. I went to sleep
again; but I have no idea how long I slept.

"When I awoke it was still quite dark, but I felt a
disagreeable sensation of cold, and it seemed to me
that the air was damp. You know the peculiar smell
of a cabin which has been wet with sea water. I covered myself up as well as I could and dozed off again,
framing complaints to be made the next day, and selecting the most powerful epithets in the language. I
could hear my room-mate turn over in the upper berth.
He had probably returned while I was asleep. Once I
thought I heard him groan, and I argued that he was
seasick. That is particularly unpleasant when one is
below. Nevertheless I dozed off and slept till early
daylight.

"The ship was rolling heavily, much more than on

the previous evening, and the gray light which came
in through the porthole changed in tint with every
movement according as the angle of the vessel's side
turned the glass seaward or skyward. It was very
cold—unaccountably so for the month of June. I
turned my head and looked at the porthole, and saw
to my surprise that it was wide open and hooked back.
I believe I swore audibly. Then I got up and shut
it. As I turned back I glanced at the upper berth.
The curtains were drawn close together; my companion had probably felt cold as well as I. It struck me
that I had slept enough. The stateroom was uncomfortable, though, strange to say, I could not smell the
dampness which had annoyed me in the night. My
room-mate was still asleep—excellent opportunity for
avoiding him, so I dressed at once and went on deck.
The day was warm and cloudy, with an oily smell on
the water. It was seven o'clock as I came out—much
later than I had imagined. I came across the doctor,
who was taking his first sniff of the morning air. He
was a young man from the West of Ireland—a tremendous fellow, with black hair and blue eyes, already
inclined to be stout; he had a happy-go-lucky, healthy
look about him which was rather attractive.

"'Fine mornin,' I remarked, by way of introduction.

"'Well,' said he, eying me with an air of ready interest, 'it's a fine morning and it's not a fine morning.
I don't think it's much of a morning.'

"'Well, no—it is not so very fine,' said I.

"'It's just what I call fuggly weather,' replied the
doctor.

" 'It was very cold last night, I thought,' I remarked. 'However, when I looked about, I found that the porthole was wide open. I had not noticed it when I went to bed. And the stateroom was damp, too.'

" 'Damp!' said he. 'Whereabouts are you?'

" 'One hundred and five—'

"To my surprise the doctor started visibly, and stared at me.

" 'What is the matter?' I asked.

" 'Oh—nothing,' he answered; 'only everybody has complained of that stateroom for the last three trips.'

" 'I shall complain too,' I said. 'It has certainly not been properly aired. It is a shame!'

" 'I don't believe it can be helped,' answered the doctor. 'I believe there is something—well, it is not my business to frighten passengers.'

" 'You need not be afraid of frightening me,' I replied. 'I can stand any amount of damp. If I should get a bad cold I will come to you.'

"I offered the doctor a cigar, which he took and examined very critically.

" 'It is not so much the damp,' he remarked. 'However, I dare say you will get on very well. Have you a room-mate?'

" 'Yes; a deuce of a fellow, who bolts out in the middle of the night and leaves the door open.'

"Again the doctor glanced curiously at me. Then he lighted the cigar and looked grave.

" 'Did he come back?' he asked presently.

" 'Yes. I was asleep, but I waked up and heard him

moving. Then I felt cold and went to sleep again. This morning I found the porthole open.'

" 'Look here,' said the doctor, quietly, 'I don't care much for this ship. I don't care a rap for her reputation. I tell you what I will do. I have a good-sized place up here. I will share it with you, though I don't know you from Adam.'

"I was very much surprised at the proposition. I could not imagine why he should take such a sudden interest in my welfare. However, his manner as he spoke of the ship was peculiar.

" 'You are very good, Doctor,' I said. 'But really, I believe even now the cabin could be aired, or cleaned out, or something. Why do you not care for the ship?'

" 'We are not superstitious in our profession, sir,' replied the doctor. 'But the sea makes people so. I don't want to prejudice you, and I don't want to frighten you, but if you will take my advice you will move in here. I would as soon see you overboard,' he added, 'as know that you or any other man was to sleep in one hundred and five.'

" 'Good gracious! Why?' I asked.

" 'Just because on the last three trips the people who have slept there actually have gone overboard,' he answered gravely.

"The intelligence was startling and exceedingly unpleasant, I confess. I looked hard at the doctor to see whether he was making game of me, but he looked perfectly serious. I thanked him warmly for his offer, but told him I intended to be the exception to the rule by which every one who slept in that particular state-room went overboard. He did not say much, but looked as grave as ever, and hinted that before we got across I should probably reconsider his proposal. In the course of time we went to breakfast, at which only an inconsiderable number of passengers assembled. I noticed that one or two of the officers who breakfasted with us looked grave. After breakfast I went into my stateroom in order to get a book. The curtains of the upper berth were still closely drawn. Not a word was to be heard. My room-mate was probably still asleep.

"As I came out I met the steward whose business it was to look after me. He whispered that the captain wanted to see me, and then scuttled away down the passage as if very anxious to avoid any questions. I went toward the captain's cabin, and found him waiting for me.

" 'Sir,' said he, 'I want to ask a favor of you.'

"I answered that I would do anything to oblige him.

" 'Your room-mate has disappeared,' he said. 'He is known to have turned in early last night. Did you notice anything extraordinary in his manner?'

"The question coming, as it did, in exact confirmation of the fears the doctor had expressed half an hour earlier, staggered me.

" 'You don't mean to say he has gone overboard?' I asked.

" 'I fear he has,' answered the captain.

" 'This is the most extraordinary thing—' I began.

" 'Why?' he asked.

" 'He is the fourth, then?' I explained. In answer to another question from the captain, I explained, without mentioning the doctor, that I had heard the story concerning one hundred and five. He seemed very much annoyed at hearing that I knew of it. I told him what had occurred in the night.

" 'What you say,' he replied, 'coincides almost exactly with what was told me by the room-mates of two of the other three. They bolt out of bed and run down the passage. Two of them were seen to go overboard by the watch; we stopped and lowered boats, but they were not found. Nobody, however, saw or heard the man who was lost last night—if he is really lost. The steward, who is a superstitious fellow, perhaps, and expected something to go wrong, went to look for him this morning, and found his berth empty, but his clothes lying about, just as he had left them. The steward was the only man on board who knew him by sight, and he has been searching everywhere for him. He has disappeared! Now, sir, I want to beg you not to mention the circumstance to any of the passengers; I don't want the ship to get a bad name, and nothing hangs about an ocean-goer like stories of suicides. You shall have your choice of any one of the officers' cabins you like, including my own, for the rest of the passage. Is that a fair bargain?'

" 'Very,' said I; 'and I am much obliged to you. But since I am alone, and have the stateroom to myself, I would rather not move. If the steward will take out that unfortunate man's things, I would as lief stay where I am. I will not say anything about the matter, and I think I can promise you that I will not follow my room-mate.'

"The captain tried to dissuade me from my intention, but I preferred having a stateroom alone to being the chum of any officer on board. I do not know whether I acted foolishly, but if I had taken his advice I should have had nothing more to tell. There would have remained the disagreeable coincidence of several suicides occurring among men who had slept in the same cabin, but that would have been all.

"That was not the end of the matter, however, by any means. I obstinately made up my mind that I would not be disturbed by such tales, and I even went so far as to argue the question with the captain. There was something wrong about the stateroom, I said. It was rather damp. The porthole had been left open last night. My room-mate might have been ill when he came on board, and he might have become delirious after he went to bed. He might even now be hiding somewhere on board, and might be found later. The place ought to be aired and the fastening of the port looked to. If the captain would give me leave, I would see that what I thought necessary was done immediately.

" 'Of course you have a right to stay where you are if you please,' he replied, rather petulantly; 'but I wish you would turn out and let me lock the place up, and be done with it.'

"I did not see it in the same light, and left the captain, after promising to be silent concerning the disappearance of my companion. The latter had had no acquaintances on board, and was not missed in the course of the day. Toward evening I met the doctor again, and he asked me whether I had changed my mind. I told him I had not.

" 'Then you will before long,' he said, very gravely.

III

"We played whist in the evening, and I went to bed late. I will confess now that I felt a disagreeable sensation when I entered my stateroom. I could not help thinking of the tall man I had seen on the previous night, who was now dead, drowned, tossing about in the long swell, two or three hundred miles astern. His face rose very distinctly before me as I undressed, and I even went so far as to draw back the curtains of the upper berth, as though to persuade myself that he was actually gone. I also bolted the door of the stateroom. Suddenly I became aware that the porthole was open and fastened back. This was more than I could stand. I hastily threw on my dressing-gown and went in search of Robert, the steward of my passage. I was very angry, I remember, and when I found him I dragged him roughly to the door of one hundred and five, and pushed him toward the open porthole.

" 'What the deuce do you mean, you scoundrel, by leaving that port open every night? Don't you know it is against the regulations? Don't you know that if the ship heeled and the water began to come in ten men could not shut it? I will report you to the captain, you blackguard, for endangering the ship!'

"I was exceedingly wroth. The man trembled and turned pale, and then began to shut the round glass plate with the heavy brass fittings.

" 'Why don't you answer me?' I said roughly.

" 'If you please, sir,' faltered Robert, 'there's nobody on board as can keep this 'ere port shut at night. You can try it yourself, sir. I ain't a-going to stop hany longer on board o' this vessel, sir; I ain't, indeed. But if I was you, sir, I'd just clear out and go and sleep with the surgeon, or something, I would. Look 'ere, sir, is that fastened what you may call securely, or not, sir? Try it, sir, see if it will move a hinch.'

"I tried the port, and found it perfectly tight.

" 'Well, sir,' continued Robert, triumphantly, 'I wager my reputation as a A1 steward, that in arf an hour it will be open again; fastened back, too, sir, that's the horful thing—fastened back!'

"I examined the great screw and the looped nut that ran on it.

" 'If I find it open in the night, Robert, I will give you a sovereign. It is not possible. You may go.'

" 'Soverin, did you say, sir? Very good, sir. Thank ye, sir. Good-night, sir. Pleasant reepose, sir, and all manner of hinchantin' dreams, sir.'

"Robert scuttled away, delighted at being released. Of course, I thought he was trying to account for his negligence by a silly story, intended to frighten me, and I disbelieved him. The consequence was that he got his sovereign, and I spent a very peculiarly unpleasant night.

"I went to bed, and five minutes after I had rolled

myself up in my blankets the inexorable Robert extinguished the light that burned steadily behind the
ground-glass pane near the door. I lay quite still in
the dark trying to go to sleep, but I soon found that
impossible. It had been some satisfaction to be angry
with the steward, and the diversion had banished that
unpleasant sensation I had at first experienced when I
thought of the drowned man who had been my chum;
but I was no longer sleepy, and I lay awake for some
time, occasionally glancing at the porthole, which I
could just see from where I lay, and which, in the
darkness, looked like a faintly luminous soup-plate
suspended in blackness. I believe I must have lain
there for an hour, and, as I remember, I was just dozing into sleep when I was roused by a draught of cold
air and by distinctly feeling the spray of the sea blown
upon my face. I started to my feet, and not having
allowed in the dark for the motion of the ship, I was
instantly thrown violently across the stateroom upon
the couch which was placed beneath the porthole. I
recovered myself immediately, however, and climbed
upon my knees. The porthole was again wide open
and fastened back!

"Now these things are facts. I was wide awake
when I got up, and I should certainly have been waked
by the fall had I still been dozing. Moreover, I
bruised my elbows and knees badly, and the bruises
were there on the following morning to testify to the
fact, if I myself had doubted it. The porthole was
wide open and fastened back—a thing so unaccount-
able that I remember very well feeling astonishment

F. Marion Crawford

rather than fear when I discovered it. I at once closed the plate again and screwed down the loop nut with all my strength. It was very dark in the stateroom. I reflected that the port had certainly been opened within an hour after Robert had at first shut it in my presence, and I determined to watch it and see whether it would open again. Those brass fittings are very heavy and by no means easy to move; I could not believe that the clamp had been turned by the shaking of the screw. I stood peering out through the thick glass at the alternate white and gray streaks of the sea that foamed beneath the ship's side. I must have remained there a quarter of an hour.

"Suddenly, as I stood, I distinctly heard something moving behind me in one of the berths, and a moment afterward, just as I turned instinctively to look—though I could, of course, see nothing in the darkness—I heard a very faint groan. I sprang across the stateroom, and tore the curtains of the upper berth aside, thrusting in my hands to discover if there were any one there. There was some one.

"I remember that the sensation as I put my hands forward was as though I were plunging them into the air of a damp cellar, and from behind the curtain came a gust of wind that smelled horribly of stagnant sea-water. I laid hold of something that had the shape of a man's arm, but was smooth, and wet, and icy cold. But suddenly, as I pulled, the creature sprang violently forward against me, a clammy, oozy mass, as it seemed to me, heavy and wet, yet endowed with a sort of supernatural strength. I reeled across the stateroom, and in an instant the door opened and the thing rushed out. I had not had time to be frightened, and quickly recovering myself, I sprang through the door and gave chase at the top of my speed, but I was too late. Ten yards before me I could see—I am sure I saw it—a dark shadow moving in the dimly lighted passage, quickly as the shadow of a fast horse thrown before a dog-cart by the lamp on a dark night. But in a moment it had disappeared, and I found myself holding on to the polished rail that ran along the bulkhead where the passage turned toward the companion. My hair stood on end, and the cold perspiration rolled down my face. I am not ashamed of it in the least: I was very badly frightened.

"Still I doubted my senses, and pulled myself together. It was absurd, I thought. The Welsh rarebit I had eaten had disagreed with me. I had been in a nightmare. I made my way back to my stateroom, and entered it with an effort. The whole place smelled of stagnant sea-water, as it had when I had waked on the previous evening. It required my utmost strength to go in and grope among my things for a box of wax lights. As I lighted a railway reading-lantern which I always carry in case I want to read after the lamps are out, I perceived that the porthole was again open, and a sort of creeping horror began to take possession of me which I never felt before, nor wish to feel again. But I got a light and proceeded to examine the upper berth, expecting to find it drenched with sea-water.

"But I was disappointed. The bed had been slept in, and the smell of the sea was strong; but the bed-

ding was as dry as a bone. I fancied that Robert had
not had the courage to make the bed after the accident
of the previous night—it had all been a hideous dream.
I drew the curtains back as far I could and examined
the place very carefully. It was perfectly dry. But
the porthole was open again. With a sort of dull be-
wilderment of horror, I closed it and screwed it down,
and thrusting my heavy stick through the brass loop,
wrenched it with all my might, till the thick metal
began to bend under the pressure. Then I hooked
my reading-lantern into the red velvet at the head of
the couch, and sat down to recover my senses if I
could. I sat there all right, unable to think of rest
—hardly able to think at all. But the porthole remained closed, and I did not believe it would now open
again without the application of a considerable force.

"The morning dawned at last, and I dressed myself
slowly, thinking over all that had happened in the
night. It was a beautiful day and I went on deck,
glad to get out in the early pure sunshine, and to smell
the breeze from the blue water, so different from the
noisome, stagnant odor from my stateroom. Instinctively I turned aft, toward the surgeon's cabin. There
he stood with a pipe in his mouth, taking his morning
airing precisely as on the preceding day.

" 'Good-morning,' said he quietly, but looking at me
with evident curiosity.

" 'Doctor, you were quite right,' said I. 'There is
something wrong about that place.'

" 'I thought you would change your mind,' he answered, rather triumphantly. 'You have had a bad

night, eh? Shall I make you a pick-me-up? I have a capital recipe.'

" 'No, thanks,' I cried. 'But I would like to tell you what happened.'

"I then tried to explain as clearly as possible precisely what had occurred, not omitting to state that I had been scared as I had never been scared in my whole life before. I dwelt particularly on the phenomenon of the porthole, which was a fact to which I could testify, even if the rest had been an illusion. I had closed it twice in the night, and the second time I had actually bent the brass in wrenching it with my stick. I believe I insisted a good deal on this point.

" 'You seem to think I am likely to doubt the story,' said the doctor, smiling at the detailed account of the state of the porthole. 'I do not doubt it in the least. I renew my invitation to you. Bring your traps here, and take half my cabin.'

" 'Come and take half of mine for one night,' I said. 'Help me to get at the bottom of this thing.'

" 'You will get to the bottom of something else if you try,' answered the doctor.

" 'What?' I asked.

" 'The bottom of the sea. I am going to leave the ship. It is not canny.'

" 'Then you will not help me to find out—'

" 'Not I,' said the doctor, quickly. 'It is my business to keep my wits about me—not to go fiddling about with ghosts and things.'

" 'Do you really believe it is a ghost?' I inquired, rather contemptuously. But as I spoke I remembered very well the horrible sensation of the supernatural which had got possession of me during the night. The doctor turned sharply on me:

" 'Have you any reasonable explanation of these things to offer?' he asked. 'No; you have not. Well, you say you will find an explanation. I say that you won't, sir, simply because there is not any.'

" 'But, my dear sir,' I retorted, 'do you, a man of science, mean to tell me that such things can not be explained?'

" 'I do,' he answered, stoutly. 'And if they could, I would not be concerned in the explanation.'

"I did not care to spend another night alone in the stateroom, and yet I was obstinately determined to get at the root of the disturbances. I do not believe there are many men who would have slept there alone, after passing two such nights. But I made up my mind to try it, if I could not get any one to share a watch with me. The doctor was evidently not inclined for such an experiment. He said he was a surgeon, and that in case any accident occurred on board he must always be in readiness. He could not afford to have his nerves unsettled. Perhaps he was quite right, but I am inclined to think that his precaution was prompted by his inclination. On inquiry, he informed me that there was no one on board who would be likely to join me in my investigations, and after a little more conversation I left him. A little later I met the captain, and told him my story. I said that if no one would spend the night with me I would ask leave to have the light burning all night, and would try it alone.

" 'Look here,' said he, 'I will tell you what I will do. I will share your watch myself, and we will see what happens. It is my belief that we can find out between us. There may be some fellow skulking on board who steals a passage by frightening the passengers. It is just possible that there may be something queer in the carpentering of that berth.'

"I suggested taking the ship's carpenter below and examining the place; but I was overjoyed at the captain's offer to spend the night with me. He accordingly sent for the workman and ordered him to do anything I required. We went below at once. I had all the bedding cleared out of the upper berth, and we examined the place thoroughly to see if there was a board loose anywhere, or a panel which could be opened or pushed aside. We tried the planks everywhere, tapped the flooring, unscrewed the fittings of the lower berth and took it to pieces—in short, there was not a square inch of the stateroom which was not searched and tested. Everything was in perfect order, and we put everything back in its place. As we were finishing our work, Robert came to the door and looked in.

" 'Well, sir—find anything, sir?' he asked with a ghastly grin.

" 'You were right about the porthole, Robert,' I said, and I gave him the promised sovereign. The carpenter did his work silently and skilfully, following my directions. When he had done he spoke.

" 'I'm a plain man, sir,' he said. 'But it's my belief you had better just turn out your things and let me run half a dozen four-inch screws through the door of this cabin. There's no good never came o' this cabin yet, sir, and that's all about it. There's been four lives lost out o' here to my own remembrance, and that in four trips. Better give it up, sir—better give it up!'

" 'I will try it for one night more,' I said.

" 'Better give it up, sir—better give it up! It's a precious bad job,' repeated the workman, putting his tools in his bag and leaving the cabin.

"But my spirits had risen considerably at the prospect of having the captain's company, and I made up my mind not to be prevented from going to the end of the strange business. I abstained from Welsh rarebits and grog that evening, and did not even join in the customary game of whist. I wanted to be quite sure of my nerves, and my vanity made me anxious to make a good figure in the captain's eyes.

IV

"The captain was one of those splendidly tough and cheerful specimens of seafaring humanity whose combined courage, hardihood, and calmness in difficulty leads them naturally into high positions of trust. He was not the man to be led away by an idle tale, and the mere fact that he was willing to join me in the investigation was proof that he thought there was something seriously wrong, which could not be accounted for on ordinary theories, nor laughed down as a common superstition. To some extent, too, his reputation was at stake, as well as the reputation of

the ship. It is no light thing to lose passengers overboard, and he knew it.

"About ten o'clock that evening, as I was smoking
a last cigar, he came up to me and drew me aside from
the beat of the other passengers who were patrolling
the deck in the warm darkness.

" 'This is a serious matter, Mr. Brisbane,' he said.
'We must make up our minds either way—to be disappointed or to have a pretty rough time of it. You
see, I can not afford to laugh at the affair, and I will
ask you to sign your name to a statement of whatever
occurs. If nothing happens to-night we will try it
again to-morrow and next day. Are you ready?'

"So we went below and entered the stateroom. As
we went in I could see Robert the steward, who stood
a little further down the passage, watching us, with
his usual grin, as though certain that something dreadful was about to happen. The captain closed the door
behind us and bolted it.

" 'Supposing we put your portmanteau before the
door,' he suggested. 'One of us can sit on it. Nothing can get out then. Is the port screwed down?'

"I found it as I had left it in the morning. Indeed,
without using a lever, as I had done, no one could
have opened it. I drew back the curtains of the upper
berth so that I could see well into it. By the captain's advice I lighted my reading-lantern, and placed
it so that it shone upon the white sheets above. He
insisted upon sitting on the portmanteau, declaring
that he wished to be able to swear that he had sat
before the door.

"Then he requested me to search the stateroom thoroughly, an operation very soon accomplished, as it consisted merely in looking beneath the lower berth and under the couch below the porthole. The spaces were quite empty.

" 'It is impossible for any human being to get in,' I said, 'or for any human being to open the port.'

" 'Very good,' said the captain, calmly. 'If we see anything now, it must be either imagination or something supernatural.'

"I sat down on the edge of the lower berth.

" 'The first time it happened,' said the captain, crossing his legs and leaning back against the door, 'was in March. The passenger who slept here, in the upper berth, turned out to have been a lunatic—at all events, he was known to have been a little touched, and he had taken his passage without the knowledge of his friends. He rushed out in the middle of the night, and threw himself overboard, before the officer who had the watch could stop him. We stopped and lowered a boat; it was a quiet night, just before that heavy weather came on; but we could not find him. Of course his suicide was afterward accounted for on the ground of his insanity.'

" 'I suppose that often happens?' I remarked, rather absently.

" 'Not often—no,' said the captain; 'never before in my experience, though I have heard of it happening on board of other ships. Well, as I was saying, that occurred in March. On the very next trip—

What are you looking at?' he asked, stopping suddenly in his narration.

"I believe I gave no answer. My eyes were riveted
upon the porthole. It seemed to me that the brass
loop-nut was beginning to turn very slowly upon the
screw—so slowly, however, that I was not sure it
moved at all. I watched it intently, fixing its position in my mind, and trying to ascertain whether it
changed. Seeing where I was looking, the captain
looked too.

" 'It moves!' he exclaimed, in a tone of conviction.
'No, it does not,' he added, after a minute.

" 'If it were the jarring of the screw,' said I, 'it
would have opened during the day; but I found it
this evening jammed tight as I left it this morning.'

"I rose and tried the nut. It was certainly loosened,
for by an effort I could move it with my hands.

" 'The queer thing,' said the captain, 'is that the
second man who was lost is supposed to have got
through that very port. We had a terrible time over
it. It was in the middle of the night, and the weather
was very heavy; there was an alarm that one of the
ports was open and the sea running in. I came below and found everything flooded, the water pouring
in every time she rolled, and the whole port swinging
from the top bolts—not the porthole in the middle.
Well, we managed to shut it, but the water did some
damage. Ever since that the place smells of sea-
water from time to time. We supposed the passenger
had thrown himself out, though the Lord only knows
how he did it. The steward kept telling me that he

could not keep anything shut here. Upon my word—
I can smell it now, can not you?' he inquired, sniffing
the air suspiciously.

"'Yes—distinctly,' I said, and I shuddered as that
same odor of stagnant sea-water grew stronger in the
cabin. 'Now, to smell like this, the place must be
damp,' I continued, 'and yet when I examined it with
the carpenter this morning everything was perfectly
dry. It is most extraordinary—hallo!'

"My reading-lantern, which had been placed in the
upper berth, was suddenly extinguished. There was
still a good deal of light from the pane of ground glass
near the door, behind which loomed the regulation
lamp. The ship rolled heavily, and the curtain of the
upper berth swung far out into the stateroom and back
again. I rose quickly from my seat on the edge of the
bed, and the captain at the same moment started to
his feet with a loud cry of surprise. I had turned
with the intention of taking down the lantern to examine it, when I heard his exclamation, and immediately afterward his call for help. I sprang toward him.
He was wrestling with all his might with the brass
loop of the port. It seemed to turn against his hands
in spite of all his efforts. I caught up my cane, a
heavy oak stick I always used to carry, and thrust it
through the ring and bore on it with all my strength.
But the strong wood snapped suddenly, and I fell
upon the couch. When I rose again the port was wide
open, and the captain was standing with his back
against the door, pale to the lips.

"'There is something in that berth!' he cried, in a

strange voice, his eyes almost starting from his head.
'Hold the door, while I look—it shall not escape us,
whatever it is!'

"But instead of taking his place, I sprang upon the
lower bed and seized something which lay in the upper
berth.

"It was something ghostly, horrible beyond words,
and it moved in my grip. It was like the body of a
man long drowned, and yet it moved and had the
strength of ten men living; but I gripped it with all
my might—the slippery, oozy, horrible thing. The
dead white eyes seemed to stare at me out of the dusk;
the putrid odor of rank sea-water was about it, and its
shiny hair hung in foul wet curls over its dead face.
I wrestled with the dead thing; it thrust itself upon
me and forced me back and nearly broke my arms; it
wound its corpse's arms about my neck, the living
death, and overpowered me, so that I, at last, cried
aloud and fell and left my hold.

"As I fell the thing sprang across me and seemed
to throw itself upon the captain. When I last saw
him on his feet his face was white and his lips set.
It seemed to me that he struck a violent blow at the
dead being, and then he, too, fell forward upon his
face, with an inarticulate cry of horror.

"The thing paused an instant, seeming to hover
over his prostrate body, and I could have screamed
again for very fright, but I had no voice left. The
thing vanished suddenly, and it seemed to my disturbed senses that it made its exit through the open
port, though how that was possible, considering the

smallness of the aperture, is more than any one can tell. I lay a long time upon the floor, and the captain lay beside me. At last I partially recovered my senses and moved, and I instantly knew that my arm was broken—the small bone of the left forearm near the wrist.

"I got upon my feet somehow, and with my remaining hand I tried to raise the captain. He groaned and moved, and at last came to himself. He was not hurt, but he seemed badly stunned.

"Well, do you want to hear any more? There is nothing more. That is the end of my story. The carpenter carried out his scheme of running half a dozen four-inch screws through the door of one hundred and five, and if ever you take a passage in the 'Kamtschatka,' you may ask for a berth in that stateroom. You will be told that it is engaged—yes—it is engaged by that dead thing.

"I finished the trip in the surgeon's cabin. He doctored my broken arm, and advised me not to 'fiddle about with ghosts and things' any more. The captain was very silent, and never sailed again in that ship, though it is still running. And I will not sail in her either. It was a very disagreeable experience and I was very badly frightened, which is a thing I do not like. That is all. That is how I saw a ghost—if it was a ghost. It was dead, anyhow."

THE INMATE OF THE DUNGEON

BY W. C. MORROW

William C. Morrow is a California writer with a strong leaning toward the tragic in literature. His most notable book, "Man: His Mark," is a melodramatic novel whose action is set in the impressive mountain scenery of California. There are but two main actors: a man who lost his beloved, and the woman who has caused his loss—for whom, nevertheless, he performs a heroic act of self-sacrifice. The same strength of style which distinguishes his novels is to be found in his short stories, of which "The Inmate of the Dungeon" is a representative selection.

THE INMATE OF THE DUNGEON

BY W. C. MORROW

AFTER the Board of State Prison Directors, sitting in session at the prison, had heard and disposed of the complaints and petitions of a number of convicts, the warden announced that all who wished to appear had been heard. Thereupon a certain uneasy and apprehensive expression, which all along had sat upon the faces of the directors, became visibly deeper. The chairman—nervous, energetic, abrupt, incisive man—glanced at a slip of paper in his hand, and said to the warden:

"Send a guard for convict No. 14,208."

The warden started and became slightly pale. Somewhat confused, he haltingly replied, "Why, he has expressed no desire to appear before you."

"Nevertheless, you will send for him at once," responded the chairman.

The warden bowed stiffly and directed a guard to produce the convict. Then, turning to the chairman, he said:

"I am ignorant of your purpose in summoning this man, but of course I have no objection. I desire, however, to make a statement concerning him before he appears."

"When we shall have called for a statement from

you," coldly responded the chairman, "you may make one."

The warden sank back into his seat. He was a tall, fine-looking man, well-bred and intelligent, and had a kindly face. Though ordinarily cool, courageous, and self-possessed, he was unable to conceal a strong emotion which looked much like fear. A heavy silence fell upon the room, disturbed only by the official stenographer, who was sharpening his pencils. A stray beam of light from the westering sun slipped into the room between the edge of the window-shade and the sash, and fell across the chair reserved for the convict. The uneasy eyes of the warden finally fell upon this beam, and there his glance rested. The chairman, without addressing any one particularly, remarked:

"There are ways of learning what occurs in a prison without the assistance of either the wardens or the convicts."

Just then the guard appeared with the convict, who shambled in painfully and laboriously, as with a string he held up from the floor the heavy iron ball which was chained to his ankles. He was about forty-five years old. Undoubtedly he once had been a man of uncommon physical strength, for a powerful skeleton showed underneath the sallow skin which covered his emaciated frame. His sallowness was peculiar and ghastly. It was partly that of disease, and partly of something worse; and it was this something that accounted also for his shrunken muscles and manifest feebleness.

There had been no time to prepare him for presentation to the Board. As a consequence, his unstockinged toes showed through his gaping shoes; the dingy suit of prison stripes which covered his gaunt frame was frayed and tattered; his hair had not been recently cut to the prison fashion, and, being rebellious, stood out upon his head like bristles; and his beard, which, like his hair, was heavily dashed with gray, had not been shaved for weeks. These incidents of his appearance combined with a very peculiar expression of his face to make an extraordinary picture. It is difficult to describe this almost unearthly expression. With a certain suppressed ferocity it combined an inflexibility of purpose that sat like an iron mask upon him. His eyes were hungry and eager; they were the living part of him, and they shone luminous from beneath shaggy brows. His forehead was massive, his head of fine proportions, his jaw square and strong, and his thin, high nose showed traces of an ancestry that must have made a mark in some corner of the world at some time in history. He was prematurely old; this was seen in his gray hair and in the uncommonly deep wrinkles which lined his forehead and the corners of his eyes and of his mouth.

Upon stumbling weakly into the room, faint with the labor of walking and of carrying the iron ball, he looked around eagerly, like a bear driven to his haunches by the hounds. His glance passed so rapidly and unintelligently from one face to another that he could not have had time to form a conception of

the persons present, until his swift eyes encountered
the face of the warden. Instantly they flashed; he
craned his neck forward; his lips opened and became
blue; the wrinkles deepened about his mouth and eyes;
his form grew rigid, and his breathing stopped. This
sinister and terrible attitude—all the more so because
he was wholly unconscious of it—was disturbed only
when the chairman sharply commanded, "Take that
seat."

The convict started as though he had been struck,
and turned his eyes upon the chairman. He drew a
deep inspiration, which wheezed and rattled as it
passed into his chest. An expression of excruciat-
ing pain swept over his face. He dropped the ball,
which struck the floor with a loud sound, and his
long, bony fingers tore at the striped shirt over his
breast. A groan escaped him, and he would have
sunk to the floor had not the guard caught him and
held him upright. In a moment it was over, and then,
collapsing with exhaustion, he sank into the chair.
There he sat, conscious and intelligent, but slouching,
disorganized, and indifferent.

The chairman turned sharply to the guard. "Why
did you manacle this man," he demanded, "when he
is evidently so weak, and when none of the others
were manacled?"

"Why, sir," stammered the guard, "surely you
know who this man is: he is the most dangerous and
desperate—"

"We know all about that. Remove his manacles."

The guard obeyed. The chairman turned to the

convict, and in a kindly manner said, "Do you know who we are?"

The convict got himself together a little and looked steadily at the chairman. "No," he replied after a pause. His manner was direct, and his voice was deep, though hoarse.

"We are the State Prison Directors. We have heard of your case, and we want you to tell us the whole truth about it."

The convict's mind worked slowly, and it was some time before he could comprehend the explanation and request. When he had accomplished that task he said, very slowly, "I suppose you want me to make a complaint, sir."

"Yes—if you have any to make."

The convict was getting himself in hand. He straightened, and gazed at the chairman with a peculiar intensity. Then firmly and clearly he answered, "I've no complaint to make."

The two men sat looking at each other in silence, and as they looked a bridge of human sympathy was slowly reared between them. The chairman rose, passed around an intervening table, went up to the convict, and laid a hand on his gaunt shoulder. There was a tenderness in his voice that few men had ever heard there.

"I know," said he, "that you are a patient and uncomplaining man, or we should have heard from you long ago. In asking you to make a statement I am merely asking for your help to right a wrong, if a wrong has been done. Leave your own wishes

entirely out of consideration, if you prefer. Assume, if you will, that it is not our intention or
desire either to give you relief or to make your case
harder for you. There are fifteen hundred human
beings in this prison, and they are under the absolute
control of one man. If a serious wrong is practiced
upon one, it may be upon others. I ask you in the
name of common humanity, and as one man of another, to put us in the way of working justice in this
prison. If you have the instincts of a man within
you, you will comply with my request. Speak out,
therefore, like a man, and have no fear of anything."

The convict was touched and stung. He looked up
steadily into the chairman's face, and firmly said,
"There is nothing in this world that I fear." Then he
hung his head, and presently he raised it and added,
"I will tell you all about it."

At that moment he shifted his position so as to bring
the beam of light perpendicularly across his face and
chest, and it seemed to split him in twain. He saw it,
and feasted his gaze upon it as it lay upon his breast.
After a time he thus proceeded, speaking very slowly,
and in a strangely monotonous voice:

"I was sent up for twenty years for killing a man.
I hadn't been a criminal: I killed him without thinking, for he had robbed me and wronged me. I came
here thirteen years ago. I had trouble at first—it
galled me to be a convict; but I got over that, because
the warden that was here then understood me and was
kind to me, and he made me one of the best men in
the prison. I don't say this to make you think I'm

complaining about the present warden, or that he didn't treat me kindly: I can take care of myself with him. I am not making any complaint. I ask no man's favor, and I fear no man's power."

"That is all right. Proceed."

"After the warden had made a good man out of me I worked faithfully, sir; I did everything they told me to do; I worked willingly and like a slave. It did me good to work, and I worked hard. I never violated any of the rules after I was broken in. And then the law was passed giving credits to the men for good conduct. My term was twenty years, but I did so well that my credits piled up, and after I had been here ten years I could begin to see my way out. There were only about three years left. And, sir, I worked faithfully to make those years good. I knew that if I did anything against the rules I should lose my credits and have to stay nearly ten years longer. I knew all about that, sir: I never forgot it. I wanted to be a free man again, and I planned to go away somewhere and make the fight all over—to be a man in the world once more."

"We know all about your record in the prison. Proceed."

"Well, it was this way. You know they were doing some heavy work in the quarries and on the grades, and they wanted the strongest men in the prison. There weren't very many: there never are very many strong men in a prison. And I was one of 'em that they put on the heavy work, and I did it faithfully. They used to pay the men for extra work

—not pay 'em money, but the value of the money in candles, tobacco, extra clothes, and things like that. I loved to work, and I loved to work extra, and so did some of the other men. On Saturdays the men who had done extra work would fall in and go up to the captain of the guard and he would give to each man what was coming to him. He had it all down in a book, and when a man would come up and call for what was due him the captain would give it to him, whatever he wanted that the rules allowed.

"One Saturday I fell in with the others. A good many were ahead of me in the line, and when they got what they wanted they fell into a new line, waiting to be marched to the cells. When my turn in the line came I went up to the captain and said I would take mine in tobacco. He looked at me pretty sharply, and said, 'How did you get back in that line?' I told him I belonged there—that I had come to get my extra. He looked at his book, and he said, 'You've had your extra: you got tobacco.' And he told me to fall into the new line. I told him I hadn't received any tobacco; I said I hadn't got my extra, and hadn't been up before. He said, 'Don't spoil your record by trying to steal a little tobacco. Fall in.' . . . It hurt me, sir. I hadn't been up; I hadn't got my extra; and I wasn't a thief, and I never had been a thief, and no living man had a right to call me a thief. I said to him, straight, 'I won't fall in till I get my extra, and I'm not a thief, and no man can call me one, and no man can rob me of my just dues.' He turned pale, and said, 'Fall in, there.' I said, 'I won't fall in till I get my dues.'

"With that he raised his hand as a signal, and the two guards behind him covered me with their rifles, and the guard on the west wall, and one on the north wall, and one on the portico in front of the arsenal, all covered me with rifles. The captain turned to a trusty and told him to call the warden. The warden came out, and the captain told him I was trying to run double on my extra, and said I was impudent and insubordinate and refused to fall in. The warden said, 'Drop that and fall in.' I told him I wouldn't fall in. I said I hadn't run double, that I hadn't got my extra, and that I would stay there till I died before I would be robbed of it. He asked the captain if there wasn't some mistake, and the captain looked at his book and said there was no mistake; he said he remembered me when I came up and got the tobacco and he saw me fall into the new line, but he didn't see me get back in the old line. The warden didn't ask the other men if they saw me get my tobacco and slip back into the old line. He just ordered me to fall in. I told him I would die before I would do that. I said I wanted my just dues and no more, and I asked him to call on the other men in line to prove that I hadn't been up.

"He said, 'That's enough of this.' He sent all the other men to the cells, and left me standing there. Then he told two guards to take me to the cells. They came and took hold of me, and I threw them off as if they were babies. Then more guards came up, and

one of them hit me over the head with a club, and I fell.
And then, sir"—here the convict's voice fell to a
whisper—"and then he told them to take me to the
dungeon."

The sharp, steady glitter of the convict's eyes failed,
and he hung his head and looked despairingly at the
floor.

"Go on," said the chairman.

"They took me to the dungeon, sir. Did you ever
see the dungeon?"

"Perhaps; but you may tell us about it."

The cold, steady gleam returned to the convict's
eyes, as he fixed them again upon the chairman.

"There are several little rooms in the dungeon.
The one they put me in was about five feet by eight.
It has steel walls and ceiling, and a granite floor.
The only light that comes in passes through a slit in
the door. The slit is an inch wide and five inches
long. It doesn't give much light, because the door is
thick. It's about four inches thick, and is made of oak
and sheet steel bolted through. The slit runs this way "
—making a horizontal motion in the air—"and it is
four inches above my eyes when I stand on tiptoe.
And I can't look out at the factory wall forty feet
away unless I hook my fingers in the slit and pull
myself up."

He stopped and regarded his hands, the peculiar appearance of which we all had observed. The ends of
the fingers were uncommonly thick; they were red
and swollen, and the knuckles were curiously marked
with deep white scars.

"Well, sir, there wasn't anything at all in the dungeon, but they gave me a blanket, and they put me on bread and water. That's all they ever give you in the dungeon. They bring the bread and water once a day, and that is at night, because if they come in the daytime it lets in the light.

"The next night after they put me in—it was Sunday night—the warden came with the guard and asked me if I was all right. I said I was. He said, 'Will you behave yourself and go to work to-morrow?' I said, 'No, sir; I won't go to work till I get what is due me.' He shrugged his shoulders, and said, 'Very well: maybe you'll change your mind after you have been in here a week.'

"They kept me there a week. The next Sunday night the warden came and said, 'Are you ready to go to work to-morrow?' and I said, 'No; I will not go to work till I get what is due me.' He called me hard names. I said it was a man's duty to demand his rights, and that a man who would stand to be treated like a dog was no man at all."

The chairman interrupted. "Did you not reflect," he asked, "that these officers would not have stooped to rob you?—that it was through some mistake they withheld your tobacco, and that in any event you had a choice of two things to lose—one a plug of tobacco, and the other seven years of freedom?"

"But they angered me and hurt me, sir, by calling me a thief, and they threw me in the dungeon like a beast. . . . I was standing for my rights, and my rights were my manhood; and that is something a man

can carry sound to the grave, whether he's bond or
free, weak or powerful, rich or poor."

"Well, after you refused to go to work what did the
warden do?"

The convict, although tremendous excitement must
have surged and boiled within him, slowly, deliberately,
and weakly came to his feet.　He placed his right foot
on the chair, and rested his right elbow on the raised
knee.　The index finger of his right hand, pointing to
the chairman and moving slightly to lend emphasis
to his narrative, was the only thing that modified
the rigid immobility of his figure.　Without a single
change in the pitch or modulation of his voice, never
hurrying, but speaking with the slow and dreary monotony with which he had begun, he nevertheless—
partly by reason of these evidences of his in-
credible self-control—made a formidable picture as he
proceeded:

"When I told him that, sir, he said he'd take me to
the ladder and see if he couldn't make me change my
mind. . . . Yes, sir; he said he'd take me to the ladder."　(Here there was a long pause.)　"And I a
human being, with flesh on my bones and the heart of
a man in my body.　The other warden hadn't tried to
break my spirit on the ladder.　He did break it, though;
he broke it clear to the bottom of the man inside of
me; but he did it with a human word, and not with
the dungeon and the ladder.　I didn't believe the
warden when he said he would take me to the ladder.
I couldn't imagine myself alive and put through at
the ladder, and I couldn't imagine any human being

who could find the heart to put me through. If I had believed him I would have strangled him then and there, and got my body full of lead while doing it. No, sir; I could not believe it.

"And then he told me to come on. I went with him and the guards. He brought me to the ladder. I had never seen it before. It was a heavy wooden ladder, leaned against the wall, and the bottom was bolted to the floor and the top to the wall. A whip was on the floor." (Again there was a pause.) "The warden told me to strip, sir, and I stripped. . . . And still I didn't believe he would whip me. I thought he just wanted to scare me.

"Then he told me to face up to the ladder. I did so, and reached my arms up to the straps. They strapped my arms to the ladder, and stretched so hard that they pulled me up clear of the floor. Then they strapped my legs to the ladder. The warden then picked up the whip. He said to me, 'I'll give you one more chance: will you go to work to-morrow?' I said, 'No; I won't go to work till I get my dues.' 'Very well,' said he, 'you'll get your dues now.' And then he stepped back and raised the whip. I turned my head and looked at him, and I could see it in his eyes that he meant to strike. . . . And when I saw that, sir, I felt that something inside of me was about to burst."

The convict paused to gather up his strength for the crisis of his story, yet not in the least particular did he change his position, the slight movement of his pointing finger, the steady gleam of his eye, or the slow monotony of his speech. I had never witnessed any scene so dramatic as this, and yet all was absolutely simple and unintentional. I had been thrilled by the greatest actors, as with matchless skill they gave rein to their genius in tragic situations; but how inconceivably tawdry and cheap such pictures seemed in comparison with this! The claptrap of the music, the lights, the posing, the wry faces, the gasps, lunges, staggerings, rolling eyes—how flimsy and colorless, how mocking and grotesque, they all appeared beside this simple, uncouth, but genuine expression of immeasurable agony!

The stenographer held his pencil poised above the paper, and wrote no more.

"And then the whip came down across my back. The something inside of me twisted hard and then broke wide open, and went pouring all through me like melted iron. It was a hard fight to keep my head clear, but I did it. And then I said to the warden this: 'You've struck me with a whip in cold blood. You've tied me up hand and foot, to whip me like a dog. Well, whip me, then, till you fill your belly with it. You are a coward. You are lower, and meaner, and cowardlier than the lowest and meanest dog that ever yelped when his master kicked him. You were born a coward. Cowards will lie and steal, and you are the same as a thief and liar. No hound would own you for a friend. Whip me hard and long, you coward. Whip me, I say. See how good a coward feels when he ties up a man and whips him like a dog. Whip me till the last breath quits my body: if you leave me alive I will kill you for this.'

"His face got white. He asked me if I meant that, and I said, 'Yes; before God, I do.' Then he took the whip in both hands and came down with all his might."

"That was nearly two years ago," said the chairman. "You would not kill him now, would you?"

"Yes. I will kill him if I get a chance; and I feel it in me that the chance will come."

"Well, proceed."

"He kept on whipping me. He whipped me with all the strength of both hands. I could feel the broken skin curl up on my back, and when my head got too heavy to hold it straight it hung down, and I saw the blood on my legs and dripping off my toes into a pool of it on the floor. Something was straining and twisting inside of me again. My back didn't hurt much; it was the thing twisting inside of me that hurt. I counted the lashes, and when I counted to twenty-eight the twisting got so hard that it choked me and blinded me; . . . and when I woke up I was in the dungeon again, and the doctor had my back all plastered up, and he was kneeling beside me, feeling my pulse."

The prisoner had finished. He looked around vaguely, as though he wanted to go.

"And you have been in the dungeon ever since?"

"Yes, sir; but I don't mind that."

"How long?"

"Twenty-three months."

"On bread and water?"

"Yes; but that was all I wanted."

"Have you reflected that so long as you harbor a

determination to kill the warden you may be kept in the dungeon? You can't live much longer there, and if you die there you will never find the chance you want. If you say you will not kill the warden he may return you to the cells."

"But that would be a lie, sir; I will get a chance to kill him if I go to the cells. I would rather die in the dungeon than be a liar and sneak. If you send me to the cells I will kill him. But I will kill him without that. I will kill him, sir. . . . And he knows it."

Without concealment, but open, deliberate, and implacable, thus in the wrecked frame of a man, so close that we could have touched it, stood Murder— not boastful, but relentless as death.

"Apart from weakness, is your health good?" asked the chairman.

"Oh, it's good enough," wearily answered the convict. "Sometimes the twisting comes on, but when I wake up after it I'm all right."

The prison surgeon, under the chairman's direction, put his ear to the convict's chest, and then went over and whispered to the chairman.

"I thought so," said that gentleman. "Now, take this man to the hospital. Put him to bed where the sun will shine on him, and give him the most nourishing food."

The convict, giving no heed to this, shambled out with a guard and the surgeon.

The warden sat alone in the prison office with No. 14,208. That he at last should have been brought face to face, and alone, with the man whom he had determined to kill, perplexed the convict. He was not manacled; the door was locked, and the key lay on the table between the two men. Three weeks in the hospital had proved beneficial, but a deathly pallor was still in his face.

"The action of the directors three weeks ago," said the warden, "made my resignation necessary. I have awaited the appointment of my successor, who is now in charge. I leave the prison to-day. In the meantime, I have something to tell you that will interest you. A few days ago a man who was discharged from the prison last year read what the papers have published recently about your case, and he has written to me confessing that it was he who got your tobacco from the captain of the guard. His name is Salter, and he looks very much like you. He had got his own extra, and when he came up again and called for yours the captain, thinking it was you, gave it to him. There was no intention on the captain's part to rob you."

The convict gasped and leaned forward eagerly.

"Until the receipt of this letter," resumed the warden, "I had opposed the movement which had been started for your pardon; but when this letter came I recommended your pardon, and it has been granted. Besides, you have a serious heart trouble. So you are now discharged from the prison."

The convict stared, and leaned back speechless. His eyes shone with a strange, glassy expression, and his white teeth glistened ominously between his parted lips. Yet a certain painful softness tempered the iron in his face.

"The stage will leave for the station in four hours," continued the warden. "You have made certain threats against my life." The warden paused; then, in a voice that slightly wavered from emotion, he continued: "I shall not permit your intentions in that regard—for I care nothing about them—to prevent me from discharging a duty which, as from one man to another, I owe you. I have treated you with a cruelty the enormity of which I now comprehend. I thought I was right. My fatal mistake was in not understanding your nature. I misconstrued your conduct from the beginning, and in doing so I have laid upon my conscience a burden which will imbitter the remaining years of my life. I would do anything in my power, if it were not too late, to atone for the wrong I have done you. If, before I sent you to the dungeon, I could have understood the wrong and foreseen its consequences, I would cheerfully have taken my own life rather than raise a hand against you. The lives of us both have been wrecked; but your suffering is in the past—mine is present, and will cease only with my life. For my life is a curse, and I prefer not to keep it."

With that the warden, very pale, but with a clear purpose in his face, took a loaded revolver from a drawer and laid if before the convict.

"Now is your chance," he said, quietly: "no one can hinder you."

The convict gasped and shrank away from the weapon as from a viper.

"Not yet—not yet," he whispered, in agony.

The two men sat and regarded each other without the movement of a muscle.

"Are you afraid to do it?" asked the warden.

A momentary light flashed in the convict's eyes.

"No!" he gasped; "you know I am not.   But I can't—not yet—not yet."

The convict, whose ghastly pallor, glassy eyes, and gleaming teeth sat like a mask of death upon his face, staggered to his feet.

"You have done it at last! you have broken my spirit.   A human word has done what the dungeon and the whip could not do. . . . It twists inside of me now. . . I could be your slave for that human word." Tears streamed from his eyes.   "I can't help crying. I'm only a baby, after all—and I thought I was a man."

He reeled, and the warden caught him and seated him in the chair.   He took the convict's hand in his and felt a firm, true pressure there.   The convict's eyes rolled vacantly.   A spasm of pain caused him to raise his free hand to his chest; his thin, gnarled fingers —made shapeless by long use in the slit of the dungeon door—clutched automatically at his shirt.   A faint, hard smile wrinkled his wan face, displaying the gleaming teeth more freely.

"That human word," he whispered—"if you had spoken it long ago, if—but it's all—it's all right—now. I'll go—I'll go to work—to-morrow."

There was a slightly firmer pressure of the hand that held the warden's; then it relaxed. The fingers which clutched the shirt slipped away, and the hand dropped to his side. The weary head sank back and rested on the chair; the strange, hard smile still sat upon the marble face, and a dead man's glassy eyes and gleaming teeth were upturned toward the ceiling.

THE OLD PARTISAN

BY OCTAVE THANET

Alice French (born at Andover, Mass., March 19, 1850) has spent her girlhood and womanhood in Iowa and Arkansas. Her fiction, most of which is descriptive of life and character in these States, has been written above the pseudonym of Octave Thanet— a name, it is said, that was suggested by some words on a passing railroad car. "The Old Partisan" depicts a ruling passion that is peculiarly American—the almost religious devotion that a plain citizen often displays toward a great political leader.

THE OLD PARTISAN

BY OCTAVE THANET

I SAT so far back in the gallery that my opinion of my delegate friend dwindled with every session. Nevertheless my unimportant seat had its advantages. I could see the vast assembly and watch the throbbing of the Republican pulse if I could not hear its heartbeats. Therefore, perhaps, I studied my neighbors more than I might study them under different circumstances. The great wooden hall had its transient and unsubstantial character stamped on every bare wooden joist and unclinched nail. It was gaudy with flags and bunting and cheap portraits. There were tin bannerets crookedly marshaled on the floor to indicate the homes of the different States. A few delegates, doubtless new to the business and over-zealous, were already on the floor, but none of the principals were visible. They were perspiring and arguing in those committee rooms, those hotel lobbies and crowded hotel rooms, where the real business of the convention was already done and neatly prepared for presentation to the nation. I had nothing to keep me from studying my neighbors. In front of me sat two people who had occupied the same seats at every session that I was present at, a young girl and an old man. The girl wore the omnipresent shirtwaist (of

pretty blue and white tints, with snowy cuffs and collar), and her green straw hat was decked with blue
corn-flowers, from which I inferred that she had an
eye on the fashions. Her black hair was thick and
glossy under the green straw. I thought that she had
a graceful neck. It was very white—whiter than her
face, which had a touch of sunburn, as if she were
often out in the open air. Somehow I concluded that
she was a shop-girl and rode a wheel. If I were
wrong it is not likely that I shall ever know.

The old man, I fancied, was not so old as he looked;
his delicate, haggard profile may have owed its sunken
lines and the dim eye to sickness rather than to years.
He wore the heavy black broadcloth of the rural politician, and his coat sagged over his narrow chest as
if he had left his waistcoat at home. On his coat
lapel were four old-fashioned Blaine badges. Inces-
santly he fanned himself.

"It can't be they ain't going to nominate him to-
day?" he asked rather than asserted, his voice breaking on the higher notes, the mere wreck of a voice.

"Oh, maybe later," the girl assured him.

"Well, I wanted to attend a Republican convention
once more before I died. Your ma would have it I
wasn't strong enough; but I knew better; you and I
knew better, didn't we, Jennie?"

She made no answer except to pat his thin, ribbed,
brown hand with her soft, white, slim one; but there
was a world of sympathy in the gesture and her silent
smile.

"I wonder what your ma said when she came downstairs and found the letter and us gone," he cackled with the garrulous glee of a child recounting successful mischief; "made me think of the times when you was little and I stole you away for the circus. Once your pa thought you was lost—'member? And once you had on your school dress and you'd tore it—she did scold you that time. But we had fun when they used to let me have money, didn't we, Jennie?"

"Well, now I earn money, we have good times, too, grandpa," said Jennie, smiling the same tender, comprehending smile.

"We do that; I don't know what I would do 'cept for you, lambie, and this is—this is a grand time, Jennie, you look and listen; it's a great thing to see a nation making its principles and its president—and such a president!"

He half turned his head as he spoke, with a mounting enthusiasm, thus bringing his flushing face and eager eyes—no longer dim—into the focus of his next neighbor's bright gray eyes. The neighbor was a young man, not very young, but hardly to be called elderly, of an alert bearing and kindly smile.

"I think him a pretty fair man myself," said the other with a jocose understatement; "I come from his town."

What was there in such a simple statement to bring a distinctly anxious look into the young girl's soft eyes? There it was; one could not mistake it.

"Well!" said the old man—there was a flattering deference in his voice. "Well, well. And—and maybe you've seen him lately?" The quavering tones sharpened with a keener feeling; it was almost as if the man were inquiring for some one on whom he had a great stake of affection. "How did he look? Was he better, stronger?"

"Oh, he looked elegant," said the Ohio man, easily, but with a disconcerted side glance at the girl, whose eyes were imploring him.

"I've been a Blaine man ever since he was run, the time Bob Ingersoll nominated him," said the old man, who sighed as if relieved. "I was at that convention and heard the speech——"

"Ah, that was a speech to hear," said a man behind, and two or three men edged their heads nearer.

The old Republican straightened his bent shoulders, his winter-stung features softened and warmed at the manifestation of interest, his voice sank to the confidential undertone of the narrator.

"You're right, sir, right; it was a magnificent speech. I can see him jest as he stood there, a stoutish, good-looking, smooth-faced man, his eyes straight ahead, and an alternate that sat next me—I was an alternate; I've been an alternate four times; I could have been a delegate, but I says, 'No, abler men than me are wanting it; I'm willing to fight in the ranks.' But I wished I had a vote, a free vote that day, I tell you. The alternate near me, he says, 'You'll hear something fine now; I've heard him speak.'"

"You did, too, I guess."

"We could hear from the first minute. That kinder fixed our attention. He had a mellow, rich kind of voice that melted into our ears. We found ourselves listening and liking him from the first sentence. At first he was as quiet as a summer breeze, but presently he began to warm up, and the words flowed like a stream of jewels. It was electrifying: it was thrilling, sir; it took us off our feet before we knew it, and when he came to the climax, those of us that weren't yelling in the aisles were jumping up and down on our chairs! I know I found myself prancing up and down on my own hat on a chair, swinging somebody else's hat and screaming at the top of my voice, with the tears running down my cheeks. God! sir, there were men there on their feet cheering their throats out that had to vote against him afterward—had to because they were instructed—no more free will than a checked trunk!" 'The light died out of his face. "Yes, sir, a great speech; never a greater ever made at a convention anywhere, never so great a speech, whoever made it: but it did no good, he wasn't nominated, and when we did nominate him we were cheated out of our victory. Well, we'll do better this day."

"We will that," said the other man, heartily; "McKinley—"

"You'll excuse me—" the old man struck in with a deprecating air, yet under the apology was something fiercely eager and anxious that glued the hearer's eyes to his quivering old face—"you'll excuse me. I—I am considerable of an invalid, and I don't keep the run of things as I used to. You see, I live with my daughter, and you know how women folks are, fretting lest things could make you sick, and my girl she

worries so, me reading the papers. Fact is I got a
shock once, an awful shock"—he shivered involuntarily and his dim eyes clouded—"and it worried her
seeing me read. Hadn't ought to; it don't worry
Jennie here, who often gets me a paper, quiet like; but
you know how it is with women—it's easier giving
them their head a little—and so I don't see many
papers, and I kinder dropped off. It seems queer, but
I don't exactly sense it about this McKinley. Is he
running against Blaine or jest for vice?"

The girl, under some feminine pretext of dropping
and reaching for her handkerchief, threw upward a
glance of appeal at the interlocutor. Hurriedly she
stepped into the conversation. "My grandfather read
a false report about—about Mr. Blaine's sickness, and
he was not well at the time and it brought on a bad
attack."

"I understand," said the listener, with a grave nod
of his head and movement of his eyes in the girl's
direction.

"But about McKinley!" the old man persisted.

"He's for Vice-President," the girl announced, her
eyes fixed on the hesitating man from Canton. I have
often admired the intrepid fashion in which a woman
will put her conscience at a moral hedge, while a man
of no finer spiritual fibre will be straining his eyes to
find a hole through which he can crawl. "McKinley
is not opposed to Blaine, is he?" she asked the man.

"The Republican party has no name that is more
loved than that of James G. Blaine," said the man,
gravely.

"That's so, that's so!" the old partisan assented eagerly; "to my mind he's a logical candidate."

The Canton man nodded, and asked if he had ever seen Blaine.

"Once, only once. I was on a delegation sent to wait on him and ask him to our town to speak—he was in Cincinnati. I held out my hand when my turn came, and the chairman nearly knocked the breath out of me by saying, 'Here's the man who gave more to our campaign fund and worked harder than any man in the county, and we all worked hard for you, too.' Well, Mr. Blaine looked at me. You know the intent way he looks. He has the most wonderful eyes; look right at you and seem to bore into you like a gimlet. I felt as if he was looking right down into my soul, and I tell you I was glad, for I choked up so I couldn't find a word, not a word, and I was ready and fluent enough in those days, too, I can tell you; but I stood there filling up, and squeezed his hand and gulped and got red, like a fool. But he understood. 'I have heard of your loyalty to Republican principles, Mr. Painter,' says he, in that beautiful voice of his, that was like a violin; and I burst in—I couldn't help it— 'It ain't loyalty to Republican principles, it's to you.' I said that right out. And he smiled, and said he, 'Well, that's wrong, but it isn't for me to quarrel with you there, Mr. Painter,' and then they pushed me along: but twice while the talk was going on I saw him look my way and caught his eye, and he smiled, and when we were all shaking hands for good-by, he shook hands with a good, firm grip, and said he, 'Good-by, Mr. Painter; I hope we shall meet again.'"

The old man drew a long sigh. "Those few moments paid for everything," he said. "I've never seen him since. I've been sick and lost money. I ain't the man I was. I never shall be put on any delegation again, or be sent to any convention; but I thought if I could only go once more to a Republican convention, and hear them holler for Blaine, and holler once more myself, I'd be willinger to die. And I told Tom Hale that, and he and Jennie raised the money. Yes, Jennie, I'm going to tell—he and Jennie put off being married a bit so's I could go, and go on plenty of money. Jennie, she worked a month longer to have plenty, and Tom, he slipped ten dollars into my hand unbeknown to her jest as we were going, so I'd always have a dime to give the waiter or the porter. I was never one of these hayseed farmers too stingy to give a colored boy a dime when he done his best. I didn't need no money for badges; I got my old badges —see!"

He pushed out the lapel of his coat, covered with those old-fashioned trade bits of tinsel and ribbon, smiling confidently. The girl had flushed crimson to the rim of her white collar; but there was not a trace of petulance in her air; and, all at once looking at him, her eyes filled with tears.

"Tom's an awful good fellow," he said, "an awful good fellow."

"I'm sure of that," said the Canton man, with the frank American friendliness, making a little bow in

Miss Jennie's direction; "but see here, Mr. Painter, do you come from Izard? Are you the man that saved the county for the Republicans, by mortgaging the farm and then going on a house-to-house canvass?"

"That's me," the old man acquiesced, blushing with pleasure; "I didn't think, though, that it was known outside—"

"Things go further than you guess. I'm a newspaper man, and I can tell you that I shall speak of it again in my paper. Well, I guess they've got through with their mail and the platform's coming in."

Thus he brushed aside the old man's agitated thanks.

"One moment," said the old man, "who—who's going to nominate him?"

For the space of an eyeblink the kindly Canton man looked embarrassed, then he said, briskly: "Foraker, Foraker of Ohio—he's the principal one. That's he now, chairman of the Committee on Resolutions. He's there, the tall man with the mustache—"

"Isn't that elderly man with the stooped shoulders and the chin beard and caved-in face Teller?" It was a man near me, on the seat behind, who spoke, tapping the Canton man with his fan, to attract his attention; already the pitiful concerns of the old man, who was "a little off" (as I had heard some one on the seat whisper), were sucked out of notice in the whirlpool of the approaching political storm.

"Yes, that's Teller," answered the Canton man, his mouth straightening and growing thin.

"Is it to be a bolt?"

The Canton man nodded, at which the other whistled and communicated the information to his neighbors, one of whom remarked, "Let 'em bolt and be d——d!" A subtle excitement seemed to communicate its vibrations to all the gallery. Perhaps I should except the old partisan; he questioned the girl in a whisper, and then, seeming to be satisfied, watched the strange scene that ensued with an expression of patient weariness. The girl explained parts of the platform to him and he assented; it was good Republican doctrine, he said, but what do they mean with all this talk against the money; were they having trouble with the mining States again? The Canton man stopped to explain—he certainly was good-humored.

During the next twenty minutes, filled as they were with savage emotion, while the galleries, like the floor, were on their chairs yelling, cheering, brandishing flags and fists and fans and pampas plumes of red, white, and blue at the little band of silver men who marched through the ranks of their former comrades, he stood, he waved his fan in his feeble old hand, but he did not shout. "You must excuse me," said he, "I'm all right on the money question, but I'm saving my voice to shout for him!"

"That's right," said the Canton man; but he took occasion to cast a backward glance which I met, and it said as plainly as a glance can speak, "I wish I were out of this!"

Meanwhile, with an absent but happy smile, the old Blaine man was keeping time to the vast waves of sound that rose and swelled above the band, above the cheering, above the cries of anger and scorn, the tremendous chorus that had stiffened men's hearts as they marched to death and rang through streets filled with armies and thrilled the waiting hearts at home:

"Three cheers for the red, white, and blue!
Three cheers for the red, white, and blue!
The army and navy forever, three cheers for the
red, white, and blue!"

But when the chairman had stilled the tumult and made his grim comment, "There appear to be enough delegates left to transact business," the old partisan cast his eyes down to the floor with a chuckle. "I can't see the hole they made, it's so small. Say, ain't he a magnificent chairman; you can hear every word he says!"

"Bully chairman," said a cheerful "rooter" in the rear, who had enjoyed the episode more than words can say, and had cheered the passing of Silver with such choice quotations from popular songs as "Goodby, my lover, good-by," and "Just tell them that you saw me," and plainly felt that he, too, had adorned the moment. "I nearly missed coming this morning, and I wouldn't have missed it for a tenner; they're going to nominate now."

The old man caught his breath; then he smiled. "I'll help you shout pretty soon," said he, while he sat down very carefully.

The "rooter," a good-looking young fellow with a Reed button and three or four gaudy badges decking his crash coat, nodded and tapped his temple furtively, still retaining his expression of radiant good-nature. The Canton man nodded and frowned.

I felt that the Canton man need not be afraid. Somehow we were all tacitly taking care that this poor, bewildered soul should not have its little dream of loyal, unselfish satisfaction dispelled.

"Ah, my countrymen," I thought, "you do a hundred crazy things, you crush *les convenances* under foot, you can be fooled by frantic visionaries—but how I love you!"

It was Baldwin of Iowa that made the first speech. He was one of the very few men—I had almost said of the two men—that we in the galleries had the pleasure of hearing; and we could hear every word.

He began with a glowing tribute to Blaine. At the first sentence, our old man flung his gray head in the air with the gesture of the war-horse when he catches the first, far-off scream of the trumpet. He leaned forward, his features twitching, his eyes burning; the fan dropped out of his limp hand; his fingers, rapping his palm, clinched and loosened themselves unconsciously in an overpowering agitation. His face was white as marble, with ominous blue shadows; but every muscle was strained; his chest expanded; his shoulders drew back; his mouth was as strong and firm as a young man's. For a second we could see what he had been at his prime.

Then the orator's climax came, and the name—the magic name that was its own campaign cry in itself.

The old partisan leaped to his feet; he waved his hands above his head; wild, strange, in his white flame of excitement. He shouted; and we all shouted with him, the McKinley man and the Reed man vying with each other (I here offer my testimony to the scope and quality of that young Reed man's voice), and the air rang about us: "Blaine! Blaine! James G. Blaine!" He shrieked the name again and again, goading into life the waning applause. Then in an instant his will snapped under the strain; his gray head tilted in the air; his gray head went back on his neck.

The Canton man and I caught him in time to ease the fall. We were helped to pull him into the aisle. There were four of us by this time—his granddaughter and the Reed "rooter," besides the Canton man and myself.

We carried him into the wide passageway that led to the seats. The Reed young man ran for water, and, finding none, quickly returned with a glass of lemonade (he was a young fellow ready in shifts), and with it we bathed the old man's face.

Presently he came back, by degrees, to the world; he was not conscious, but we could see that he was not going to die.

"He'll be all right in no time," declared the Reed man. "You had better go back and get your seats, and keep mine!"

I assured both men that I could not return for more than a short time, having an engagement for luncheon.

"That's all right," said the Reed man, turning to the Canton man. "I ain't shouting when Foraker comes; you are. You go back and keep my seat; I'll come in later on Hobart."

So the kindly Canton man returned to the conven-

tion for which he was longing, and we remained in
our little corner by the window, the young girl fanning the old man, and the young man on the watch
for a boy with water. He darted after one; and then
the girl turned to me.

No one disturbed us. Below, the traffic of a great
city roared up to us and a brass band clanged mer-
rily. The crowd hurried past, drawn by the tidings
that "the fight was on"; it choked the outlets and
suffocated the galleries.

"He's been that way ever since he read, suddenly,
that Blaine was dead," she said, lowering her voice
to keep it safe from his failing ears; "he had a kind
of a stroke, and ever since he's had the notion that
Blaine was alive and was going to be nominated, and
his heart was set on going here. Mother was afraid;
but when—when he cried to go, I could not help taking him—I didn't know but maybe it might help him;
he was such a smart man and such a good man: and
he has had trouble about mortgaging the farm; and
he worked so hard to get the money back, so mother
would feel all right. All through the hot weather he
worked, and I guess that's how it happened. You
don't think it's hurt him? The doctor said he might
go. He told T——, a gentleman friend of mine, who
asked him."

"Oh, dear, no," said I; "it has been good for him."

I asked for her address, which fortunately was
near, and I offered her the cab that was waiting for me.
I had some ado to persuade her to accept it; but when
I pointed to her grandfather's pale face she did accept

it, thanking me in a simple but touching way, and, of course, begging me to visit her at Izard, Ohio.

All this while we had been sedulously fanning the old man, who would occasionally open his eyes for a second, but gave no other sign of returning consciousness.

The young Reed man came back with the water. He was bathing the old man's forehead in a skilful and careful way, using my handkerchief, when an uproar of cheering shook the very floor under us, and the rafters overhead.

"Who is it?" the old man inquired feebly.

"Foraker! Foraker!" bellowed the crowd.

"He's nominated him!" muttered the old man; but this time he did not attempt to rise. With a smile of great content he leaned against his granddaughter's strong young frame and listened, while the cheers swelled into a deafening din, and immeasurable tumult of sound, out of which a few strong voices shaped the chorus of the "Battle Cry of Freedom," to be caught up by fifteen thousand throats and pealed through the walls far down the city streets to the vast crowd without.

The young Reed "boomer," carried away by the moment, flung his free hand above his head and yelled defiantly: "Three cheers for the man from Maine!" Instantly he caught at his wits, his color turned, and he lifted an abashed face to the young girl.

"But, really, you know, that ain't giving nothing away," he apologized, plucking up heart. "May I do it again?"

The old partisan's eye lighted. "Now they're shouting! That's like old times! Yes, go it again, boy! Blaine! Blaine! James G. Blaine!"

He let us lead him to the carriage, the rapturous smile still on his lips. The "rooter" and I wormed our way through the crowd back to the seat which the kind Canton man had kept for us.

We were quite like old acquaintances now; and he turned to me at once, "Was there ever a politician or a statesman, since Henry Clay, loved so well as James G. Blaine?"

THE RETURN

BY I. K. FRIEDMAN

Isaac Kahn Friedman (born in Chicago, November 3, 1870) is one of the increasing number of American authors who draw their strength from knowledge of the plain and poor people, and sympathy with their condition. "The Return" is the echo of an old-world tragedy, the murder by an avaricious peasant couple of their own son, who had returned in disguise, after a long absence, to surprise his parents with his wealth. Mr. Friedman has added a realistic effect to the motive by giving it a modern setting in Italian American life, and has concentrated the emotional interest by reducing the murderers to one—and that the mother.

THE RETURN

BY I. K. FRIEDMAN

ANGELO PASCELLA stepped into Rosaura Pascella's wine room, and seating himself at one of his mother's tables, placed his carpet-bag on the floor and called for pranzo con mezzo foglietta de vino; dinner with wine. The card-playing, eating, drinking, arguing Italians ceased their diversions long enough to take a look at the new-comer.

He was a swarthy, healthy, prosperous looking fellow, whose twenty-five years perched carelessly on his shoulders, as if perfectly willing to make room for a twenty-sixth. There was nothing in his looks, dress or manner that entitled him to a second glance, and no suspicion of vexing mystery arose in the minds of Rosaura's patrons to spoil the flavor of the spaghetti importati, or to interrupt the flow of wine and words and cards.

Madre Pascella, whose small shrewd eyes were boring through the stranger's carpet-sack to inventory the contents thereof, seeing a prospective patron in the stranger, hastened to wait on him herself, after soundly scolding the servant for not paying better attention to the wants of her customers—this rather to impress the stranger than to reprove the servant.

Angelo, on his part, marveled much at the little

THE RETURN

BY I. K. FRIEDMAN

ANGELO PASCELLA stepped into Rosaura
Pascella's wine room, and seating himself at
one of his mother's tables, placed his carpet-
bag on the floor and called for *pranzo con mezza bot-
tliglia de vino*, dinner with wine. The card-playing,
eating, drinking, arguing Italians ceased their diversions long enough to take a look at the new-comer.

He was a swarthy, healthy, prosperous looking fellow, whose twenty-five years perched carelessly on
his shoulders, as if perfectly willing to make room for
a twenty-sixth. There was nothing in his looks, dress
or manner that entitled him to a second glance, and
no suspicion of vexing mystery arose in the minds of
Rosaura's patrons to spoil the flavor of the *sphagetti
importati*, or to interrupt the flow of wine and words
and cards.

Madre Pascella, whose small shrewd eyes were boring through the stranger's carpet-sack to inventory
the contents thereof, seeing a prospective patron in
the stranger, hastened to wait on him herself, after
soundly scolding the servant for not paying better attention to the wants of her customers—this rather to
impress the stranger than to reprove the servant.

Angelo, on his part, marveled much at the little

change that had taken place in his mother's appearance in the thirteen long years of his absence from home. She had grown somewhat stouter, the masculine growth on her upper lip was darker and thicker (those who spoke behind her back called it *un mostacchio*), her hair had lost its raven-like blackness, her face was a little more wrinkled, and that was all. Rosaura Pascella came of a stock that withers and dries, rather than dies.

The place, unlike its owner, was much the worse for wear; the plaster on the ceiling and walls was ready at any minute to fall on the floor, and seemed to beg for the support of props to prevent a tumble so disastrous. The floor had sagged under the heavy weight of the refrigerator and the clumsy pine bar; and both bar and refrigerator had arrived at that point of decrepitude where painting and repairing are too expensive to be practicable. The benches, tables and chairs—some minus an arm, some minus a leg, and some minus both—were the same ones around which Antonio had romped and played when a boy.

"Evidently the madre has not prospered since I left home; everything is going to rack and ruin," he reflected on looking around. Then, thinking of his own material success, "I shall put things to rights in less than no time."

When the mother placed the *pranzo* on the table, her son found it difficult to keep from throwing his arms around her, kissing her and crying, *"Mia carissima."* But he held the reward of a more brilliant and sudden surprise before his eyes, and restrained himself.

He did not know whether to feel sad or glad because she did not recognize him after an absence of only thirteen years. He knew her, forsooth! He gladdened himself with the reflection that he had out-handsomed her recollection, and ate on in silence, his eyes fixed on his plate. Ah! but the dish of spaghetti was fine, a motherly welcome in itself; and he smacked his lips and smiled contentedly. She was standing behind him with her arms folded, waiting for a chance to speak; she saw the smile and broke in abruptly, "How do you like it?"

"Fine," he answered, "just like my mother used to make," and he looked her straight in the eyes.

She bowed acknowledgment like one used to being complimented, and for whom one compliment is of as little value as another.

"I see," said she, pointing to the bag, "that you are from a distance."

"Yes, from New Orleans"—the words slipped from his lips inadvertently and he wished that he could recall them.

"Ehi! New Orleans!" The mere mentioning of the name changed her from an inquisitive questioner into a most voluble informer. She had a son there in the fruit business with her brother. A fine lad he was, too! He had left home when a boy of twelve and had been gone thirteen years. It was her only child; how she yearned to see him again, her boy! He might know him, his name was Angelo Pascella?

Angelo shook his head.

"No?" she thought every Italian in New Orleans must know her boy. He had prospered, he was rich, he was influential. He had promised over and over again in his letters to come home and spend a few days with his old mother, but the years had gone by and still he did not come. Ah! if he only knew the pleasure his return would bring her, but young men were forgetful and—

Some one at the further end of the room called for a bottle of wine, and her chatter was interrupted.

Angelo looked through the room wistfully to see if he could not discover some old friends of his boyhood days. They were all gone, the old familiar faces, or, at least, none of them was there. A feeling of the transitoriness of things, of separation from the life of which he had once been a component part, touched him with a vague sense of loneliness. His coming home had made him homesick, and he yearned to grasp his sack and start for New Orleans again. Then he blamed himself for not revealing his identity—a word from him and presto! all would change; his mother's arms would entwine lovingly about his neck, and his old friends would come crowding on the scene as if raised by magic. He would do it, surprise or no; but the sudden announcement ought to be surprise enough.

A diminutive, round-shouldered, bow-legged Italian entered the room and arrested Angelo's attention. He had seen a face like that somewhere, but he could not associate it with any particular place or time. But the legs? There was only one pair of legs in the world that bowed like those; surely enough, it must be little Pietro del Re, the tailor. Many an hour had he passed in the little tailor's basement shop, an ever welcome guest, listening to stories and descriptions of Italy and its wars.

He caught Pietro's eye and beckoned to him. "Would he have a glass of wine?" In a few minutes they were talking of the golden memories of the days gone by. Angelo felt his way carefully, and when the opportune moment came he discovered his identity. Pietro gave his head a jerk which made the rings in his ears dance. "What!" he exclaimed, "you don't say, you—!"

The sentence was never finished save in the mind of the speaker, for Angelo clapped his hands over the mouth of the surprised tailor. "Hush!" whispered he, "I want to surprise her, and you will spoil it all." This mysterious action did not escape the attention of the madre, who was watching them from behind the bar.

"And you mean to say that she don't know you?" he jerked his thumb over his shoulder to designate the "she."

Angelo shook his head. "No, but I think I will tell her later, when the others are gone and we are left alone."

Pietro proposed a better scheme. Angelo's was not half dramatic enough to suit the imaginative tailor's conception of what a theatrical surprise should be. Angelo must go directly to bed; and he, Pietro, would immediately betake himself home. In the morning he would arise early and gather all the old friends, Cassaretto, Barretti, Salvino, De Stefano, and a host of others whom Angelo had known since his boyhood and about whom he had just been questioning Pietro. They would all assemble at the Osteria dell Gallo (the Inn of the Cock), and apprise the madre who her guest really was. Then she would rush upstairs, enter her son's room and have him wake in her arms; and when the mother and son came downstairs the crowd would give them a rousing welcome.

"Come vi piace?" he asked.

Angelo rolled a cigarette, lighted it, and thought awhile. *"Molto moltissimo,"* he answered, blowing the cloud of thin smoke away.

The tailor shook hands, and arose for an immediate transaction of his part of the bargain.

At the doorway Rosaura stopped him—"Who is the man, why did he put his hand over your mouth to prevent you from speaking?"

An imaginative mind is of service in more ways than one; Pietro manufactured a very plausible lie on the spur of the moment. "He is a rich man, a very rich man, his pockets are lined with gold. When he told me how much he had, 'What! so much as that!' I was about to cry, and up goes his hand over my mouth. You see, Madre Pascella, he knows me to be an honest man; of the others he is not so sure. Goodnight."

Rosaura was still reflecting on how much truth there might be in the tailor's lie when Angelo ap-

proached and asked to be shown to his room. Here
was an opportunity to make this stranger show the
material with which his pockets were lined, and to
prove him a Crœsus, or Pietro del Re a liar.

"The rules of the house are to pay in advance,"
she said authoritatively, her hands on her hips.

The stranger smiled quietly, drew a fat roll of bills
from the inside pocket of his vest and paid the amount
demanded in a way that said, "And I wouldn't care if
it were a little higher."

The sight of it made her eyes ache and the palms of
her hands itch. There was more than enough in that
one roll to pay her year's rent, and in the morning
Carlo Neppi, the landlord, would be around clamor-
ing for his money; and Neppi was terrible when the
rent was not ready, all counted out in dimes and quarters and dollar bills—he would throw her into the
streets, and give her a shrug of his shoulders for
sympathy.

She lit a kerosene lamp, and opened the door that
shut the saloon from the winding stairway which led
to the lodging-house above. As they were moving
down the narrow hallway toward the room designated for Angelo, he gave way to a sudden impulse,
caught her round her ample waist and kissed her.
"Go away, fool!" she cried, shoving him vigorously
against the wall. She entered the room, put the lamp
on the wash-stand, and made her exit without even
wishing him good-night.

It was the room he had occupied when a boy; the
wash-stand, the bed, the stool, all looked as if they

had been waiting for him, and a Murillo Madonna, a cheap, dust-mellowed lithograph, beamed a welcome home from her place on the wall.   There was little enough in that bare room about which old memories could cluster; but they clung all the more closely to the small space available, like vines that put forth their creepers to mass their foliage about a single nail in an old wall.

Just below his window, which looked on the street, the signboard (a cock with the inscription "Osteria dell Gallo") was creaking loudly as it swayed back and forth in the wind.   Angelo regulated the creaking to the refrain, "Wel-come home, wel-come home," and his imagination made the inanimate cock crow the words softly.   The refrain soon lulled him to sleep.

Downstairs Rosaura was bubbling over with impatience; it seemed to her that midnight, the hour for closing, would never come, and that the loiterers would never go.

"It is past twelve; come, pay; it is very late, I must close or disobey the ordinance," she said to Enrico Grassi, who was telling her for the tenth time how Paolo Cherino had cheated him out of the last game of *morra,* and how Paolo, and not he, should pay for the last drinks.

"In a minute, just a minute, and I have done," repeated the excited Enrico.   "When a man has only a half thumb and bends it half-way, it would take the devil himself to tell whether it was up or down. 'Four,' says I! 'Three,' says Paolo, 'you pay.' Now Madre, I leave it with you if—"

"I care not whether it was up or down, Paolo has gone and you must pay!" cried the bored and impatient hostess.

"Well," said Enrico, with a shrewd smile, "you are like the rest of them, you are in the conspiracy to cheat me. Charge it!" and out he went with a slam of the door.

"It was worth the price of two glasses of wine to be rid of the fellow," she reflected philosophically, as she locked the door and turned the lamps out.

She moved up the stairs as carefully as if each inch of the way were connected by wire with bells, and the slightest jar would start the bells ringing and awaken some restless sleeper.

When in her room she removed her shoes and walked cautiously, on tiptoe, to the door that divided Angelo's room from her own, and pressed her ear against it. She heard the sleeper's deep and regular breathing, significant of one who has a light heart and an easy conscience for bedfellows. "He sleeps too soundly," she thought, "for a man with so much money."

She drew the bolt quietly, bent her knee against the panel of the door, waited a second in breathless suspense; then pressed forward quickly and turned the knob; the door opened as noiselessly as if the hinges had been oiled.

His bed was just opposite the door, and she could see every line of his youthful face by the light cast from the lamp that she had left burning low on a chair in the centre of her own room.

She advanced to his bedside slowly, slowly; the distance was but a few feet; to her it seemed as many miles. He had his vest buttoned over his woolen nightgown; it was the object of her search, and she noticed it before anything else. She bent over him so closely that she could feel the moisture of his breath on her hot cheek.

As Rosaura stood thus, holding her stiletto in her right hand, and firmly and gently unbuttoning his vest with her left hand, it seemed to her that she had seen the man before. So forcibly did the idea strike her that she paused in the very heat and excitement of the action to scan the sleeper's features more closely.

He turned on his side as if troubled by her searching stare and buried his face in the pillow.

She raised her stiletto, ready to strike if he awoke. His breathing continued regular and rounded as the ticking of an oscillating pendulum.

Then with one quick movement of the stiletto she ripped his vest down the back, and the heavier half of the garment, the half with the purse, she removed by a single tug.

In an over-anxiety to secure her treasure without awakening him, she let the stiletto slip and it pricked him in the back. He awoke with a start. Fearful lest he cry aloud, she grasped him by the throat with her long, knotty, masculine fingers, and the battle began for the supremacy between mother and son.

The son was the stronger, but the mother had all the advantages of position, forewarning and forearming. He used his strong arms for levers and tried to raise his body to a sitting posture. Her grasp tightened, and he felt the life-breath being choked out of him as she forced him on his back. He swung his left arm out in a half circle and struck her a staggering blow on the temple; she reeled, stretched out her long arm and caught the bed-post to save herself from falling.

Angelo sprang to his feet, and was on the floor in almost the time it took Rosaura's arm to reach out and grasp for support. He recognized his assailant and stood terror-stricken, dumfounded, paralyzed. *"Madre mia, madre mia!"* he gasped plaintively, beseechingly. The stiletto was drawn back, flashed, and leaped straight to his heart.

She crept on her hands and knees to the hall door, opened it and listened. The living were as silent as the murdered; the dead and the sleeping could tell no tales.

Pietro's sleep was by no means as sound as that of Angelo . He tossed about restlessly the whole night, laying his plan of attack for the great surprise on the morrow; for Pietro was a simple soul who made the most of one of those rare opportunities that gave him half a chance to appear of importance in the community.

He had made his plans a score of times, and changed them just as often; he would go for Antonio Salvino first and have him summon Gustavo de Stefano, and Gustavo and Antonio could summon those who lived south of the Osteria; while he, himself, could gather those who lived in another direction.

No, he would go first to Gaetano Negrini's, that
would save time, for although Gaetano lived a little
further away, he was much the younger man and
could move much the quicker. To have them assemble there together at seven o'clock to the minute,
that was a task which would require skilful manœu-
vring! Rather than be one minute late, Pietro preferred being three hours ahead of time, and the dawn
had preceded him only by a few minutes when he
made his way toward Negrini's domicile.

As he passed the Osteria he was surprised beyond
measure to see Rosaura assisting two burly, desperate-
appearing Italians (entire strangers to Pietro) to
shove a long pine box on a rickety express wagon.

"Something always goes wrong," he growled. "I
wonder what business she has to nose about at this
hour! Something to do with Angelo, I'll wager. She
always finds out everything, the Madre."

"A distinguished-looking visitor we had last night,"
he began tentatively.

She was so surprised to see him there that she
almost let her end of the box fall.

"Oh, it's you, is it, Pietro? And what are you
doing around at this time of day?" She shouted
some unnecessary directions to the assistants to hide
her discomposure.

"I was about to ask the same question of you,"
answered Pietro guardedly.

"That's my affair," she retorted sharply.

The timid tailor stood abashed, and for want of
something better to relieve his embarrassment, he re-

peated abstractedly, "A distinguished-looking visitor we had last night."

She flushed perceptibly and relaxed her hold on the box. "Take care!" cried one of the men.

"What visitor?" She shifted her position so that her back was turned to the interrogator.

"Why, the young man, the good-looking chap with the carpet-bag."

"Oh, he—how should I know who he was? He went away last night." Her dark face flushed again and she felt the blood beat at her temples; she blessed her good sense for having turned her back to his face.

At last the box was on the wagon, and the two desperadoes jumped on the seat and drove rapidly toward the south.

"Gone away! A nice trick to serve me! All my pains for nothing. I wonder if she tells the truth?" he muttered.

Rosaura stood on the edge of the curb watching the wagon until it passed from sight, then she turned toward the house. Pietro stood thinking what tactics he would employ to gain the truth.

"You there yet?" she said, turning around. "I thought you had gone long ago."

"I—I am not sure whether I understand," answered Pietro, apologetically. "Did you say he went away?"

"Of course I said so. Have you grown deaf; do you want me to repeat it a dozen times?" She was again the master of her expression, or rather of her inexpression.

"Did he tell you where he was going? Did he leave his name? Did he tell you when he would return?"

"Why should he tell me such things; what am I to him? I gave him his lodging and he paid me; there our business ended."

"But, Madre Pascella, I know who he was; I will give you ten guesses, and if you guess right, I will treat to a bottle of your best when he returns; and if you don't guess the treat is yours. Come, now," said Pietro in one breath, anxious to surprise Rosaura and have a part of his glory at least, since the full measure had been denied him.

The blood left her dark cheeks and she blanched visibly. Had he suspected something? Was he trying to bulldoze her into a confession and hush-money? She would show him with what kind of a *man* he was dealing.

"Guess, guess! Do you think I have nothing better to do than to stand here on the sidewalk and waste my precious time guessing with an old fool when I have breakfast to get for twenty?" She pushed him to one side and started toward the door.

The awed tailor (it takes nine tailors to make a man, the world over), fearing lest some one else, waiting inside with the surprise all ready, might cheat him out of his hard-earned reward, and seeing his dream of glory fade into nothingness, hastened to say: "Madre Pascella, it was your son Angelo; he told me so last night in the wine room. That's why

he put his hand over my mouth. 'Angelo, you!' I
was about to cry. 'Hush, you fool,' says he, and up
goes his hand over my mouth.   Yes, it was Angelo,
and I alone am in the secret; in me alone—"

   "Dio del Cielo!" cried Rosaura, and fell swooning
to the ground.

A PURPLE RHODODENDRON

BY JOHN FOX, JR.

John Fox, Jr. (born in Bourbon County, Kentucky, in 1863) has achieved deserved popularity by strong, direct character studies of the original types to be found in his native State. These are generally "mountain men" of the backwoods regions, where the vendetta still flourishes; but occasionally, as in the present selection, Mr. Fox presents a type of the "Kentucky gentleman," whom the abnormally developed sentiment of chivalry, in combination with habits of self-indulgence, brings to a tragic though quixotic end.

A PURPLE RHODODENDRON

BY JOHN FOX, JR.

THE purple rhododendron is rare. Up in the Gap here, Bee Rock, hung out over Roaring Rock, blossoms with it—as a gray cloud purples with the sunrise. This rock was tossed lightly on edge when the earth was young, and stands vertical. To get the flowers you climb the mountain to one side, and, balancing on the rock's thin edge, slip down by roots and past rattlesnake dens till you hang out over the water and reach for them. To avoid snakes it is best to go when it is cool, at daybreak.

I know but one other place in this southwest corner of Virginia where there is another bush of purple rhododendron, and one bush only is there. This hangs at the throat of a peak not far away, whose ageless gray head is bent over a ravine that sinks like a spear thrust into the side of the mountain. Swept only by high wind and eagle wings as this is, I yet knew one man foolhardy enough to climb to it for a flower. He brought one blossom down: and to this day I do not know that it was not the act of a coward; yes, though Grayson did it, actually smiling all the way from peak to ravine, and though he was my best friend—best loved then and since—I believe he was the strangest

man I have ever known, and I say this with thought;
for his eccentricities were sincere.   In all he did I can
not remember having even suspected anything theatrical but once.

We were all Virginians or Kentuckians at the
Gap, and Grayson was a Virginian.   You might have
guessed that he was a Southerner from his voice and
from the way he spoke of women—but no more.
Otherwise, he might have been a Moor, except for his
color, which was about the only racial characteristic he
had.   He had been educated abroad and, after the English habit, had traveled everywhere.   And yet I can
imagine no more lonely way between the eternities than
the path Grayson trod alone.

He came to the Gap in the early days, and just why
he came I never knew.   He had studied the iron question a long time, he told me, and what I thought reckless speculation was, it seems, deliberate judgment to
him.   His money "in the dirt," as the phrase was,
Grayson got him a horse and rode the hills and waited.
He was intimate with nobody.   Occasionally he would
play poker with us and sometimes he drank a good
deal, but liquor never loosed his tongue.   At poker his
face told as little as the back of his cards, and he won
more than admiration—even from the Kentuckians,
who are artists at the game; but the money went from
a free hand, and, after a diversion like this, he was apt
to be moody and to keep more to himself than ever.
Every fortnight or two he would disappear, always
over Sunday.   In three or four days he would turn up
again, black with brooding, and then he was the last

man to leave the card-table or he kept away from it altogether. Where he went nobody knew; and he was not the man anybody would question.

One night two of us Kentuckians were sitting in the club, and from a home paper I read aloud the rumored engagement of a girl we both knew—who was famous for beauty in the Bluegrass, as was her mother before her and the mother before her—to an unnamed Virginian. Grayson sat near, smoking a pipe; and when I read the girl's name I saw him take the meerschaum from his lips, and I felt his eyes on me. It was a mystery how, but I knew at once that Grayson was the man. He sought me out after that and seemed to want to make friends. I was willing, or rather he made me more than willing; for he was irresistible to me, as I imagine he would have been to anybody. We got to walking together and riding together at night, and we were soon rather intimate; but for a long time he never so much as spoke the girl's name. Indeed, he kept away from the Bluegrass for nearly two months; but when he did go he stayed a fortnight.

This time he came for me as soon as he got back to the Gap. It was just before midnight, and we went as usual back to Imboden Hill, through moon-dappled beeches, and Grayson turned off into the woods where there was no path, both of us silent. We rode through tremulous, shining leaves—Grayson's horse choosing a way for himself—and, threshing through a patch of high, strong weeds, we circled past an amphitheatre of deadened trees whose crooked arms were tossed out into the moonlight, and halted on the spur. The moon was poised over Morris's farm; South Fork was shining under us like a loop of gold, the mountains lay about in tranquil heaps, and the moon-mist rose luminous between them. There Grayson turned to me with an eager light in his eyes that I had never seen before.

"This has a new beauty to-night!" he said; and then "I told her about you, and she said that she used to know you—well." I was glad my face was in shadow —I could hardly keep back a brutal laugh—and Grayson, unseeing, went on to speak of her as I had never heard any man speak of any woman. In the end, he said that she had just promised to be his wife. I answered nothing. Other men, I knew, had said that with the same right, perhaps, and had gone from her to go back no more. And I was one of them. Grayson had met her at White Sulphur five years before, and had loved her ever since. She had known it from the first, he said, and I guessed then what was going to happen to him. I marveled, listening to the man, for it was the star of constancy in her white soul that was most lustrous to him—and while I wondered the marvel became a commonplace. Did not every lover think his loved one exempt from the frailty that names other women? There is no ideal of faith or of purity that does not live in countless women to-day. I believe that; but could I not recall one friend who walked with Divinity through pine woods for one immortal spring, and who, being sick to death, was quite finished —learning her at last? Did I not know lovers who believed sacred to themselves, in the name of love, lips that had been given to many another without it? And

now did I not know—but I knew too much, and to Grayson I said nothing.

That spring the "boom" came. Grayson's property quadrupled in value and quadrupled again. I was his lawyer, and I pleaded with him to sell; but Grayson laughed. He was not speculating; he had invested on judgment; he would sell only at a certain figure. The figure was actually reached, and Grayson let half go. The boom fell, and Grayson took the tumble with a jest. It would come again in the autumn, he said, and he went off to meet the girl at White Sulphur.

I worked right hard that summer, but I missed him, and I surely was glad when he came back. Something was wrong; I saw it at once. He did not mention her name, and for a while he avoided even me. I sought him then, and gradually I got him into our old habit of walking up into the Gap and of sitting out after supper on a big rock in the valley, listening to the run of the river and watching the afterglow over the Cumberland, the moon rise over Wallen's Ridge and the stars come out. Waiting for him to speak, I learned for the first time then another secret of his wretched melancholy. It was the hopelessness of that time, perhaps, that disclosed it. Grayson had lost the faith of his childhood. Most men do that at some time or other, but Grayson had no business, no profession, no art in which to find relief. Indeed, there was but one substitute possible, and that came like a gift straight from the God whom he denied. Love came, and Grayson's ideals of love, as of everything else, were morbid and quixotic. He believed that he owed it to the woman he should marry never to have loved another. He had loved but one woman, he said, and he should love but one. I believed him then literally when he said that his love for the Kentucky girl was his religion now—the only anchor left him in his sea of troubles, the only star that gave him guiding light. Without this love, what then?

I had a strong impulse to ask him, but Grayson shivered, as though he divined my thought, and, in some relentless way, our talk drifted to the question of suicide. I was not surprised that he rather defended it. Neither of us said anything new, only I did not like the way he talked. He was too deliberate, too serious, as though he were really facing a possible fact. He had no religious scruples, he said, no family ties; he had nothing to do with bringing himself into life; why—if it was not worth living, not bearable— why should he not end it? He gave the usual authority, and I gave the usual answer. Religion aside, if we did not know that we were here for some purpose, we did not know that we were not, and here we were anyway, and our duty was plain. Desertion was the act of a coward, and that Grayson could not deny.

That autumn the crash of '91 came across the water from England, and Grayson gave up. He went to Richmond, and came back with money enough to pay off his notes, and I think it took nearly all he had. Still, he played poker steadily now—for poker had been resumed when it was no longer possible to gamble in lots—he drank a good deal, and he began just at this time to take a singular interest in our volunteer police guard. He had always been on hand when there was trouble, and I sha'n't soon forget him the day Senator Mahone spoke, when we were punching a crowd of mountaineers back with cocked Winchesters. He had lost his hat in a struggle with one giant; he looked half crazy with anger, and yet he was white and perfectly cool, and I noticed that he never had to tell a man but once to stand back. Now he was the first man to answer a police whistle. When we were guarding Talt Hall, he always volunteered when there was any unusual risk to run. When we raided the Pound to capture a gang of desperadoes, he insisted on going ahead as spy; and when we got restless lying out in the woods waiting for daybreak, and the captain suggested a charge on the cabin, Grayson was by his side when it was made. Grayson sprang through the door first, and he was the man who thrust his reckless head up into the loft and lighted a match to see if the murderers were there. Most of us did foolish things in those days under stress of excitement, but Grayson, I saw, was weak enough to be reckless. His trouble with the girl, whatever it was, was serious enough to make him apparently care little whether he were alive or dead. And still I saw that not yet even had he lost hope. He was having a sore fight with his pride, and he got body-worn and heartsick over it. Of course he was worsted, and in the end, from sheer weakness, he went back to her once more.

I shall never see another face like his when Grayson came back that last time. I never noticed before that there were silver hairs about his temples. He stayed in his room, and had his meals sent to him. He came out only to ride, and then at night. Waking the third morning at daybreak, I saw him through the window galloping past, and I knew he had spent the night on Black Mountain. I went to his room as soon as I got up, and Grayson was lying across his bed with his face down, his clothes on, and in his right hand was a revolver. I reeled into a chair before I had strength enough to bend over him, and when I did I found him asleep. I left him as he was, and I never let him know that I had been to his room; but I got him out on the rock again that night, and I turned our talk again to suicide. I said it was small, mean, cowardly, criminal, contemptible! I was savagely in earnest, and Grayson shivered and said not a word. I thought he was in better mind after that. We got to taking night rides again, and I stayed as closely to him as I could, for times got worse and trouble was upon everybody. Notes fell thicker than snowflakes, and, through the foolish policy of the company, foreclosures had to be made. Grayson went to the wall like the rest of us. I asked him what he had done with the money he had made. He had given away a great deal to poorer kindred; he had paid his dead father's debts; he had played away a good deal, and he had lost the rest. His faith was still imperturbable. He had a dozen rectangles of "dirt," and from these, he said, it would all come back some day. Still, he felt the sudden poverty keenly, but he faced it as he did any other physical fact in life——dauntless. He used to be fond of saying that no one thing could make him miserable. But he would talk with mocking earnestness about some much dreaded combination; and a favorite phrase of his—which got to have peculiar significance—was "the cohorts of hell," who closed in on him when he was sick and weak, and who fell back when he got well. He had one strange habit, too, from which I got comfort. He would deliberately walk into and defy any temptation that beset him. That was the way he strengthened himself, he said. I knew what his temptation was now, and I thought of this habit when I found him asleep with his revolver, and I got hope from it now, when the dreaded combination (whatever that was) seemed actually to have come.

I could see now that he got worse daily. He stopped his mockeries, his occasional fits of reckless gayety. He stopped poker—resolutely—he couldn't afford to lose now; and, what puzzled me, he stopped drinking. The man simply looked tired, always hopelessly tired; and I could believe him sincere in all his foolish talk about his blessed Nirvana: which was the peace he craved, which was end enough for him.

Winter broke. May drew near; and one afternoon, when Grayson and I took our walk up through the Gap, he carried along a huge spy-glass of mine, which had belonged to a famous old desperado, who watched his enemies with it from the mountain-tops. We both helped capture him, and I defended him. He was sentenced to hang—the glass was my fee. We sat down opposite Bee Rock, and for the first time Grayson told me of that last scene with her. He spoke without bitterness, and he told me what she said,

word for word, without a breath of blame for her.
I do not believe that he judged her at all; she did not
know—he always said; she did not *know;* and then,
when I opened my lips, Grayson reached silently for
my wrist, and I can feel again the warning crush of
his fingers, and I say nothing against her now.

I asked Grayson what his answer was.

"I asked her," he said, solemnly, "if she had ever
seen a purple rhododendron."

I almost laughed picturing the scene—the girl bewildered by his absurd question—Grayson calm, su-
perbly courteous. It was a mental peculiarity of his
—this irrelevancy—and it was like him to end a matter of life and death in just that way.

"I told her I should send her one. I am waiting
for them to come out," he added; and he lay back
with his head against a stone and sighted the telescope
on a dizzy point, about which buzzards were circling.

"There is just one bush of rhododendron up there,"
he went on. "I saw it looking down from the Point
last spring. I imagine it must blossom earlier than
that across there on Bee Rock, being always in the
sun. No, it's not budding yet," he added, with his
eye to the glass. "You see that ledge just to the left?
I dropped a big rock from the Point square on a rat-
tler who was sunning himself there last spring. I can
see a foothold all the way up the cliff. It can be done,"
he concluded, in a tone that made me turn sharply
upon him.

"Do you really mean to climb up there?" I asked,
harshly.

"If it blossoms first up there—I'll get it where it blooms first." In a moment I was angry and half sick with suspicion, for I knew his obstinacy; and then began what I am half ashamed to tell.

Every day thereafter Grayson took that glass with him, and I went along to humor him. I watched Bee Rock, and he that one bush at the throat of the peak —neither of us talking over the matter again. It was uncanny, that rivalry—sun and wind in one spot, sun and wind in another—Nature herself casting the fate of a half-crazed fool with a flower. It was utterly absurd, but I got nervous over it—apprehensive, dismal.

A week later it rained for two days and the water was high. The next day the sun shone, and that afternoon Grayson smiled, looking through the glass, and handed it to me. I knew what I should see. One purple cluster, full blown, was shaking in the wind. Grayson was leaning back in a dream when I let the glass down. A cool breath from the woods behind us brought the odor of roots and of black earth; up in the leaves and sunlight somewhere a wood-thrush was singing, and I saw in Grayson's face what I had not seen for a long time, and that was peace—the peace of stubborn purpose. He did not come for me the next day, nor the next; but the next he did, earlier than usual.

"I am going to get that rhododendron," he said. "I have been half-way up—it can be reached." So had I been half-way up. With nerve and agility the flower could be got, and both these Grayson had. If

he had wanted to climb up there and drop, he could
have done it alone, and he would have known that I
should have found him. Grayson was testing himself again, and, angry with him for the absurdity of
the thing and with myself for humoring it, but still
not sure of him, I picked up my hat and went. I
swore to myself silently that it was the last time I
should pay any heed to his whims. I believed this
would be the last. The affair with the girl was over.
The flower sent, I knew Grayson would never mention her name again.

Nature was radiant that afternoon. The mountains had the leafy luxuriance of June, and a rich, sun-
lit haze drowsed on them between the shadows starting out over the valley and the clouds so white that
the blue of the sky looked dark. Two eagles shot
across the mouth of the Gap as we neared it, and high
beyond buzzards were sailing over Grayson's rhododendron.

I went up the ravine with him and I climbed up
behind him—Grayson going very deliberately and
whistling softly. He called down to me when he
reached the shelf that looked half-way.

"You mustn't come any further than this," he said.
"Get out on that rock and I'll drop them down to
you."

Then he jumped from the ledge and caught the
body of a small tree close to the roots, and my heart
sank at such recklessness and all my fears rose again.
I scrambled hastily to the ledge, but I could get no
further. I might possibly make the jump he had

made—but how should I ever get back? How would he? I called angrily after him now, and he wouldn't answer me. I called him a fool, a coward; I stamped the ledge like a child—but Grayson kept on, foot after hand, with stealthy caution, and the purple cluster nodding down at him made my head whirl. I had to lie down to keep from tumbling from the ledge; and there on my side, gripping a pine bush, I lay looking up at him. He was close to the flowers now, and just before he took the last upward step he turned and looked down that awful height with as calm a face as though he could have dropped and floated unhurt to the ravine beneath.

Then with his left hand he caught the ledge to the left, strained up, and, holding thus, reached out with his right. The hand closed about the cluster, and the twig was broken. Grayson gave a great shout then. He turned his head as though to drop them, and, that far away, I heard the sibilant whir of rattles. I saw a snake's crest within a yard of his face, and, my God! I saw Grayson loose his left hand to guard it! The snake struck at his arm, and Grayson reeled and caught back once at the ledge with his left hand. He caught once, I say, to do him full justice; then, without a word, he dropped—and I swear there was a smile on his face when he shot down past me into the trees.

I found him down there in the ravine with nearly every bone in his body crushed. His left arm was under him, and outstretched in his right hand was the shattered cluster, with every blossom gone but one. One white half of his face was unmarked, and on it was still the shadow of a smile. I think it meant more than that Grayson believed that he was near peace at last. It meant that Fate had done the deed for him and that he was glad. Whether he would have done it himself, I do not know; and that is why I say that though Grayson brought the flower down —smiling from peak to ravine—I do not know that he was not, after all, a coward.

That night I wrote to the woman in Kentucky. I told her that Grayson had fallen from a cliff while climbing for flowers; and that he was dead. Along with these words, I sent a purple rhododendron.

THE TIPSTER

BY EDWIN LEFEVRE

Edwin Lefevre (born in Colon, South America, January 23, 1871, of an American father and South American mother) studied mining engineering at Lehigh University, but on leaving college entered into financial journalism. Being fond of good stories, he collected many anecdotes of the sharp deals of Wall Street financiers, and this stimulated his invention to originate fictitious characters and incidents having a basis in human nature acted upon by the passion of gain. "The Tipster" has been selected by the author for reproduction in the present series as representative of his work. It first appeared in "McClure's Magazine."

THE TIPSTER

I

GILMARTIN was still laughing professionally at the prospective buyer's funny story when the telephone on his desk buzzed. He said: "Excuse me for a minute, old man," to the customer—Hopkins, the Connecticut manufacturer.

"Hello; who is this?" he spoke into the transmitter. "Oh, how are you?—Yes—I was out—Is that so?—Too bad—Too bad—Yes; just my luck to be out. I might have known it!—Do you think so?—Well, then, sell the zoo Occidental common—You know best.—What about Trolley?—Hold on?—All right; just as you say—I hope so—I don't like to lose, and—Ha! ha!—I guess so—Good-by."

"It's from my brokers," explained Gilmartin, hanging up the receiver. "I'd have saved five hundred dollars if I had been here at half-past ten. They called me up to advise me to sell out, and the price is off all over three points. I could have got out at a profit this morning; but no, sir; not I. I had to be away, trying to buy some camphor."

Hopkins was impressed. Gilmartin perceived it and went on, with an air of comical wrath which he thought was preferable to indifference. "It isn't the

THE TIPSTER

BY EDWIN LEFEVRE

I

GILMARTIN was still laughing professionally at the prospective buyer's funny story when the telephone on his desk buzzed. He said: "Excuse me for a minute, old man," to the customer —Hopkins, the Connecticut manufacturer.

"Hello; who is this?" he spoke into the transmitter. "Oh, how are you?—Yes—I was out—Is that so?—Too bad—Too bad—Yes; just my luck to be out. I might have known it!—Do you think so?— Well, then, sell the 200 Occidental common—You know best—What about Trolley?—Hold on?—All right; just as you say—I hope so—I don't like to lose, and—Ha! ha!—I guess so—Good-by."

"It's from my brokers," explained Gilmartin, hanging up the receiver. "I'd have saved five hundred dollars if I had been here at half-past ten. They called me up to advise me to sell out, and the price is off over three points. I could have got out at a profit this morning; but no, sir; not I. I had to be away, trying to buy some camphor."

Hopkins was impressed. Gilmartin perceived it and went on, with an air of comical wrath which he thought was preferable to indifference: "It isn't the money I mind so much as the tough luck of it. I didn't make my trade in camphor after all and I lost in stocks, when if I'd only waited five minutes more in the office I'd have got the message from my brokers and saved my five hundred. Expensive, my time is, eh?" with a woful shake of the head.

"But you're ahead of the game, aren't you?" asked the customer, interestedly.

"Well, I guess yes. Just about twelve thousand."

That was more than Gilmartin had made; but having exaggerated, he immediately felt very kindly disposed toward the Connecticut man.

"Whew!" whistled Hopkins, admiringly. Gilmartin experienced a great tenderness toward him. The lie was made stingless by the customer's credulity. This brought a smile of subtle relief to Gilmartin's lips. He was a pleasant-faced, pleasant-voiced man of three-and-thirty. He exhaled health, contentment, neatness, and an easy conscience. Honesty and good-nature shone in his eyes. People liked to shake hands with him. It made his friends talk of his lucky star; and they envied him.

"I bought this yesterday for my wife; took it out of a little deal in Trolley," he told Hopkins, taking a small jewel-box from one of the desk's drawers. It contained a diamond ring, somewhat showy, but obviously quite expensive. Hopkins's semi-envious admiration made Gilmartin add, genially: "What do you say to lunch? I feel I am entitled to a glass of 'fizz' to forget my bad luck of this morning." Then, in an exaggeratedly apologetic tone: "Nobody likes to lose five hundred dollars on an empty stomach!"

"She'll be delighted, of course," said Hopkins, thinking of Mrs. Gilmartin. Mrs. Hopkins loved jewelry.

"She's the nicest little woman that ever lived. Whatever is mine is hers; and what's hers is her own. Ha! ha! But," becoming nicely serious, "all that I'll make out of the stock market I'm going to put away for her, in her name. She can take better care of it than I; and, besides, she's entitled to it, anyhow, for being so nice to me."

That is how he told what a good husband he was. He felt so pleased over it that he went on, sincerely regretful: "She's visiting friends in Pennsylvania or I'd ask you to dine with us." And they went to a fashionable restaurant together.

Day after day Gilmartin thought persistently that Maiden Lane was too far from Wall Street. There came a week in which he could have made four very handsome "turns" had he but been in the brokers' office. He was out on business for his firm and when he returned the opportunity had gone, leaving behind it vivid visions of what might have been; also the conviction that time, tide, and the ticker wait for no man. Instead of buying and selling quinine and balsams and essential oils for Maxwell & Kip, drug brokers and importers, he decided to make the buying and selling of stocks and bonds his exclusive business. The hours were easy; the profits would be great. He would make enough to live on. He would not let the Street take away what it had given. That was the great secret: to know when to quit! He would be content with a moderate amount, wisely invested in gilt-edged bonds. And then he would bid the Street good-by forever.

Force of long business custom and the indefinable fear of new ventures for a time fought successfully his increasing ticker-fever. But one day his brokers wished to speak to him, to urge him to sell out his entire holdings, having been advised of an epoch-making resolution by Congress. They had received the news in advance from a Washington customer. Other brokers had important connections in the Capital and therefore there was no time to lose. They dared not assume the responsibility of selling him out without his permission. Five minutes—five eternities!—passed before they could talk by telephone with him; and when he gave his order to sell, the market had broken five or six points. The news was "out." The news agencies' slips were in the brokers' offices and half of Wall Street knew. Instead of being among the first ten sellers Gilmartin was among the second hundred.

II

The clerks gave him a farewell dinner. All were there, even the head office-boy to whom the two-dollar subscription was no light matter. The man who probably would succeed Gilmartin as manager, Jenkins, acted as toastmaster. He made a witty speech which ended with a neatly turned compliment. Moreover, he seemed sincerely sorry to bid good-by to the

man whose departure meant promotion—which was
the nicest compliment of all. And the other clerks—
old Williamson, long since ambition-proof; and young
Hardy, bitten ceaselessly by it; and midde-aged Jameson, who knew he could run the business much better
than Gilmartin; and Baldwin, who never thought of
business in or out of the office—all told him how good
he had been and related corroborative anecdotes that
made him blush and the others cheer; and how sorry
they were he would no longer be with them, but how
glad he was going to do so much better by himself;
and they hoped he would not "cut" them when he met
them after he had become a great millionaire. And
Gilmartin felt his heart grow soft and feelings not all
of happiness came over him. Danny, the dean of the
office boys, whose surname was known only to the
cashier, rose and said, in the tones of one speaking of
a dear departed friend: "He was the best man in the
place. He always was all right." Everybody laughed;
whereupon Danny went on, with a defiant glare at the
others: "I'd work for him for nothin' if he'd want me,
instead of gettin' ten a week from any one else." And
when they laughed the harder at this he said, stoutly:
"Yes, I would!" His eyes filled with tears at their
incredulity, which he feared might be shared by Mr.
Gilmartin. But the toastmaster rose very gravely and
said: "What's the matter with Danny?" And all
shouted in unison: "He's all right!" with a cordiality
so heartfelt that Danny smiled and sat down, blushing happily. And crusty Jameson, who knew he could
run the business so much better than Gilmartin, stood

up—he was the last speaker—and began: "In the ten years I've worked with Gilmartin, we've had our differences and—well—I—well—er—oh, DAMN IT!" and walked quickly to the head of the table and shook hands violently with Gilmartin for fully a minute, while all the others looked on in silence.

Gilmartin had been eager to go to Wall Street. But this leave-taking made him sad. The old Gilmartin who had worked with these men was no more and the new Gilmartin felt sorry. He had never stopped to think how much they cared for him nor indeed how very much he cared for them. He told them, very simply, he did not expect ever again to spend such pleasant years anywhere as at the old office; and as for his spells of ill-temper—oh, yes they needn't shake their heads; he knew he often was irritable—he had meant well and trusted they would forgive him. If he had his life to live over again he would try really to deserve all that they had said of him on this evening. And he was very, very sorry to leave them. "Very sorry, boys; very sorry. *Very* sorry!" he finished lamely, with a wistful smile. He shook hands with each man—a strong grip, as though he were about to go on a journey from which he might never return —and in his heart of hearts there was a new doubt of the wisdom of going to Wall Street. But it was too late to draw back.

They escorted him to his house. They wished to be with him to the last possible minute.

III

Everybody in the drug trade seemed to think that
Gilmartin was on the highroad to Fortune. Those
old business acquaintances and former competitors
whom he happened to meet in the street-cars or in thea-
tre lobbies always spoke to him as to a millionaire-to-be,
in what they imagined was correct Wall Street jargon,
to show him that they too knew something of the great
game. But their efforts made him smile with a sense
of superiority, at the same time that their admiration
for his cleverness and their good-natured envy for his
luck made his soul thrill joyously. Among his new
friends in Wall Street also he found much to enjoy.
The other customers—some of them very wealthy men
—listened to his views regarding the market as at-
tentively as he, later, felt it his polite duty to listen to
theirs. The brokers themselves treated him as a "good
fellow." They cajoled him into trading often—every
one hundred shares he bought or sold meant $12.50
to them—and when he won, they praised his unerring
discernment. When he lost they soothed him by
scolding him for his recklessness—just as a mother
will treat her three-year-old's fall as a great joke in
order to deceive the child into laughing at its misfortune. It was an average office with an average
clientèle.

From ten to three they stood before the quotation
board and watched a quick-witted boy chalk the price
changes, which one or another of the customers read
aloud from the tape as it came from the ticker. The

higher stocks went the more numerous the customers became, being allured in great flocks to the Street by the tales of their friends, who had profited greatly by the rise. All were winning, for all were buying stocks in a bull market. They resembled each other marvelously, these men who differed so greatly in cast of features and complexion and age. Life to all of them was full of joy. The very ticker sounded mirthful; its clicking told of golden jokes. And Gilmartin and the other customers laughed heartily at the mildest of stories without even waiting for the point of the joke. At times their fingers clutched the air happily, as if they actually felt the good money the ticker was presenting to them. They were all neophytes at the great game—lambkins who were bleating blithely to inform the world what clever and formidable wolves they were. Some of them had sustained occasional losses; but these were trifling compared with their winnings.

When the slump came all were heavily committed to the bull side. It was a bad slump. It was so unexpected—by the lambs—that all of them said, very gravely, it came like a thunderclap out of a clear sky. While it lasted, that is, while the shearing of the flock was proceeding, it was very uncomfortable. Those same joyous, winning stock-gamblers, with beaming faces, of the week before, were fear-clutched, losing stock-gamblers, with livid faces, on what they afterward called the day of the panic. It really was only a slump; rather sharper than usual. Too many lambs had been over-speculating. The wholesale dealers in securities—and insecurities—held very little of their own wares, having sold them to the lambs, and wanted them back now—cheaper. The customers' eyes, as on happier days, were intent on the quotation board. Their dreams were rudely shattered; the fast horses some had all but bought joined the steam yachts others almost had chartered. The beautiful homes they had been building were torn down in the twinkling of an eye. And the demolisher of dreams and dwellings was the ticker, that instead of golden jokes was now clicking financial death.

They could not take their eyes from the board before them. Their own ruin, told in mournful numbers by the little machine, fascinated them. To be sure, poor Gilmartin said: "I've changed my mind about Newport. I guess I'll spend the summer on my own *Hotel de Roof!*" And he grinned; but he grinned alone. Wilson, the dry goods man, who laughed so joyously at everybody's jokes, was now watching, as if under a hypnotic spell, the lips of the man who sat on the high stool beside the ticker and called out the prices to the quotation boy. Now and again Wilson's own lips made curious grimaces, as if speaking to himself. Brown, the slender, pale-faced man, was outside in the hall, pacing to and fro. All was lost, including honor. And he was afraid to look at the ticker, afraid to hear the prices shouted, yet hoping— for a miracle! Gilmartin came out from the office, saw Brown and said, with sickly bravado: "I held out as long as I could. But they got *my* ducats. A sporting life comes high, I tell you!" But Brown did not heed him, and Gilmartin pushed the elevator button impatiently and cursed at the delay. He not only had lost the "paper" profits he had accumulated during the bull market, but all his savings of years had crumbled away beneath the strokes of the ticker that day. It was the same with all. They would not take a small loss at first, but had held on, in the hope of a recovery that would "let them out even." And prices had sunk and sunk until the loss was so great that it seemed only proper to hold on, if need be a year, for sooner or later prices must come back. But the break "shook them out," and prices went just so much lower because so many people had to sell, whether they would or not.

IV

After the slump most of the customers returned to their legitimate business—sadder, but it is to be feared not much wiser men. Gilmartin, after the first numbing shock, tried to learn of fresh opportunities in the drug business. But his heart was not in his search. There was the shame of confessing defeat in Wall Street so soon after leaving Maiden Lane; but far stronger than this was the effect of the poison of gambling. If it was bad enough to be obliged to begin lower than he had been at Maxwell & Kip's, it was worse to condemn himself to long weary years of work in the drug business when his reward, if he remained strong and healthy, would consist merely in being able to save a few thousands. But a few lucky weeks in the stock market would win him back all he had lost—and more!

He should have begun in a small way while he was learning to speculate. He saw it now very clearly. Every one of his mistakes had been due to inexperience. He had imagined he knew the market. But it was only now that he really knew it, and therefore it was only now, after the slump had taught him so much, that he could reasonably hope to succeed. His mind, brooding over his losses, definitely dismissed as futile the resumption of the purchase and sale of drugs, and dwelt persistently on the sudden acquisition of stock market wisdom. Properly applied, this wisdom ought to mean much to him. In a few weeks he was again spending his days before the quotation board, gossiping with those customers who had survived, giving and receiving advice. And as time passed the grip of Wall Street on his soul grew stronger until it strangled all other aspirations. He could talk, think, dream of nothing but stocks. He could not read the newspapers without thinking how the market would "take" the news contained therein. If a huge refinery burned down, with a loss to the "Trust" of $4,000,000, he sighed because he had not foreseen the catastrophe and had sold Sugar short. If a strike by the men of the Suburban Trolley Company led to violence and destruction of life and property, he cursed an unrelenting Fate because he had not had the prescience to "put out" a thousand shares of Trolley. And he constantly calculated to the last fraction of a point how much money he would have made if he had sold short just before the calamity at the very top prices and had covered his stock at the

bottom. Had he only known! The atmosphere of
the Street, the odor of speculation surrounded him
on all sides, enveloped him like a fog, from which
the things of the outside world appeared as though
seen through a veil. He lived in the district where
men do not say "Good-morning" on meeting one another, but "How's the market?" or, when one asks:
"How do you feel?" receives for an answer: "Bull-
ish!" or "Bearish!" instead of a reply regarding the
state of health.

At first, after the fatal slump, Gilmartin impor-
tuned his brokers to let him speculate on credit, in a
small way. They did. They were kindly enough
men and sincerely wished to help him. But luck ran
against him. With the obstinacy of unsuperstitious
gamblers he insisted on fighting Fate. He was a
bull in a bear market; and the more he lost the more
he thought the inevitable "rally" in prices was due.
He bought in expectation of it and lost again and
again, until he owed the brokers a greater sum than
he could possibly pay; and they refused point blank
to give him credit for another cent, disregarding his
vehement entreaties to buy a last hundred, just one
more chance, the last, because he would be sure to
win. And, of course, the long-expected happened
and the market went up with a rapidity that made the
Street blink; and Gilmartin figured that had not the
brokers refused his last order, he would have made
enough to pay off the indebtedness and have left, in
addition, $2,950; for he would have "pyramided" on
the way up. He showed the brokers his figures,

accusingly, and they had some words about it and he left the office, almost tempted to sue the firm for conspiracy with intent to defraud; but decided that it was "another of Luck's sockdolagers" and let it go at that, gambler-like.

When he returned to the brokers' office—the next day—he began to speculate in the only way he could —vicariously. Smith, for instance, who was long of 500 St. Paul at 125, took less interest in the deal than did Gilmartin, who thenceforth assiduously studied the news slips and sought information on St. Paul all over the Street, listening thrillingly to tips and rumors regarding the stock, suffering keenly when the price declined, laughing and chirruping blithely if the quotations moved upward, exactly as though it were his own stock. In a measure it was as an anodyne to his ticker fever. Indeed, in some cases his interest was so poignant and his advice so frequent—he would speak of *our* deal—that the lucky winner gave him a small share of his spoils, which Gilmartin accepted without hesitation—he was beyond pride-wounding by now—and promptly used to back some miniature deal of his own on the Consolidated Exchange or even in "Percy's"—a dingy little bucket shop, where they took orders for two shares of stock on a margin of 1%; that is, where a man could bet as little as two dollars.

Later, it often came to pass that Gilmartin would borrow a few dollars when the customers were not trading actively. The amounts he borrowed diminished by reason of the increasing frequency of their refusals. Finally, he was asked to stay away from

the office where once he had been an honored and
pampered customer.

He became a Wall Street "has been" and could be
seen daily on New Street, back of the Consolidated
Exchange, where the "put" and "call" brokers con-
gregate. The tickers in the saloons nearby fed his
gambler's appetite. From time to time luckier men
took him into the same be-tickered saloons, where he
ate at the free lunch counters and drank beer and
talked stocks and listened to the lucky winners' narra-
tives with lips tremulous with readiness to smile and
grimace. At times the gambler in him would assert
itself and he would tell the lucky winners, wrathfully,
how the stock he wished to buy but couldn't the week
before had risen 18 points. But they, saturated with
their own ticker fever, would nod absently, their
soul's eyes fixed on some quotation-to-be; or they
would not nod at all, but in their eagerness to look at
the tape, from which they had been absent two long
minutes, would leave him without a single word of
consolation or even of farewell.

V

One day, in New Street, he overheard a very well-
known broker tell another that Mr. Sharpe was "going to move up Pennsylvania Central right away."
The overhearing of the conversation was a bit of rare
good luck that raised Gilmartin from his sodden
apathy and made him hasten to his brother-in-law,
who kept a grocery store in Brooklyn. He implored
Griggs to go to a broker and buy as much Pennsyl-

vania Central as he could—that is, if he wished to live in luxury the rest of his life. Sam Sharpe was going to put it up. Also, he borrowed ten dollars.

Griggs was tempted. He debated with himself many hours, and at length yielded with misgivings. He took his savings and bought one hundred shares of Pennsylvania Central at 64, and began to neglect his business in order to study the financial pages of the newspapers. Little by little Gilmartin's whisper set in motion within him the wheels of a ticker that printed on his day-dreams the mark of the dollar. His wife, seeing him preoccupied, thought business was bad; but Griggs denied it, confirming her worst fears. Finally, he had a telephone put in his little shop, to be able to talk to his broker.

Gilmartin, with the ten dollars he had borrowed, promptly bought ten shares in a bucket shop at 63⅞; the stock promptly went to 62⅞; he was promptly "wiped"; and the stock promptly went back to 64½.

On the next day a fellow-customer of Gilmartin of old days invited him to have a drink. Gilmartin resented the man's evident prosperity. He felt indignant at the ability of the other to buy hundreds of shares. But the liquor soothed him, and in a burst of mild remorse he told Smithers, after an apprehensive look about him as if he feared some one might overhear: "I'll tell you something, on the dead q. t., for your own benefit."

"Fire away!"

"Pa. Cent. is going 'way up."

"Yes?" said Smithers, calmly.

"Yes; it will cross par sure."

"Umph!" between munches of a pretzel.

"Yes. Sam Sharpe told"—Gilmartin was on the point of saying a "friend of mine," but caught himself and went on, impressively—"told me, yesterday, to buy Pa. Cent., as he had accumulated his full line, and was ready to whoop it up. And you know what Sharpe is," he finished, as if he thought Smithers was familiar with Sharpe's powers.

"Is that so?" nibbled Smithers.

"Why, when Sharpe makes up his mind to put up a stock, as he intends to do with Pa. Cent., nothing on earth can stop him. He told me he would make it cross par within sixty days. This is no hearsay, no tip. It's cold facts. I don't *hear* it's going up; I don't *think* it's going up; I *know* it's going up. Understand?" And he shook his right forefinger with a hammering motion.

In less than five minutes Smithers was so wrought up that he bought 500 shares and promised solemnly not to "take his profits," *i. e.* sell out, until Gilmartin said the word. Then they had another drink and another look at the ticker.

"You want to keep in touch with me," was Gilmartin's parting shot. "I'll tell you what Sharpe tells me. But you must keep it quiet," with a sidewise nod that pledged Smithers to honorable secrecy.

Had Gilmartin met Sharpe face to face, he would not have known who was before him.

Shortly after he left Smithers he buttonholed another acquaintance, a young man who thought he knew Wall Street, and therefore had a hobby—manipulation. No one could induce him to buy stocks by telling him how well the companies were doing, how bright the prospects, etc. That was bait for "suckers," not for clever young stock operators. But any one, even a stranger, who said that "they"—the perennially mysterious "they," the "big men," the mighty "manipulators" whose life was one prolonged conspiracy to pull the wool over the public's eyes— "they" were going to "jack up" these or the other shares, was welcomed and his advice acted upon. Young Freeman believed in nothing but "their" wickedness and "their" power to advance or depress stock values at will. Thinking of his wisdom had given him a chronic sneer.

"You're just the man I was looking for," said Gilmartin, who hadn't thought of the young man at all.

"Are you a deputy sheriff?"

"No." A slight pause for oratorical effect. "I had a long talk with Sam to-day."

"What Sam?"

"Sharpe. The old boy sent for me. He was in mighty good humor too. Tickled to death. He might well be—he's got 60,000 shares of Pennsylvania Central. And there's going to be from 50 to 60 points profit in it."

"H'm!" sniffed Freeman, sceptically, yet impressed by the change in Gilmartin's attitude from the money-borrowing humility of the previous week to the confident tone of a man with a straight tip. Sharpe was notoriously kind to his old friends—rich or poor.

"I was there when the papers were signed," Gilmartin said, hotly. "I was going to leave the room,
but Sam told me I needn't. I can't tell you what it
is about; really I can't. But he's simply going to put
the stock above par. It's 64½ now, and you know
and I know that by the time it is 75 the newspapers
will all be talking about inside buying; and at 85
everybody will want to buy it on account of important
developments; and at 95 there will be millions of bull
tips on it and rumors of increased dividends, and
people who would not look at it thirty points lower
will rush in and buy it by the bushel. Let me know
who is manipulating a stock, and to h——l with dividends and earnings. Them's *my* sentiments," with a
final hammering nod, as if driving in a profound
truth.

"Same here," assented Freeman, cordially. He
was attacked on his vulnerable side.

Strange things happen in Wall Street. Sometimes tips come true. It so proved in this case.
Sharpe started the stock upward brilliantly—the
movement became historic in the Street—and Pa.
Cent. soared dizzily and all the newspapers talked of it
and the public went mad over it and it touched 80
and 85 and 88 and higher, and then Gilmartin made
his brother-in-law sell out and Smithers and Freeman. Their profits were: Griggs, $3,000; Smithers,
$15,100; Freeman, $2,750. Gilmartin made them
give him a good percentage. He had no trouble with
his brother-in-law. Gilmartin told him it was an in-
violable Wall Street custom and so Griggs paid, with

an air of much experience in such matters. Freeman was more or less grateful. But Smithers met Gilmartin, and full of his good luck repeated what he had told a dozen men within the hour: "I did a dandy stroke the other day. Pa. Cent. looked to me like higher prices and I bought a wad of it. I've cleaned up a tidy sum," and he looked proud of his own penetration. He really had forgotten that it was Gilmartin who had given him the tip. But not so Gilmartin, who retorted, witheringly:

"Well, I've often heard of folks that you put into good things and they make money and afterward they come to you and tell how damned smart they were to hit it right. But you can't work that on me. I've got witnesses."

"Witnesses?" echoed Smithers, looking cheap. He remembered.

"Yes, wit-ness-es," mimicked Gilmartin, scornfully. "I all but had to get on my knees to make you buy it. And I told you when to sell it, too. The information came to me straight from headquarters and you got the use of it, and now the least you can do is to give me twenty-five hundred dollars."

In the end he accepted eight hundred dollars. He told mutual friends that Smithers had cheated him.

VI

It seemed as though the regeneration of Gilmartin had been achieved when he changed his shabby raiment for expensive clothes. He paid his tradesmen's bills and moved into better quarters. He spent his

money as though he had made millions. One week
after he had closed out the deal his friends would have
sworn Gilmartin had always been prosperous. That
was his exterior. His inner self remained the same
—a gambler. He began to speculate again, in the
office of Freeman's brokers.

At the end of the second month he had lost not only
the $1,200 he had deposited with the firm, but an
additional $250 he had given his wife and had been
obliged to "borrow" back from her, despite her assur-
ances that he would lose it. This time the slump was
really unexpected by all, even by the magnates—the
mysterious and all-powerful "they" of Freeman's—
so that the loss of the second fortune did not reflect
on Gilmartin's ability as a speculator, but on his luck.
As a matter of fact, he had been too careful and had
sinned from over-timidity at first, only to plunge later
and lose all.

As the result of much thought about his losses Gilmartin became a professional tipster. To let others
speculate for him seemed the only sure way of winning. He began by advising ten victims—he learned
in time to call them clients—to sell Steel Rod preferred, each man 100 shares; and to a second ten he
urged the purchase of the same quantity of the same
stock. To all he advised taking four points' profit.
Not all followed his advice, but the seven clients who
sold it made between them nearly $3,000 overnight.
His percentage amounted to $287.50. Six bought,
and when they lost he told them confidentially how
the treachery of a leading member of the pool had

obliged the pool managers to withdraw their support from the stock temporarily, whence the decline. They grumbled; but he assured them that he himself had lost nearly $1,600 of his own on account of the traitor.

For some months Gilmartin made a fair living, but business became very dull. People learned to fight shy of his tips. The persuasiveness was gone from his inside news and from his confidential advice from Sharpe and from his beholding with his own eyes the signing of epoch-making documents. Had he been able to make his customers alternate their winnings and losses he might have kept his trade. But, for example, "Dave" Rossiter, in Stuart & Stern's office, stupidly received the wrong tip six times in succession. It wasn't Gilmartin's fault, but Rossiter's bad luck.

At length, failing to get enough clients in the ticker district itself, Gilmartin was forced to advertise in an afternoon paper, six times a week, and in the Sunday edition of one of the leading morning dailies. They ran like this:

WE MAKE MONEY

for our investors by the best system ever devised. Deal with genuine experts. Two methods of operating; one speculative, the other ensures absolute safety.

NOW

is the time to invest in a certain stock for ten points sure profit. Three points margin will carry it. Remember how correct we have been on other stocks. Take advantage of this move.

IOWA MIDLAND.

Big movement coming in this stock. It's very near at hand. Am waiting daily for word. Will get it in time. Splendid

opportunity to make big money. It costs only a 2-cent stamp
to write to me.

_____

CONFIDENTIAL INFORMATION.

Private secretary of banker and stock operator of world-wide
reputation has valuable information. I don't wish your money.
Use your own broker. All I want is a share of what you will
surely make if you follow my advice.

_____

WILL ADVANCE $40 PER SHARE.

A fortune to be made in a railroad stock. Deal pending which
will advance same $40 per share within three months. Am in
position to keep informed as to developments and the operations
of a pool. Parties who will carry for me 100 shares with a New
York Stock Exchange house will receive the full benefit of information. Investment safe and sure. Highest references given.

He prospered amazingly. Answers came to him
from furniture dealers on Fourth Avenue and dairy-
men up the State and fruit growers in Delaware and
factory workers in Massachusetts and electricians in
New Jersey and coal miners in Pennsylvania and shop-
keepers and physicians and plumbers and undertakers
in towns and cities near and far. Every morning
Gilmartin telegraphed to scores of people—at their
expense—to sell, and to scores of others to buy the
same stocks. And he claimed his commissions from
the winners.

Little by little his savings grew; and with them
grew his desire to speculate on his own account. It
made him irritable not to gamble.

He met Freeman one day in one of his dissatisfied
moods. Out of politeness he asked the young cynic
the universal query of the Street:

"What do you think of 'em?" He meant stocks.

"What difference does it make what *I* think?" sneered Freeman, with proud humility. "I'm nobody." But he looked as if he did not agree with himself.

"What do you *know?*" pursued Gilmartin mollifyingly.

"I know enough to be long of Gotham Gas. I just bought a thousand shares at 180." He really had bought a hundred only.

"What on?"

"On information. I got it straight from a director of the company. Look here, Gilmartin, I'm pledged to secrecy. But, for your own benefit, I'll just tell you to buy all the Gas you possibly can carry. The deal is on. I know that certain papers were signed last night, and they are almost ready to spring it on the public. They haven't got all the stock they want. When they get it, look out for fireworks."

Gilmartin did not perceive any resemblance between Freeman's tips and his own.

He said, hesitatingly, as though ashamed of his timidity:

"The stock seems pretty high at 180."

"You won't think so when it sells at 250. Gilmartin, I don't *hear* this; I don't *think* it; I *know* it!"

"All right; I'm in," quoth Gilmartin, jovially. He felt a sense of emancipation now that he had made up his mind to resume his speculating. He took every cent of the nine hundred dollars he had made from telling people the same things that Freeman told him now, and bought a hundred Gotham Gas at $185 a share.

Also he telegraphed to all his clients to plunge in the stock.

It fluctuated between 184 and 186 for a fortnight. Freeman daily asseverated that "they" were accumulating the stock. But, one fine day, the directors met, agreed that business was bad, and having sold out most of their own holdings, decided to reduce the dividend rate from 8 to 6 per cent. Gotham Gas broke seventeen points in ten short minutes. Gilmartin lost all he had. He found it impossible to pay for his advertisements. The telegraph companies refused to accept any more "collect" messages. This deprived Gilmartin of his income as a tipster. Griggs had kept on speculating and had lost all his money and his wife's in a little deal in Iowa Midland. All that Gilmartin could hope to get from him was an occasional invitation to dinner. Mrs. Gilmartin, after they were dispossessed for non-payment of rent, left her husband, and went to live with a sister in Newark who did not like Gilmartin.

His clothes became shabby and his meals irregular. But always in his heart, as abiding as an inventor's faith in himself, there dwelt the hope that some day, somehow, he would "strike it rich" in the stock market.

One day he borrowed five dollars from a man who had made five thousand in Cosmopolitan Traction. The stock, the man said, had only begun to go up, and Gilmartin believed it and bought five shares in "Percy's," his favorite bucket shop. The stock began to rise slowly but steadily. The next afternoon

"Percy's" was raided, the proprietor having disagreed with the police as to price.

Gilmartin lingered about New Street, talking with other customers of the raided bucket shop, discussing whether or not it was a "put up job" of old Percy himself, who, it was known, had been losing money to the crowd for weeks past. One by one the victims went away and at length Gilmartin left the ticker district. He walked slowly down Wall Street, then turned up William Street, thinking of his luck. Cosmopolitan Traction had certainly looked like higher prices. Indeed, it seemed to him that he could almost hear the stock shouting, articulately: *"I'm going up, right away, right away!"* If somebody would buy a thousand shares and agree to give him the profits on a hundred, on ten, on one!

But he had not even his carfare. Then he remembered that he had not eaten since breakfast. It did him no good to remember it now. He would have to get his dinner from Griggs in Brooklyn.

"Why," Gilmartin told himself with a burst of curious self-contempt, "I can't even buy a cup of coffee!"

He raised his head and looked about him to find how insignificant a restaurant it was in which he could not buy even a cup of coffee. He had reached Maiden Lane. As his glance ran up and down the north side of that street, it was arrested by the sign:

MAXWELL & KIP

At first he felt but vaguely what it meant. It had grown unfamiliar with absence. The clerks were com-

ing out.   Jameson, looking crustier than ever, as
though he were forever thinking how much better than
Jenkins he could run the business; Danny, some inches
taller, no longer an office boy, but spick and span in a
blue serge suit and a necktie of the latest style, exhal-
ing health and correctness; Williamson, grown very
gray and showing on his face thirty years of routine;
Baldwin, happy as of yore at the ending of the day's
work, and smiling at the words of Jenkins—Gilmartin's successor, who wore an air of authority, of
the habit of command which he had not known in the
old days.

Of a sudden Gilmartin was in the midst of his old
life.   He saw all that he had been, all that he might
still be.   And he was overwhelmed.   He longed to
rush to his old associates, to speak to them, to shake
hands with them, to be the old Gilmartin.   He was
about to step toward Jenkins, but stopped abruptly.
His clothes were shabby, and he felt ashamed.   But,
he apologized to himself, he could tell them how he
had made a hundred thousand and had lost it.   And
he even might borrow a few dollars from Jenkins.

Gilmartin turned on his heel with a sudden impulse
and walked away from Maiden Lane quickly.   All
that he thought now was that he would not have them
see him in his plight.   He felt the shabbiness of his
clothes without looking at them.   As he walked, a great
sense of loneliness came over him.

He was back in Wall Street.   At the head of the
Street was old Trinity; to the right the Sub-Treasury;
to the left the Stock Exchange.

From Maiden Lane to the Lane of the Ticker—such had been his life.

"If I could only buy some Cosmopolitan Traction!" he said. Then he walked forlornly northward, to the great Bridge, on his way to Brooklyn, to eat with Griggs, the ruined grocery man.

END OF VOLUME THREE